CHARLIE N. HOLMBERG

AUTHOR OF THE PAPER MAGICIAN

Interior design by Cora Johnson
Edited by Kristy Stewart and Lisa Shepherd

Cover design by Melissa Williams Design

Published by Mirror Press, LLC

ISBN-13: 978-1-947152-22-9

To Danny, my sister and dear friend.
I don't often write characters inspired by
real-life people, but you were the first.

CHAPTER 1

To the ears of Gentry's father, gold cried louder than his children did.

"You jest." Gentry wrung the index finger of her left hand in the fist of her right. Her pa had spoken a great deal of the mining in California as of late, but he'd never speculated about hunting for gold himself. Never out loud. Now that he'd said it, she couldn't stop hearing it.

"There ain't time for jesting." Butch Abrams set a heavy hand on his eldest daughter's shoulder. "We're out here, settled in the middle of nowhere . . . there's more to life than deserts and Mormons."

Gentry shook off her pa's touch. "But we haven't yet been here two years! We just finished planting, and what about your job at the mill?" *Don't cry,* she chided herself, swallowing against the hard, sore orb in her throat. *Not in front of Pearl. Not in front of Pearl.*

Pearl, the youngest at twelve, stood from the wicker chair before the woodstove, worrying her lip. Her hair, the same blonde Ma's had been, wisped from its braid and curled about her face. Rooster, Gentry's brother, leaned against the wall by the door, his arms folded, his eyes cast to the floor. He was almost as tall as Pa, but he wasn't a man, not yet. Not yet.

Her father sighed. "I'm leaving in the morning."

"So soon?" Pearl croaked.

"You can't leave in the morning." Gentry's windpipe constricted against her will, squeezing the words into a whine. She swallowed again and let go of her mangled finger. "You can't *leave*. What are we supposed to do in the meantime? The trip is so long . . ." How long? How far was it to San Francisco? Her family had put down roots right in the middle of Utah Territory, or *Deseret*, as the Mormons called it. At least two weeks' travel by horse, surely. Two weeks before their father could even hope to find work.

"What if they don't hire you?" Gentry tried. "You'd be gone more than a month, and we—"

"Already been hired." Her father spoke too quickly. His temper flared in the vein pulsing down the center of his forehead. "Got the letter yesterday."

"And you didn't tell us?"

"Now listen, young lady." Shadows bloomed over her face. He lifted a thick finger toward Gentry's nose. "I don't report to you. You ain't my supervisor, my father, or my wife."

No, his wife—their mother—died the day after they finished the house, and the babe who'd killed her lived a day's ride away.

Gentry pressed her lips together.

Her father straightened and dropped the accusing finger. "You're twenty now; you can keep an eye on things." He hesitated. "I'll send wages as soon as I can. All will be well. And Rooster still has work."

"It's only part-time." Rooster's voice sounded low and too old for a seventeen-year-old boy. It prickled the skin on Gentry's back.

"It'll work out. I've done the numbers," their father assured them. He turned to Pearl and smiled, but Gentry thought the expression too tight. That vein still pulsed down

2

his forehead. "It'll be all right, hear? And you can take my bed; I won't be needing it. And you'll all help each other and keep things afloat." He turned back to Gentry. "I'll write. And I'll send wages. You work on finding a nice, wealthy man to marry."

He meant it as a joke, but Gentry didn't laugh. She bit her tongue to keep from scowling. "I don't want you sending wages. I don't want your space. I want you to stay."

"Nope." He shook his head, his eyes nearly closed. A gesture that said *I've made up my mind, and your silly talk won't change it.* "I've got to report soon or they'll give the position to someone else."

Rooster asked, "Which company is it?"

Butch Abrams eyed his son. "Boston. Best one."

Gentry took a deep breath. *Don't cry. Not in front of Pearl.* "Pa—"

"Gentry, so help me, I'll switch you like you was a little girl, hear?"

Gentry pinched her mouth shut. Shaking his head once more, her father passed between her and Pearl into the second room of the house—it had only two—where the beds lay. He shut the door behind him. Time to think, he'd tell them, were he in a less foul mood. Time to pack.

Time to leave.

~~~

He didn't say goodbye.

Gentry hadn't slept well. Not because she shared a bed with both her siblings. Not because Pearl, wedged in the middle, kept rolling over and swatting Gentry with a limp arm. Her mind ran circles around itself, like it always did when fueled with anxiety. As though if she thought the same thoughts enough times, they'd flit away and leave her be.

She watched her father rise without lighting a candle, watched the shadows of his clothes as he dressed, listened to him spit and scratch his beard. She watched him pick up his suitcase and step out of the room, his footsteps quieter than she'd ever heard them. She listened as he reached the front door, opened it, and closed it. Then Gentry rose, her chestnut braid falling over her shoulder, and followed his path. She opened the door, stood in its doorway, and watched as her pa mounted Rose, one of their two mares, and rode south, away from the rising sun. Away from *them.*

She didn't think he'd do it. That he'd *actually* do it. A small piece of her chest tore out and followed him, leaving a hollow ache in her heart. When her pa didn't look back, the ache filled with bitterness that he had taken the piece with him at all. Gentry pressed a thumb to the spot on her chest, holding her breath against the familiarity of it—so similar to when Ma died.

She stood there in her nightgown until her father became a blurred dot against the mountains. Until they swallowed him and the rising sun changed the peaks from blue to brown, pouring its too-hot light over the little town of Dry Creek. The nearest neighbor's cocks crowed—the Abrams didn't own any chickens, not anymore—and Gentry finally stepped inside, slamming the door behind her.

Rooster was pulling on his work shirt as she came—one of the sleeves needed to be patched, but if he was going to Hoss's farm now, there wouldn't be time to mend it until this evening.

Rooster said nothing, but after he clipped on his suspenders and stomped his feet into his boots, Pearl rolled over in bed and asked, "Is Pa gone?"

"Yes." Gentry said. Quick and simple, avoiding her gaze. She slipped into the bedroom and dressed, nearly pulling a stitch as she yanked on her worn, brown-striped petticoat. Her scalp ached once she finished brushing her hair and pinning it into a too-tight bun. In the kitchen, she stoked the coals in the tiny woodstove hard enough to puff clouds of ash into the air. She pulled a cast-iron skillet from the cupboards and slammed it on the stove. Gripping the handle for a long moment, Gentry sucked in a deep breath.

She knew they were watching her. Her siblings. Who else was there to look up to? Who knew how long their father would be away? Gentry pried her fingers off the skillet's handle one by one, each joint resisting.

This will be good, she told herself. *Pa will find success out there and send wages home. We'll be comfortable. Maybe even move out there, if work goes well. Wouldn't that be something, to live by the ocean again?*

Gentry allowed herself a few more deep breaths before fetching a bowl and the dwindling bag of flour. She'd filled in her ma's shoes just fine, hadn't she? She'd fill their pa's for a little while too.

Rooster passed behind her on his way to the door.

"You're not staying for breakfast?" Gentry asked.

"I want to get there early."

He felt it too, then. Get to the farm early—try to earn a little extra. Gentry couldn't fault him that. She crossed the tiny kitchen and tore off the heel of the last loaf of bread she'd made. She tossed it to Rooster, who said a quick *thanks* and stepped out the door.

Gentry stirred flapjack batter and made a few cakes for herself and Pearl. She set Pearl's on a plate on the kitchen table, which crowded too close to the washbasin and drawers, then ate hers plain as she mixed the start of bread dough and left it on the table to rise.

Pearl came out of the bedroom, her hair, too, pulled into a bun. She looked younger today, like she was eight instead of twelve. She always looked young in Gentry's eyes, though. Like they refused to acknowledge her baby sister was growing up.

Hands on hips, Gentry examined their small home, noting what needed to be cleaned and what needed to be mended. She peered out the far window to the garden they'd planted. She prayed for rain. This place was so . . . dry.

The Abrams had meant to settle in California, but her ma discovered she was pregnant just after they left, and the babe ailed her so that they stopped the journey seven hundred miles early. At least one of them would make it now. Pa hadn't even suggested moving the family as a whole—there just wasn't the money for such a trip, not yet. After being forced to settle in the middle of Utah Territory, Pa had compensated by squandering what money they had left on bricks and glass for their tiny house. They'd never recovered from the self-inflicted destitution.

Walls of brick instead of wood, and Gentry felt no safer within them.

The only thing to do was carry on as though their father hadn't left, as well as they could. Mending, then laundry, then crops, then back to the bread. *Not so difficult,* she thought.

Glancing at the pile of mending, however, she noted a pair of her father's slacks that he'd left behind. They had a hole in the right pocket. *Then finances,* she thought with a frown. She had to figure out what they had and what they could stretch until Pa sent his first wages. If he made good time, maybe they'd hear from him next month.

The sun was already too hot by the time Gentry hung the laundry to dry. A bonnet kept it off her hair and face as she walked the rows of the garden. They weren't farmers, not in trade, but her pa had purchased a decent-sized plot for food. They'd added variety to the planting this year, hoping to get a better harvest than last. Turnips, potatoes, carrots. Heartier crops, ones that withstood the climate and filled a belly faster. Gentry pulled a few weeds as she patrolled the rows.

The plot didn't go all the way to the thin fence that surrounded it—there was half a row's worth of space on the west side. Extra potatoes—those grew quickly enough—or maybe a berry bush . . . no, potatoes were a safer bet, and Gentry needed to feel safe.

Gentry went to the stable where Bounder, the other mare, still rested. She set Pearl to tending her while she moved their gardening supplies, minus the plow, to Rose's empty stall. She took the hoe, sweat dripping down the curve of her spine, and worked breaking up the sunhardened soil along the fence.

Dust from the labor floated through the air, soiling the hem of her dress and sticking to the sweat along her hairline. She ached for Virginia, for its seascented air and green summers, for air that didn't dry out her sinuses and make her skin thirst. But the work gave her focus and eased the tension in her gut, and the dry heat was more tolerable than Virginia's bogging humidity.

She'd worked the hoe halfway up the line before a shadow blocked the sun from her work and a familiar voice called, "Ho, Gentry!"

Straightening, Gentry rubbed her sleeve over her brow and peered at Hoss Howland, their neighbor to the north. He *was* a farmer. Hoss had hired Rooster as a farmhand during harvest last year and offered him a job at the start of spring. Hoss was a thick man, stout, yet still an inch or so taller than her father. A wide-brimmed hat shaded his head, and a neatly trimmed beard of chestnut shaded his face. His trousers and shirt had soft earth stains marking them, and what skin they showed was heavily tanned from years of outdoor labor. If Gentry was not mistaken, Hoss had turned forty-one at the end of winter.

"Morning, Hoss." Gentry shaded her eyes from the sun.

"Afternoon," he corrected her with a grin. "I hear your father's set out for California."

Gentry's smile faded, but she forced her mouth to hold some semblance of it. "That he did, first thing this morning."

"How long's his contract?"

Gentry shook her head and leaned on the hoe. "I'm not sure. Not too long." She hoped.

Hoss nodded, looking up the line of earth Gentry still had to break. "You should have a man helping you with this."

"Rooster is—"

"No, no, never mind it," he said, though he didn't give Gentry much time to wonder at his words. "About Rooster, though."

Gentry's shoulders inched downward. "He isn't causing trouble, is he?"

Hoss laughed—it was a hearty sound that built her smile back up. Gentry appreciated the cheer. Pa didn't laugh anymore, except when he managed to get his hands on some liquor. "That boy couldn't cause trouble if he wanted to. Don't you worry. I'm actually thinking to give him more hours on the farm, but I don't want to take him away if you need him here."

Gentry's eyes widened. She would never say no to more work and more money for the family. "Not at all. Keep him as long as you like."

She hesitated, studying Hoss. She knew him fairly well after living down the road from him for nearly two years. She narrowed her eyes. "Hoss Howland."

He raised an eyebrow.

Gentry lifted the hoe and replanted it firmly by her feet. "If you think we're in need of charity—"

Hoss held up both hands in protest. "Not at all. I admit, I've been ... thinking about it since Rooster told me this morning. But I have been thinking of getting more workers as the beans are coming in. Honest." His voice grew heavier. "I wouldn't lie to you, Gentry."

Gentry glanced away at those words. No, not at the words, but the way Hoss's gaze softened when he said them. Maybe, were he not twice her age, Gentry might have had the courage to meet those eyes.

She looked out over the crops. So much work to do. "Thank you. Rooster will take the work."

"Already has," Hoss said. "But I wanted to check with you as well."

"As you rightly should. Now get on. There's only so much daylight left."

"Days'll only be getting longer." Hoss nodded and smacked his palm on the fence twice before pulling away. "Good day, Miss Abrams."

"To you too."

Later, while supper cooked in the oven and Pearl set the table, Gentry sat on a wicker chair with her father's old ledger. The covers were bent on both sides, and the graphite had been smeared, but most of his numbers were legible. If there was one thing Gentry thanked her father for, it was keeping a good record of their finances. She only wished he'd gone over them with her before leaving.

The number of minuses in the far column made her stomach clench.

She started a new page, counting what was in the savings box—what her father hadn't taken for his trip—and estimated

Rooster's new wages against their land debts and needs. She added the numbers three times. It wouldn't be enough to sustain them, but it would get them through this first month just fine, if they were careful. See them to the first wages from her father. Gentry wasn't sure how much a gold miner made, but if so many were crossing the country to try their hands at it, there had to be a few pretty pennies in the work, especially if her father found a new vein.

Still, those numbers gnawed at Gentry. She added them a fourth time.

"How's it looking?" Rooster asked as he came through the front door, toweling off his wet hair. He'd taken a bath out in the stables after work. Hoss's farm often left him filthy.

"We'll be all right for a month," she said, "if Pa's wages come in. I don't know how long it'll take before he sends money to us. Did he tell you?" She bit her lip, hopeful.

Rooster's mouth tilted into a half frown. "He didn't give me any more details than he did you or Pearl."

Pearl nodded as she set a water cup between her and Gentry's plates.

Gentry took a deep breath.

"I'd think . . ." Rooster set a hand on the edge of the table and leaned on it, throwing the towel over his shoulder. "I'd think six weeks, maybe. Eight if they make him pay for his own lodging."

Gentry's stomach clenched tighter. The smell of supper almost became nauseating. "They'd hire men from clear out here and make them pay their own board?"

Rooster shrugged. "Everyone's going out to California. Not like the companies are desperate for workers. Companies save every cent they can. It's about profit, Gen."

Gentry scanned the numbers and tapped her pencil against her lips. "We won't have much to harvest that early."

Pearl said, "Maybe we can ask Hannah."

Gentry shut the ledger. "We're not going to ask Hannah."

Hannah Hinkle, that was. One of the Mormons up north in American Fork. The one who had found Gentry sobbing on the side of the road as she struggled to find a family for the half brother her father didn't want. Though she was barely older than Gentry, she had adopted little Caleb and had kept in touch with the family ever since.

Gentry knew that if she asked Hannah for assistance, Hannah would do everything she could to help. Too much, even. But no. They hadn't come to that. Yet.

"They'll take the china," Rooster said.

Gentry turned toward him.

"The Mormons, I mean," he explained. "Some of the other hands were talking about it. They're taking ceramics and gold and the like for that big temple they're building in Salt Lake City. We could probably sell to them."

"Ma's china." Gentry's stomach loosened a little.

"What? No!" Pearl objected. "That was *Ma's*. And Grandma's. We can't get rid of it."

"We don't use it, Pearl." Gentry hated the way her voice begged.

"We do at Christmas," she protested.

"We don't need it," Rooster said.

"It's good china too," Gentry added, more to her brother than her sister. "It's gold-rimmed." Leaf-thin, but that had to be worth something. "Hannah would know where to take it."

Pearl's eyebrows nearly crossed, she scrunched them so tightly. "Why don't you sell them your necklace too, if we need so much money?"

Gentry's fingers immediately went to the empty locket around her neck, its heart-shaped pendant and fine chain. She didn't know how many carats the thing was, but it didn't matter. Her ma had given this to her as she lay on the birthing bed, bleeding out her life. Gentry didn't care if it were made of diamonds, they couldn't be desperate enough to sell it, even to the highest bidders.

No, not that. She pulled her hand away. *Not yet.*

Gentry sighed. "You can come with me, Pearl. We can head up tomorrow, even. Look around town. Visit Caleb."

Frowning, Pearl nodded and went to pull the cast iron cooking pot out of the coals. Cornbread and gravy from yesterday's chicken tonight. Tomorrow, Gentry would boil the carcass and scrape every last fiber of meat from its bones. It should make enough soup for three.

"How much do you think we can get?" Gentry asked her brother.

Rooster shrugged. "As much as you can squeeze out of them."

〰

"We can sew," Pearl suggested as Bounder made her slow trot over the narrow dirt roads north. "Sew some dresses and bonnets, sell them."

Gentry tugged the reins slightly right, steering Bounder and their wagon around a depression in the road. "Every woman knows how to sew." She took a deep breath in an attempt to tame the nerves that had been brewing in her stomach all day. One day to get to Hannah's, albeit unannounced, and one day to get to Salt Lake City. Would it be worth the trip? "I don't think there'd be a demand for anything we piece together, not out here." In Virginia, maybe. But all the women in Utah Territory were homebodies with dozens of children, and they sewed every piece of clothing they wore. "We couldn't afford the fabric, anyway."

"We could open a hotel."

Gentry laughed. "Oh Pearl, that's a wonderful idea, but we don't have enough money to buy the sheets for one bed, let alone to build an entire building full of them. Someday, maybe."

With all the miners heading west for gold, they'd certainly get plenty of customers. She wondered where their pa had slept last night. Had he found a house or barn to lay his head, or did he camp out in the rough beside Rose? Gentry doubted there were many hotels between Dry Creek and San Francisco.

If only she could muster the same confidence her father had.

They rode for a few hours in silence clipped by bursts of conversation, stopping once while Pearl relieved herself behind some sagebrush. As they neared the squeeze between the two mountain ranges, Pearl asked, "What's that smell?"

Gentry hadn't noticed anything out of the ordinary, but when she sniffed, she smelled it too. Something like rotten eggs. She scanned their arid surroundings. There were no villages or farms here, just a long, horse-pounded dirt road. "I don't know. A skunk?"

Bounder shook her head, uneasy.

"It doesn't smell like a skunk."

No, it didn't. Sweat slicked Gentry's palms.

The smell grew stronger until it filled the air all around the wagon, and Gentry couldn't turn her nose from it. The air felt hotter too. She inched closer to Pearl.

They came around a bend, and a burst of steam from the road ahead made Gentry jump in her seat, half a cry escaping her lips.

"Whoa!" She jerked back on Bounder's reins.

Pearl stood on the wagon seat. "What in the . . . ?"

Gentry stared ahead as another, smaller burst—a geyser—erupted from the road ahead of them. The earth had sunk into small craters, and in many of them glowed bright blue or yellow water. Unnatural colors that weren't a mere reflection of the sky. The awful, rotting smell wafting from the pits burned her eyes and nose. Bounder hoofed the ground. She'd never seen—or smelled—the like.

Gentry stood in the wagon seat, careful with her balance, to get a better look. The steaming pools ate up the entire road and stretched out into the wild clear to the Wasatch Mountains on one side and a good mile or so toward the large lake on the other. Gentry had heard stories of acidic geysers in the unorganized territory north of them, but nothing in the Utah lands. And certainly not on this road—Gentry had been up and down its length a dozen times.

One of the pools began to bubble.

Pearl, with her sleeve over her nose, said, "We have to go back."

Gnawing on her lip, Gentry looked over her shoulder to the box of china sitting in the wagon bed. They were almost to American Fork, but she wouldn't dare put her sister's life in peril.

"No." She sat down and tugged on Pearl's skirt until her sister did the same. "It's all right . . . if we leave it alone, it will leave us alone."

"It stinks."

"We'll go around."

"There's no road. What if it goes out to the lake?"

"I don't think it does . . . and the ground is flat enough." The dry earth was speckled with sagebrush, a few trees making their stand here and there. Her eyes found a smooth enough path through it; they'd just need to backtrack a little.

Clicking her tongue, Gentry turned Bounder around,

moving them at a trot until she pulled off the road. She didn't want to break a wheel or hurt the horse's legs. This would have to be slow.

"I wish Pa were here," Pearl muttered.

"Me too." Gentry tried to ignore the uneasy feeling in her gut. "Me too."

CHAPTER 2

The ground was fairly level, and both Bounder and the wagon had little problem navigating it. However, to Gentry's dismay, the safe path was a long one, and the strange pools stretched farther north than she thought. By the time she turned the wagon back toward the road, the heavy sun sat on the Oquirrh Mountains' peaks.

Bounder snorted, shook her long mane, and planted her hooves.

"C'mon girl, just a little farther," Gentry prodded, snapping the reins. Bounder moved forward a few steps, then stopped again, hoofing the ground. Gentry's insides twisted into a tight cord that made her shiver. *Please, just go. Please don't make this harder.*

She could do this. They were almost there. She could lead them to American Fork, sell the china, and make it back in good time. They would be all right.

Gentry could be mother and father, just for a little while.

"She's tired," Pearl said.

"No, it's not that." Gentry worried her lip. "C'mon, girl." She shook the reins, almost whipping them. "Giddyup."

Bounder took one step, then backtracked two, straining against her trace.

Gentry clenched her jaw. Glanced to the sun. They could still make it in time. Going back wasn't an option anymore.

She stopped chewing her lip—*not in front of Pearl*—and handed her sister the reins.

"But—"

"It's fine," Gentry assured her, sliding down from the seat. "Keep your eye ahead in case there's a dip or something I don't see."

"What about Indians?"

"There are no Indians around here," she promised, though she found herself scanning the Oquirrhs just in case. Everything had begun to grow shadows. Swallowing, she grabbed Bounder's bridle and tugged her forward.

"Come on, it's safe." Gentry gave it a few good tugs. Bounder took a step forward, then another, at least somewhat content to use Gentry as a shield against whatever had spooked her. There were no wolves in these parts, and she heard no rattlesnakes, but maybe the mare had smelled a mountain lion . . .

Gentry tugged harder, urging the horse back toward the road.

The sky betrayed her, and the sun set faster than it ought to. The mountains cast their great lumbering shadows over the desert. If Gentry reached the road, they could make it to Hannah's before too long, even if they had to ride in the dark.

Pearl lit their lamp and hung it off the side of the wagon as the last dregs of sunlight guided their path.

Gentry tripped, but when she looked back, the ground was smooth, free even of weeds.

Hot air puffed from Bounder's nostrils. Gentry rubbed her nose before grabbing the noseband of the bridle and tugging the horse forward.

Gentry stumbled again.

"Gentry—"

"I'm fine."

"No. I think," Pearl squeaked, "I think it's moving."

"What's moving?"

But then Gentry saw it—saw sagebrush bob like kelp on the sea, the soft movement before a wave came in. The brush farther out bobbed first, then closer, closer.

Bounder tore her bridle from Gentry's hands and reared. Pearl screamed.

"Whoa! Whoa!" Gentry cried, sidestepping to avoid dancing hooves. A soft cracking like a newly fed fire reached her ears, and the ground waved beneath her feet and the wagon. She faltered and grabbed Bounder's trace.

"Gentry!" Pearl cried.

"Hold on!" The ground rippled. Gentry's heart lodged against the back of her tongue, hammering, mad. The earth gurgled. She groped for the wagon. She had to get to Pearl.

Bounder whinnied and reared again. She teetered to one side. The trace bowed as the wagon tipped.

Pearl screamed and grabbed the wagon's side.

A loud *crash* sounded as the box of china slid from the wagon bed and toppled to the ground.

"No!" Gentry cried as Bounder found her footing, righting the wagon. Gentry leaned hard into the horse, the ground bubbling more and more, bucking as though water boiled beneath it. Gentry scrambled for the back of the wagon. "Hold her!" she shouted.

"I'm trying!" Pearl scrambled for the reins.

Pieces of gold-rimmed china lay scattered over the earth. Gentry lunged for them, picking up the shards.

The desert opened a fist-sized mouth and swallowed one of them.

Gentry's eyes bugged. Her pulse radiated in her skull.

The ground bucked again and sucked on her knees.

She screamed.

"Gentry!" Pearl called.

"Get off me!" Gentry cried, swiping at the rippling dust. She tried to stand, but a new wave hit, knocking her onto all fours. Her fingers slipped into the loosening earth. Bounder whinnied in her ears.

More pieces of china sank into the soil.

Then the soil reached up and *grabbed* her.

Cool tendrils like uneven fingers scraped across her neck, wrapping around the necklace there. Gentry screamed and beat at it, turning the earthy limb back to dust. A new hand came up, grabbing the heart-shaped pendant. The chain *snapped* under the weight.

Pearl screamed. The wagon shot toward Gentry—

Another arm wrapped around Gentry's waist, but when Gentry struck it, it remained solid. She lurched backward as the wagon rolled over the spot where she had been, crunching another china plate under its wheel. The dirt claw around her necklace disintegrated, raining earth over the front of Gentry's blouse, leaving the broken chain in her fist.

Finding purchase beneath her feet, Gentry pulled from the new grip and turned to see a man—a man who shone, gold, lightning-shaped lines tracing his neck. She blinked, and the patterns vanished.

He looked down at her with gold eyes and smiled. "You'll be all right. Hold on."

"My sister!" she cried.

He released her and grabbed the back of the wagon, stumbling over the rocking earth. He stretched his left hand out toward the ground, and for a moment Gentry thought she saw it again on his forearm—zigzagging lines of golden light— but they vanished as quickly as they came.

The earth belched and stilled.

"Easy, girl." The man jogged to Bounder. Gentry moved to stop him—the mare was still spooked—but he uttered something under his breath that pricked the horse's ears. She held still, and he pressed his nose to hers, speaking in low tones Gentry couldn't decipher. The mare huffed but was content enough to listen.

Gentry clutched her necklace and stared at him. Stared at the quieted desert. In the distance, a cricket chirped.

"Pearl," she whispered, running on shaky legs to the wagon seat. "Pearl, are you all right?"

Her sister still held the reins, her knuckles white and hands quivering. She met Gentry's eyes and gave a firm nod.

"Thank you," Gentry said to the man by Bounder. The light was dim, but he appeared young, though older than her by a handful of years. "I—"

A seagull squawked, avoiding her feet. Gentry started. A seagull out here, at night?

It wasn't alone. Several of the large, white-and-gray birds lingered around the site, their wings folded back, their webbed feet clumsy against the rocky earth. Many of them studied her, cocking their heads this way and that. There had to be at least two dozen of them.

"You'll be fine now. Though I highly recommend taking the road." The man patted Bounder between the eyes.

Gentry studied him—what features she could see between the twilight and the lantern. He was about Hoss's height and had golden hair swept back from his face. His eyes weren't as golden as she'd thought, but close. The color of browning butter. He wore a simple white shirt and black slacks, but she noticed gold studs in his ears—three in one lobe, four in the other. She'd never seen someone with piercings like that, and certainly not a man.

He grinned at her.

"I-I was," she stuttered, "but . . . the road. There are pools all along it—acidic pools that steam and spray water—"

She thought he'd think her mad, but he merely rubbed his chin and looked toward the Wasatch Mountains. Toward the road. "You don't say? That's quite a problem. Best be on your way before full night falls. The road is just ahead."

"It's—" Gentry began, but as her eyes moved past her savior, she saw the road. Downhill a little, but she saw the two lines formed by wagon tracks and a few lights in the distance—American Fork.

"But I swear it wasn't so close." She jumped as the seagulls around the wagon all took off at once, a spray of feathers and squawks. Gentry shied from them, watching their ascent into the indigo sky. When she looked back, the man was gone.

She turned on her heel, scanning the shadowed area.

"Where did he go?" Pearl asked, relaxing her grip on the reins.

"I . . . don't know." Gentry held her broken necklace in her shaking hand for a moment before pocketing it. Taking several deep breaths, she tried to piece her thoughts together, but they were as broken as the china.

The china. Gentry returned to the back of the wagon and frantically began sifting through the dirt for fragments. How many of the plates had broken? She thought she saw a shadow move in the corner of her vision and started, but when she turned, there was nothing there.

She needed to get Pearl to Hannah's.

Dropping the china fragments into the box of plates, she gritted her teeth, forbidding herself to cry. Not now. *Not in front of Pearl.*

"All right," she said, but the word was airy against the lump forming in her throat. She hefted the box back into the wagon. "Let's go."

As she came around to the wagon seat, she looked back into the bewildering darkness and whispered, "Thank you."

~~~

Lanterns, lamps, and candles alike chased away darkness in clumps from American Fork. The hum of people moving between homes and talking low buzzed like tired insects. It made Gentry nostalgic for Virginia and its fireflies.

"They must have felt the shake," Gentry murmured to Pearl, leading Bounder and their wagon up a dirt road. Her hands trembled, but she tried to still them for her sister's sake.

She saw a man being carried from his house by two others, who supported one of his legs. The glow of a lantern shimmered on wetness on his trousers. Blood.

Gentry urged Bounder forward. *Oh God, please let the Hinkles be all right. Please let them be unscathed.* If they were hurt, or worse . . .

Gentry held her breath. *Caleb.*

The house appeared quickly, and Gentry pulled Bounder before it and threw the brake of the wagon. The lights were on within. There was no damage on the outside that Gentry could see through the dark, but that did little to settle her.

"Pearl, hurry," she urged, trudging to the house. She knocked on the door until her knuckles hurt.

Carolyn Hinkle, Hannah's sister-wife, answered. No sign of injury. Gentry sighed.

"Good heavens, what are you two doing here so late?" She shone her candle over Gentry, and, perhaps noticing Gentry's dirt-covered blouse, exclaimed, "Oh my, come in, come in."

Gentry thanked Carolyn, but she didn't think the older woman heard her. Carolyn turned back into the house so quickly her candle almost went out. "Hannah! The Abrams girls are here!"

"What?" came a high, soft voice from the back of the house. It was a large house, four times the size of Gentry's. Thuds of feet on stairs sounded, and Hannah, dressed in a white print dress, her curly hair poking out from its pins, appeared in the front room.

"Goodness!" she ran toward them. She embraced Gentry first, then Pearl. Hannah was of a height with Gentry and only two years older. "I didn't know you were coming! And the quake! Did you feel it?"

"Are you well?" Gentry asked, looking her over, peering into the rest of the house.

Hannah nodded. "Just some furniture slipped, a few broken dishes."

Broken dishes. Gentry's bones turned to lead within her. "I'm so sorry to bother you. I'm so relieved you're well."

"Bother? No bother at all. And better off than you two, by the looks of it." She took Gentry's hand and lifted it, examining her dirt-streaked dress. It was evident that she and Pearl had, fortunately, not sustained any injuries themselves. "I said you were always welcome, and I meant it, and we haven't retired yet, see?" She smiled, gesturing to her dress. "You must have set out awfully late to get here after dark. The quake, though. Is your horse well? Rooster?"

"Bounder is fine, but I need to board her and brush her down." Guilt crawled up Gentry's ribs like spider legs. "Rooster is at home. I'm sorry to put you out—"

"No more apologizing. We'll take care of everything."

"Caleb?"

Hannah smiled. "He's well. Slept through it."

Carolyn said, "So odd. I've never been in a quake before." She rubbed her arms, perhaps feeling chilled.

"I . . . I don't know what it was," Gentry admitted. And she didn't. She still felt the cool, sandy fingers of the earth grappling for her necklace, which now rested securely in her pocket. Every time she blinked, she saw lightning traces of gold on the back of her eyelids.

She would have thought she imagined it, had Pearl not been a witness.

Hannah smiled. "Let's get you cleaned up and see to the horse. Carolyn, is there any milk left?"

"I'll pour two glasses." The first wife retreated into the kitchen.

Pearl asked, "Caleb is still sleeping?"

Hannah nodded. "But we'll see him in the morning. Do you have spare clothes? Night things?"

"We do," Gentry answered.

"This way." Hannah led them to her bedroom, though Gentry and Pearl both knew the way. "There's already a bowl of water and a cloth on the dresser. I'll send Willard after Bounder when he gets back, and then we'll catch up, hm?"

Gentry assumed Hannah and Carolyn's husband was one of the many scurrying about the streets, helping with the damage the quake caused. "Thank you. So much." Gentry felt weights leave her shoulders and dissipate into the ether as the words passed her lips.

"You're very welcome." Hannah smiled and shut the door.

~~~

Gentry knew the tale sounded absurd, but Hannah kept her expression level, despite Pearl's overly detailed outbursts, which Gentry wished she'd kept to herself. The day's events were far-fetched enough as it was.

Hannah said, "A man just showed up out of nowhere?"

Gentry sipped at the warmed milk in her hands. She

hadn't had milk since . . . well, since the last time she'd stayed at the Hinkle residence. "I don't know where he came from, but he showed up, and the earth stopped shaking."

"Good timing, I suppose." Hannah stifled a yawn.

Pearl added, "Then he vanished with the seagulls."

Hannah blinked. "Seagulls? Were you out by the lake?"

"No, but there *were* seagulls," Gentry said. A lot of seagulls.

"Frightful. And the road like that . . . well, we'll see to it in the morning. You two can take my bed."

Gentry stiffened. "Oh Hannah, we couldn't possibly . . ."

"Gentry Abrams." Hannah put her hands on her hips. "When have you ever been able to win an argument against me? It's too late to be trying, besides." She grinned. "Sleep, and we'll worry about the road and the china when we're not burning through candles."

Pearl leapt from her chair and hugged Hannah, arms around her neck. Setting the cup of milk down, Gentry said, "Thank you."

Gentry and Pearl, after slipping on their nightcaps, crawled into a bed that was a little softer and a little wider than the one they shared at home. Pearl fell asleep quickly, and Gentry lay awake staring at the wall, thoughts of finances and china and family churning through her head to the rhythm of her sister's snores.

When she closed her eyes, she dreamed of seagulls.

～

Broken. All but two plates and a saucer.

Gentry stared into the box. She'd set the larger shards of the gold-rimmed china on the rag rug beside her. She sat on the floor in the Hinkles' front room, box full of broken china in front of her.

Her ma's china. Smashed. Useless.

Gentry's eyes stung. She dug her fingernails into her palms and blinked rapidly. *Don't cry. Not in front of Pearl and Hannah.* Pearl was already sniffling on the chair in the corner.

Gentry was the mother *and* the father now. She had to be the post that supported the fence. *Do. Not. Cry.*

She let out a long breath and pressed a hand against her eyes.

"It's all right," Hannah offered. "We'll make it work."

Willard Hinkle, Carolyn and Hannah's husband, stepped into the room. He was a man nearing forty, almost Hoss's age, with a long mustache and round, silver spectacles. Gentry didn't look at him, only listened to his footsteps and the silence that followed them.

"We're morose today," he said. Gentry felt his eyes on her and on the mess she'd strewn about his carpet. "What's this?"

Hannah answered. Gentry silently thanked her for it, as the returned lump in her throat would have made her own voice squeak. "Gentry and Pearl were hoping to sell some of the china, but their wagon jostled on the way here and the box fell."

Gentry swallowed. "Don't they break it up anyway? For that temple?"

Willard frowned. "I'm afraid not. True, some ceramics were used in Kirtland, but . . . not for this one."

Gentry bit the inside of her lip, her insides feeling like a dried sponge. A moment of silence fell over them. From the corner of her eye, she saw Hannah tilt her head and widen her eyes at her husband.

"But we can make use of it somehow, perhaps," Willard added after a few more stale seconds. "Might be able to find someone to buy the whole pieces."

"Some women might like the broken bits for jewelry,"

Hannah suggested. "Especially the bits with gold trim." She turned to Gentry. "So many of them sold what they had to make the trip out here. There might be interest, especially if you're willing to trade."

"Not sure what we could trade for, but . . ."

Willard said, "I'm going to Salt Lake City to look at some land and get some estimates; I could take it with me. No harm done."

Gentry felt as though someone had blown a very large bubble inside her chest. "Truly?"

Willard nodded. "I'll take it and see what I can get for it. Look around and see if I can sell the whole pieces for more, but there are a lot of poor folk in these parts, so I can't make any promises."

"Yes, please. Anything will do." Gentry quickly gathered the broken pieces and returned them to the box.

"Mind your fingers. Goodness," Hannah said.

Pearl asked, "Are you moving?"

"Oh no, dear," replied Hannah. "I think I mentioned Willard's printing press in Providence, before we came out here. He's hoping to put together a new one."

"It's good work, and we could use a newspaper, hm?" Willard chuckled. When Gentry finished loading the box, he stooped down and picked it up. Gentry shot to her feet to hold the door open for him and closed it after.

A whine sounded down the hall. Gentry perked up.

"Caleb?" she asked.

Hannah nodded, standing. "I'll fetch him."

Caleb, of course, shied away from both Gentry and Pearl, at least at first. Though he was their half brother, he seldom interacted with them. He was well past walking now and had a dozen words to his vocabulary, as well as a near-full set of teeth in his small mouth. Gentry watched as Hannah fed him bits of bread, wrinkling her nose and singing some Mormon song to him. Caleb's tan hands reached for the slice in Hannah's hand after a few minutes, unsatisfied with the offered morsels.

Though they shared a mother, little Caleb didn't look much like Gentry or her siblings. They all had brown eyes, yes, but Caleb's were too dark, as was the case with his skin and hair. That's how Pa had known Ma had been unfaithful. That was why Pa wouldn't keep Caleb after she died.

After his breakfast, Caleb warmed up and let Gentry and Pearl play with him. They rolled a knitted ball back and forth until Caleb's older sister fetched him, as well as two of Carolyn's children. They shared lunch together, and Gentry helped Hannah with the laundry while Pearl took the children outside to play and to tend Bounder. It wasn't until after supper that Gentry stepped away, finding Carolyn in the kitchen.

"I don't know the chances," Gentry fished her ma's necklace from her pocket, "but is there a jeweler nearby?"

She held the chain's ends in her hands. The clasps were still intact, but the ring that held one of them in place was missing. Bent out of shape and dropped somewhere in the desert.

Gentry's fingers grew clammy around the gold. As clammy as her mother's had been as she huffed after delivering Caleb, this locket pressed against the dip in her collarbone. Gentry blinked the image away and tensed the muscles in her stomach to keep her resolve.

"A jeweler? Ha! Few around here can afford it." She glanced over her shoulder at the necklace in Gentry's hands. "Oh dear, what happened?"

The ground reached up and snatched it off my neck, she thought, but she swallowed the words. She wasn't sure that *had* happened, after all. Last night was a blur of confusion. It was easier to pretend it didn't happen than to acknowledge it, but Gentry had never been good at pretending.

She'd seen the ground roll like the ocean off Virginia's coast before a storm. Clearing her throat, she said, "It got caught and snapped."

Carolyn studied it. "Just needs a new ring to connect the clasp. Do you have it?"

Gentry shook her head. What if the chain was irreparable? She certainly couldn't afford to replace the missing gold link unless Pa really did make it big in California.

"Hmm . . . Agnes Snow might have something to hold it in place. If you head down the road," she pointed northward, "to the second right, she's in the triangle-shaped house. Only one on the road. She does all sorts of beading. If nothing else, she can tie a thread around it until you find something better."

"Thank you." The words mingled with a breath of relief. After letting Hannah and Pearl know of her errand, she followed Carolyn's path, nodding to the people in the street—some she recognized, some she didn't. All were Mormon, or so she guessed. One usually couldn't tell a Mormon from a non-Mormon—they didn't wear priest collars or kippah or the like—but most settlers in this area were of their sect.

Gentry turned the corner, noticing three women gibbering beside a man with graying hair. There was nothing to say matrimony tied them—by all means, they were likely stopped for a bit of conversation. The Hinkles were the only polygamous family she knew. Still, Gentry tried to imagine her own future husband, then thought of sharing him with another woman, or two. She frowned, unable to fathom giving her whole heart to a husband who only gave part of his back. And how did he keep them all? Pa had barely supported one wife and her children, even when the wife left the equation.

Agnes's home was not difficult to find. While American

Fork seemed a little bigger every time Gentry visited, it was still sparse, with wide bits of land between houses, though still not as empty as Dry Creek. Gentry knocked on the front door, and an old woman with a cane answered—the very Agnes she was seeking. After Gentry explained herself, Agnes invited her in and, with a pair of pliers, hooked a small nickel ring through the chain and clasp. Gentry had a few pennies on her, but Agnes merely shooed Gentry and her abundant thanks away.

A breeze swept through Gentry's hair as she stepped outside, taking with it the bite of the desert sun. Gentry tied her bonnet about her neck, but didn't bother putting it on her head. She stared off beyond the town to the wide, dry world around her, cupped by mountains, and sighed. Best to enjoy her time here while she could. Willard Hinkle wouldn't be back until tomorrow. Then it was back to Dry Creek and the empty spot at the supper table.

She missed her father. They hadn't been as close since Ma's passing. Or, perhaps, since Caleb's birth, as they had been one in the same. Her father had focused more on work than on family after that, on what needed to be done more than who needed a shoulder to cry on. But he had still been there, sturdy and strong. Gentry prayed he wouldn't be gone too long. Barring that, she hoped he'd find success in California.

Be there for them, Gentry, she thought, but the words sounded in her ma's voice, the cadence out of rhythm with Gentry's footsteps. *Don't overlook Pearl. Don't forget Rooster.*

Maybe she could do something nice for them when she got back. Rooster should take Pa's bed, of course. He was too old to be sleeping with his sisters. Maybe, if the china sold well enough, Gentry could get some honey and make some cakes.

Rooster loved Ma's honey cakes, and it had been so long since any of them had tasted the sweets. Yes, Gentry would do that, even if she had to beg honey from Hoss. Perhaps if she flashed her ankles . . .

Gentry chuckled, shaking her head. What silly thoughts to think, but it felt good to laugh.

She pulled her ma's necklace from her pocket, inspecting the new link. It didn't match, of course, but no one would see it, especially if she had a bonnet on. No one noticed the backs of necklaces. Unclasping it, she strung it around her neck, relishing the familiar weight against her collar.

She looked up, noticing she'd gone too far down the road; she was nearly to the small cemetery. Lost in her thoughts. Ma used to chide her for it.

She turned around to head back, peering down the slightly curved road to see the lengthening shadows coming off houses and people alike.

One of them moved.

Gentry froze, staring at it. Waiting for it to move again, for surely it had been a trick of the light.

A dark, triangular swatch of darkness shifted back and forth. The shadow of a shed. Like it . . . breathed.

Swallowing, Gentry crossed the street and quickened her pace, putting distance between the shed and herself. She stepped in a puddle, but it didn't splash about her shoes as it should.

It hadn't rained in weeks.

Looking down, Gentry saw the puddle wriggle and stretch. Small, white holes opened in it, and the dark stuff glared with dozens of eyes.

Gentry shrieked and raced backward, bits of the thing sticking to her shoe.

"Are you all right, miss?" asked a male voice. Gentry spun

toward a balding man with a sack over his shoulder, but around his feet danced creatures of the wildest kind. Long, translucent bird legs stemmed from slender, pear-shaped bodies. They had half a dozen arms soft as cat tails and faces without eyes or mouth. He didn't seem to notice.

Blood fled Gentry's extremities. She gritted her teeth, her eyes bugging, and backed away.

"Miss?" he asked.

She shook her head. "Y-you don't *see* them?"

The man's brow skewed. "See what?"

She shook her head harder, turned around, and ran down the street, toward the cemetery. The man didn't follow.

She stopped at the short fence around the graves, many of them new, and gripped the wood under her hands, taking in deep breath after deep breath. Wisps of hair stuck to her temples with perspiration.

Anxiety. It was just anxiety. Gentry closed her eyes hard enough to see spots, then blinked the spots away. She focused on the heavy rhythm of her pulse.

A red smile the length of her arm grinned at her from atop one of the graves, set in a violet, raindrop-shaped body twice her size. A massive, grinning blob.

Gentry screamed.

The blob lunged.

She ran.

Direction fled her mind. Gentry bolted down the street until it wasn't street anymore, just flattened wild and crossing trails. The shadows grew as the sun set, spraying orange and salmon across the sky.

Something gray and translucent bubbled from the ground before her. Gentry stopped hard and slid, falling to her knees, scraping her palms on half-earthed pebbles. Sweat beaded along her spine as she scrabbled back to her feet and ran away from it. Her heart palpitated like a plucked fiddle string against the percussion of her breaths and footfalls.

The sun vanished as she ran, and Gentry made the grave mistake of looking up. It was not a cloud that passed overhead, but a giant navy beast, flying through the sky as though tethered to a kite string, tendrils of its dark body squiggling out in the air with no apparent end. Behind it dragged twilight.

The earth rumbled beneath her feet.

"No, no, no! Go away!" She tried to outrun the sky demon above her. Her thoughts flickered back to Pearl and Hannah, to refuge with them, but then she spied the beast from the cemetery following her.

She *ran*.

The farther she ran, the more they came: black birds with noodle-like wings, insects with too many or too few legs that stood knee-height or taller, shapeless ghosts that sang eerily into the descending darkness, following her with their eyes. Gentry clamped her hands over her ears and sprinted as hard as her tiring legs would carry her, racing atop her toes, ignoring the sting in her ribs and the burning in her lungs. She stumbled down a dip in the ground, half twisting her ankle as she went. A single tear fled her eyelashes as she forced weight upon it and ran, raced—

She hit something and shoved it back. Tried to run through it, but hands clasped her wrists and pulled her palms away from her ears.

"Calm down, calm down!" a male voice broke through the jumble of her thoughts. "What's wrong?"

Gentry shook her head, twisting in the man's grip, looking back over the spirits and ethereal creatures. She panted, desperate for air. "They're ... they're everywhere. Can't you see them?"

A serpent passed close to her feet, a foot off the ground. Gentry's muscles seized. "Go *away!*"

"*You* see them?" the voice asked, and a bell of familiarity rang inside her mind. She turned back toward the man, meeting his bright, astonished eyes. "They won't hurt you."

"Y-you see them?" she gasped.

His blond eyebrows pulled together. "I'm surprised *you* do, miss. You didn't see them yesterday."

Gentry took a shaky step back, and the stranger released her wrists. She studied him—his blond hair, swept back from his face. His eyes, the color of browning butter. His simple clothes and the gold studs in his ears.

"You!" She nearly tripped over herself. "You . . . you're from last night . . ."

The man took her hands—her palms stung against his fingers—and pulled her toward a great boulder in the earth. Shimmers like small lightning bugs skittered over its face. He waved his hand and they scattered—only then did Gentry recognize their translucent bodies, their misshapen forms. More of the . . . monsters.

"They won't hurt you," he repeated. "At least, they shouldn't."

"*Shouldn't?*"

"Shhh, look." He turned her around and gestured to the valley before them, at the swirling spirits and beasts roaming it. The great kite-thing had already fled, leaving twilight behind.

Gentry stepped back until her shoulders hit the boulder. She leaned heavily against it, catching her breath, trying to steady herself. "Wh-what are they?"

"Wild magic," the golden man said. "No one has bespelled it, so it shouldn't have any purpose with you besides mild curiosity. Not this close to other humans."

"Other ... humans ..." She eyed him, head to toe to head, ensuring that he was *human* and not ... wild magic. "I don't understand."

"Of course you don't." He grinned. "Few do, especially our kind. Your kind."

"What's the difference?" Her question sounded sharper than she'd intended, but her breath was coming back, and she put its full force into the words.

"Our kind. Whites, Anglos, what have you." His tone was as casual as it would be over a cup of tea. "Your kind, the religious folk."

"I'm not a Mormon," she snapped.

"I ... didn't say you were." His smiled faded for just a moment. A second later, it came back in full strength. "What did you say your name was?"

"I didn't." Another serpent curled around the boulder. She bit down on a shriek as it neared her leg.

"You've obviously done something to draw their attention," he said, his manner too easy for Gentry's liking. "It won't hurt you. Shoo."

He kicked a booted foot at it, and the strange creature changed direction, slithering toward the Oquirrhs.

"I—it's Gentry." She sucked in a deep breath. "My name. Gentry Abrams."

"Isn't that a boy's name?"

"Well I certainly didn't choose it!" She ached for something to climb to distance herself from the cacophony of ... *this.* "I don't understand any of this! Magic doesn't exist!"

The man laughed. "Either it does, or we're both crazy, Gentry."

He paused, looking at her neck. No, her necklace. His face wrinkled for a second, then slid back into place. "Ah, I bet that's it. May I?"

She touched the heart pendant. "May you *what*?"

He stepped around her and pinched the chain of her necklace. His too-familiar touch made her skin heat like the summer sun. She would have jerked away if not for fear of snapping the delicate chain

He unclasped the necklace. The moment he pulled it from her skin, the monsters disappeared.

Gentry gasped, spun. Winced at her ankle.

Gone. Every last one. Before her stretched quiet, *peaceful* desert. Vanished with the lifting of her necklace. The sky held only fading colors and stretching twilight. She couldn't see any houses or the lights of the town. How far had she run?

"How did you—?"

"I think they enchanted it when they took it." He let the gold chain dangle from his fingers.

"What are *they*?" she whispered.

"Wild magic. It's here. It's always here, if you're in the right place," the man answered. "Fewer in the cities, always more at night."

"But I . . . they were on the road, in the cemetery . . ."

"You're from American Fork?" he asked.

She shook her head. "J-just visiting. Please, give it back to me."

The man held up the necklace, studying it for a moment. "Are you sure?"

She nodded too quickly. "I want to know where they are."

"They're mostly harmless." He handed her the necklace. Gentry clasped it, and her vision changed. The ghosts filled it again. There were more of them deeper in the valley, away from town. Dancing, shifting, shapeless shadows.

"You're all right?" he asked, looking at her hands. Her palms were scraped and bloody.

Gentry didn't answer, not right away. She took a limping

step away from the boulder, then another, peering around it toward American Fork. Or where American Fork should be.

A realization struck her. She turned back to the man.

"You see them."

He nodded.

"You said . . . last night. They were there?"

He smiled.

"You stopped them, didn't you." Her own words sounding somehow foreign to her ears. "You . . . shooed them away."

"Something like that." He stepped forward and took her hand, the one that didn't clutch the necklace, and opened it. As he examined it, Gentry noticed a seagull atop the boulder.

When she turned her gaze back to him, she found herself looking into his eyes. The twilight hid her flushing cheeks.

"I won't hurt you, either," he promised. "Since we're already out here and sharing secrets, why don't I take care of this, hm?"

He held her hand to her face. Now that Gentry's attention wasn't solely focused on the spirits—the wild magic—she noticed the sting of her palms.

She nodded once. It was enough.

The man stepped back, still holding her hand, and waved his arm through the air.

From behind the boulder soared dozens—no, *hundreds*—of seagulls, soaring into the air in a sea of white and gray, some diving down, others turning in sharp curves. The wind their wings created rustled Gentry's hair and fluttered about her skirt. Her eyes widened at the sight of the man's forearm. Patterns of lightning glowed gold beneath his skin. No—those were his *veins*.

The birds spiraled, forming shapes, their individual bodies blurring together, hardening into something distinctly not *bird*.

Within moments, a white-and-gray mottled *house* loomed before them, hovering above the ground just as the ethereal serpents had.

CHAPTER 3

G entry was going to faint.

She stumbled back, nearly tripping as the house formed before her, solid and . . . house-like. As though it had been carved from marble. Other than the color, one would never have guessed it was made from—

"Seagulls," she whispered, and she pinched herself. She was going mad. She knew it. Something deep inside her brain had snapped.

Something else not-normal purred softly behind her. She jumped and swatted away a small, hovering blob-thing.

The man gestured to the door. "After you."

She swallowed and thought of Pearl. But Pearl wasn't alone. She'd be fine. But would she be worrying? Did she think Gentry was merely chatting with Agnes?

But Gentry was alone. With a man. Whom she assumed was unmarried and whose motives were not abundantly clear.

"How do I know you're not going to kill me?" she blurted.

The man laughed. His laugh had a nice sound to it, a sort of easy genuineness that cut through some of the taut threads connecting Gentry's rational brain to the rest of her body. "I'm harmless, especially to a pretty face." He stepped into the house and patted the door frame. It sounded solid enough. "See? Safe."

Was he referring to the house or himself? Gentry inched forward, unsure of how to handle the compliment regarding her appearance. Was he trying to put her at ease, or did he really think . . . not that it mattered. In a place as sparse at this, it wasn't hard to be pretty. There were only so many single women to look at.

She stepped into the house and looked around. Pale lights shone in the corners, but there were no candles or lamps. Where did that light come from?

The man—his eyes more golden now—slipped by her and guided her to sit on a white-and-gray block in the front room. He went to another, higher block and knocked on it. "Come now, Turkey," he chided. "My pack, please."

The block grew feathers, ruffled them, then spat out an old leather pack. Gentry's breath hitched at the sight of it. The seagull house had hidden compartments in it? *Surely this is a dream.*

"Thank you," the man said.

It took Gentry a moment to relocate her breath. When she did, she asked, "T-turkey?"

"Thinks he's bigger than he is, and half the time you want to shoot him." The man winked. He sat on the floor by Gentry's feet and shuffled through the pack until he found some sort of ointment and some thin bandages. Oh. For her.

She shifted on her bird-bench. "It's not so bad—"

"Hush. It will help."

Hesitant, Gentry opened her left hand. The cuts looked angry in the bright, unearthly light. He dabbed them with the ointment. She studied his face while he focused on her hands. She gauged him at about twenty-five, twenty-six. His nose was strong without being prominent. Some of the gold from his eyes had faded, but maybe that was a trick of the light too.

He had four gold studs in each ear instead of the three and four he wore yesterday. Gentry had never seen a man with pierced ears, and while his now normal-colored eyes calmed her, the piercings were confusing.

"Um," she said as he wrapped a short length around her palm, *What did you do to your ears? How did you turn seagulls into marble?* "What was your name?"

"One moment." He lightly dabbed ointment across her palm. Gentry flinched, but the stranger kept her fingers in a soft yet firm grip, and in moments the sting of the cuts subsided to a warm buzz.

Surely he can't be bad, she told herself as he cut a strip of bandage, wrapped it around her hand, and tied it in an almost cute bow. Then he offered his own hand. Gentry awkwardly shook it.

"Winn," he said.

"Win what?"

"My name." A bright, wide grin stretched his lips. "Winn. Nice to meet you, Gentry Abrams."

"Well, Winn"—he moved to her other hand, and she relaxed somewhat—"can you explain this to me?"

She held up the necklace with her wrapped hand.

"Earth spirits. Last night." He applied ointment to her unbound palm. "They stay away from roads and cities. You were traveling over highly magicked ground, Gentry. They're stirring because of the mining, and they sensed your gold."

The words buzzed through Gentry's brain like angry flies. "Wait, what?"

"Gold." He tied a bandage into a second little bow on her other hand. Leaning back, he met her eyes. "It's what they feed on. Gold."

"That makes no sense."

"I don't make the rules." He grinned. "But there were strong spirits migrating through here yesterday. I think they mistakenly enchanted that necklace of yours, which might explain why the others are bothering you. They know you can see them, and that's an exciting prospect."

The center of Gentry's forehead began to pulse. Sighing, she put her elbows on her knees and rubbed her temples. "None of this makes sense."

"That's because you don't want it to," he said, "and it won't until you stop trusting what others have told you and start believing in what you feel."

She eyed him.

"Hagree proverb," he said, referring to the Indians in the most western parts of Utah Territory.

He sat straight, took her necklace, and placed it on her fingers above her bandage. He placed her other hand on top of it. "Don't you feel it?"

Gentry only felt her own pulse, which radiated in the scrapes along her palms. She glanced down to his hands.

"Sorry." He grinned all the more and released her.

"Winn."

"Hm?"

"How do you know all this? Do all . . . this?" She gestured to the house around them.

"That, dear Gentry, is a long story. Perhaps for another night." He stood and stretched. "You don't perchance know an Ira Maheux, do you?"

Gentry shook her head.

"Ah, well." He stretched his arms overhead for a moment before settling them onto his hips. "Just visiting. Where's home then, if I might ask?"

Gentry glanced to the bandages on her hand. Twice this

man had been kind to her. She didn't think it was a coincidence. "Dry Creek."

"I don't know it."

"It's small. Barely worth a dot on the map." She pocketed the necklace. She couldn't bring herself to wear it, not right now. "South and a little west. A day's ride." Her face fell at the prospect of morning. She began wringing her left index finger, but she winced when she tugged on the scraped skin of her palms. "Are the . . . spirits . . . gone from there?"

"I imagine so. But the road is fine, now."

She straightened. "You saw that? The ponds?"

Winn rubbed his chin. Something about the movement made him look older. "Yes. Nasty stuff. Happening more and more."

Gentry stood, then wobbled a little with the movement of the house. Was it going somewhere? She placed a hand on the wall to steady herself, then pulled it back when an unseen beak nipped at her. "There are more ponds like that?"

Winn sighed. "Ponds, quakes, sometimes even storms. It's a mess."

"Why are they happening?" Gentry still smelled the harsh stink of sulfur in her sinuses, felt the earthy claws grappling for her neck. She shivered.

Winn noticed. "Cold?"

She shook her head.

"The magic in this world—what's left of it—feeds off gold," he said, softer. "When we pull too much of it out of the earth, it offsets the balance."

Gentry reached into her pocket and touched her necklace. Did he mean California? The mines? They were . . . offsetting the balance? Causing these pools and quakes that threatened her friends and family?

Was her father all right?

Chewing her lip, she turned to Winn and studied him, his hair that could have been made of gold thread, his gold-flecked eyes watching her. They crinkled as he smiled. She blushed, and he laughed.

"Well, Gentry Abrams," he said as though her first and last name were all one word, "will it be American Fork or Dry Creek?"

She perked. "You can take me there?"

"I would hardly be a gentleman if I didn't."

A small smile tugged on Gentry's mouth. "American Fork, please. My sister is there. The house off of Chipman Road, if you know it."

"I'll get you as close as I can. Might startle a few night owls." The house shifted. Based on the pressure in her belly, it felt like over and up. The unearthly light within dimmed to a twilightesque blue. Gentry peered out the window, but she saw only the occasional lantern. The valley had grown too dark to see anything but emerging stars.

After a minute or so, Winn offered his hand. Gentry eyed him. Did he want to shake it again?

"So you don't fall," he said.

Gentry clasped his hand. The moment she did, the floor gave out from beneath her. She shrieked as birds reformed and broke apart from each other, carrying the scent of salt water and brine shrimp on their wings. The walls collapsed, then the roof, turning into a torrent of feathers and webbed feet.

Gentry bit down another scream as wings whipped by her. Her free hand gripped Winn's arm, and she protected her face against his chest.

Seconds later, the storm died down, and Gentry felt solid ground beneath her feet.

Lifting her head, Gentry searched for the birds. A few of them waddled over dark ground, moonlight glinting off their eyes. She recognized the edge of American Fork—the turnery. Chipman Road was perhaps a five-minute walk.

If any of the town's residents saw the unbecoming of the bird-house, they stayed hidden.

"You all right?"

Gentry immediately released Winn and stepped back, though he kept his hold on her hand. "I . . . yes, thank you."

He grinned. "Until we meet again."

"Again?" Gentry chirped, but the word wasn't loud enough to carry past her lips. Did he expect another coincidence, or was a reunion *intended*? Her stomach fluttered at the thought.

Winn actually bowed to her, and, at the bow's lowest point, kissed her hand. Jitters burned an uneven trail up her arm.

Then he turned and walked away—only a dozen steps or so before the birds flocked again, a tornado of bodies that swallowed the golden man and hid him in the shadows of the mountains.

~~~

Gentry kept the necklace in her pocket for the sake of her sanity. Even without the ghosts, her hands trembled when she touched it.

"Oh, I was getting worried." Hannah lay a hand on her chest when Gentry came through the door of the Hinkle house. She sat in a chair in the front room nursing her baby girl, Rachel, who was only four months old. "Pearl was about to head to Agnes's to see what kept you so long."

Gentry's fingers brushed the bandages about her hands. "Oh . . . yes. She's quite chatty."

"Agnes? Really?" Hannah asked. "She must have taken a liking to you, I suppose. Was she helpful?"

"Oh, yes. All fixed."

"Your hands!"

"I fell," she answered too quickly, though that much was the truth. She didn't know how to explain Winn and the spirits without sounding completely loony, so she didn't, for now. "But I'm patched up. Can I, uh, help with anything before bed? Where's Pearl?" She struggled to adjust to the here and now. She felt like she'd just fallen from a storybook. Everything around her appeared so ordinary.

"She's just out of the bath. Should be in your room."

"*Your* room, Hannah."

The woman smiled. "All the same, in the end. Willard should be home tomorrow. I've been praying for you, Gentry, and I think we'll get good news."

"Thank you," she said. "I'll go . . . find Pearl."

~~~

Sleep played games of hide-and-seek with Gentry that night. When it hid, she lay awake in Hannah's bed listening to Pearl's breathing and thinking of magic. She stared hard at the shadows in the corners of the room, waiting for them to move or blink, but they remained still. She ran her fingers over the bandaging around her hands, thinking of Winn and his house of birds. She broke apart and repieced his words: magic, gold, spirits, mining. Mining?

Her thoughts turned to her father and wondered at the connection.

When sleep sought her, she had torrential dreams that were more pictures and colors than anything with a semblance of story. Swirling seagulls, golden gardens, clusters of kite-like spirits dragging across the sky.

Gentry woke early, not willing to play another round of hide-and-seek, and went to the kitchen to set the table for breakfast. Doing what she could to earn her keep. Carolyn was up not long after, and Gentry helped her grate potatoes for hash browns and form dough into biscuits. The Hinkle family barely fit around their kitchen table. A few more years and they'd have to get a second.

Gentry tried not to think of the empty space at her own.

After everyone had roused and Gentry broke a biscuit into pieces for Caleb, Willard returned home. Carolyn greeted him first, then Hannah, both with equal fondness. Gentry tried not to think on the oddness of it and cast Pearl a withering look when Pearl opened her mouth to comment. She, thankfully, closed it without much sound.

"Mr. Hinkle." Gentry wrung her finger again. She caught herself and stashed her hands behind her back. "Were you successful with the china?" Her voice softened with each word, ending the sentence in a near-whisper. How would she explain herself to Rooster if she came home poorer than when she left?

"Ah, yes, nearly forgot." Willard opened a small suitcase and fished around in it until he found an envelope. "I don't know how much you were hoping for, but I did manage to sell all of it."

Gentry glanced to Pearl, who frowned. Her sister had wanted to save at least one piece of china, for sentimentality.

Gentry took the envelope and opened it. There were several coins within, totaling about two dollars.

A heaving sigh escaped her mouth, and a warm shiver coursed from her shoulders into her hands. "Thank you." She closed the envelope and smiled. "This will help. Thank you, truly."

Willard grinned. "It's no problem. How long are you two staying?"

Gentry turned to Pearl. "Not long, I'm afraid. We'll need to leave soon to get back before dusk."

Pearl frowned. "But the road—"

"It's fine now." A crispness formed in her chest. "I mean, I heard it was." All truth.

"Hmm." A wrinkled formed between Hannah's eyebrows. She studied Gentry, who averted her eyes to a spot on the carpet. "I guess the water receded. Place is so dry, probably sucked it right back up. Here, let me pack you a lunch."

"Oh, thank you!" Pearl followed Hannah into the kitchen. It was no secret that the Hinkles had nicer food than the Abrams. Gentry shook her head and stowed the money in the pocket of her skirt. Half an hour later, she drove herself and her sister back to Dry Creek.

~~~

Rooster arrived at the house at the same time Gentry and Pearl did, with the sun starting its descent in the sky. His clothes were dirtier than usual, the bridge of his nose sunburned, and his hair heavy with sweat. Hoss strode beside him, dusty and suntanned.

"What took so long?" he asked, wiping his hands on a handkerchief not much cleaner than the rest of him. "Hoss here was about to set out looking for you."

"The road flooded." Pearl hopped off the wagon the moment it came to a stop. "It flooded and it smelled terrible, and we had to go around, and then an earthquake shook us and broke all the china."

Hoss laughed. "That's some imagination."

Pearl's brows touched. "It's no imagination, Mr. Howland. I swear it."

"Don't swear," Rooster chided.

"It's true." Gentry slid from the wagon herself. Hoss moved as though to help her, but he only made it a step before she touched the ground. "A geyser opened up on the road, and we had to go around."

Hoss's eyes widened. "A geyser?"

Gentry nodded, moving to Bounder and scratching the mare under her forelock. "And we broke the china, but still managed to sell it. Willard Hinkle took it into town for me. We had to wait for his return until we could head back."

"Caleb?" Rooster asked.

Gentry smiled. "He's getting big." She glanced at Hoss. She didn't want to talk about money, or her bastard brother, with him standing there. Rooster must have sensed it, for he didn't ask more.

"We got two dollars!" Pearl shouted.

Gentry rubbed her thumb and forefinger into her eyes.

"Well that's something." Hoss smiled. Eyes on Gentry, he added, "Can I help you with anything? Stable the horse for you?"

"I can do it." Rooster led Bounder and the wagon toward the stable.

"Thank you for keeping an eye on him," Gentry said to Hoss.

"Just glad to see you and Miss Pearl all in one piece. We were right worried." Hoss removed his hat and ran his fingers back through his hair.

Gentry fiddled with the ties of her bonnet. "Well, I'll not have you wandering around in the dark, Hoss Howland. Thank you for seeing to us. I'll send Rooster by in the morning."

Hoss tipped his hat. "Good day to you." He smiled at Pearl before turning and heading back for his farm, passing a glance back to Gentry once he hit the road. The gesture made a spot between her shoulder blades itch.

Kneading tightness from her abdomen, she headed into the house, Pearl following behind. Finding her father's ledger, Gentry filled in the new income. The numbers were looking better.

Not good, but better.

~~~

Her father hadn't written while Gentry and Pearl were gone, but such was to be expected—he wouldn't be to California yet. Gentry hoped he would write along the way, but it had only been a few days. Letters would come. Just one letter would lend Gentry strength for her new role.

As Gentry worked the garden the next day, Pearl weeding beside her, a squawk brought her attention to the fence. There, balancing on the farthest post, stood a seagull regarding her with one eye, its beak slightly open as though it were panting. Gentry straightened, wondering at it—seagulls didn't frequent Dry Creek—but when she moved toward it, the bird flapped its wings and took off.

She watched it go, searching for more of its kind, but the gull appeared to be solitary. Surely it wasn't one of Winn's. And what purpose would Winn have sending a gull this way?

Until we meet again, he had said. Gentry had mentioned living in Dry Creek, but there were few enough people in town that it wouldn't be too hard to find a specific person. All he'd have to do was ask Mr. Olson at the mercantile.

Her skin prickled. She looked at Pearl, wondering if she should mention her bizarre visit, but decided against it. Had it not been for the bandages on her hands, which were now discarded, she would have thought she'd hit her head on the way back from Agnes's and dreamed it all.

Her necklace weighed down her pocket. She still chose ignorance over wearing it.

Gentry counted it a blessing that her father had taken Rose. It left only one horse to care for. Feeding Bounder took more out of their budget then feeding themselves did, but all that would get easier once the garden started to produce. There were wild grass and weeds about that Bounder grazed on between meals of hay and bran, though unfortunately the mare had no interest in sagebrush, and that they had aplenty.

The weather cooled significantly the following day, much to Gentry's pleasure. The day after all three of them over-slept—storm clouds in the sky had dulled the sunlight.

Gentry woke with a start. "Rooster, Rooster! You'll be late!"

Rooster lifted his head from his pillow on the other bed. It took a few seconds, but realization struck him. He swore and jumped out of bed, pulling on his dirty trousers from the day before and pounding his feet into his boots.

Gentry didn't fear Rooster's job was in jeopardy—Hoss was a kind and reasonable man, and even if he weren't, Gentry knew a few kind words from her would smooth anything over. Still, the job was indispensable.

Gentry dressed herself and yelled after Rooster, "Did you get something to eat?"

"I'll pick from my lunch," he called back, and he bolted out the door. The satchel that bounced at his hip, containing his noontime meal, looked too flat, too light. Pa's lunches had never looked so small.

Gentry sighed. Turning to the window, she peered out to the heavy storm clouds. They could certainly use a good rain, though the clouds had a strange texture to them, almost like curdled milk, and a nearly burgundy hue. Gentry had never seen clouds like those before. Not in Utah Territory, not in Virginia, and not in the places in between.

Thunder rumbled far beyond the mountains.

Returning to the room where Pearl was brushing her hair, Gentry opened the drawer of the shared nightstand and retrieved her ma's necklace. She glanced about the house with it in her hand, seeing nothing out of the ordinary. Stepping outside—the air smelled stale and rainy—she noticed a few glimmering shapes far toward the Wasatch Mountains, moving away from her. A fading spot of blue in the sky. Then nothing.

Rooster returned as Gentry scrubbed the last breakfast dish. "Hoss is calling it quits today." He hung his hat on a nail near the door. "The storm looks bad."

Gentry pinched her lips together but nodded. A day without pay. She'd have to write that in her ledger. One day shouldn't be so bad. They would survive.

As if sensing her thoughts, Rooster said, "I think I'll go to the mill this weekend, see if they're hiring extra help."

The mill, where her father had worked before setting out west. "You think Pa's position is still open?"

Rooster shrugged. "Worth a shot." A grin spread on his face. "Besides, maybe Pattie Benson will be there."

Gentry rolled her eyes. "All right, lover boy, why don't you bring in some water before the heavens drown us in it?"

Her words were ominous, for not half an hour later, the sky tore open and poured out its sorrows.

The storm banged with thunder that made Pearl shriek and assaulted the town with a downpour so heavy Gentry could barely see out the windows. Within minutes, puddles formed over the earth. Their roof began to leak in one corner. Rooster set a bucket under the drip.

"The plants," Gentry murmured. She hurried into the bedroom and pulled the blankets off her bed, rolled them in her arms, and rushed outside.

The rain bit her skin like horseflies. Large drops careened from the clouds and slapped the ground. Gentry should have grabbed her bonnet—rain skewed her vision.

She was soaked by the time she reached the garden gate. Unfurling the blankets, she set them over the crops. Several smaller plants had already been beaten down. She hadn't grabbed enough to cover all the crops, and she couldn't, not unless she wanted every blanket in the house muddied. She set out the two she had over the more fragile crops, then stood, her heels sinking half an inch into fresh mud.

The sound of the storm was heavy and constant, like someone shushing into both her ears without pausing for breath. How long would it last? Would the other plants survive? Would the roof leak more? Was the stable roof strong enough to withstand it? What if the rain caused a flood?

Gentry drew in wet air until her lungs stretched to their limits, then let it out all at once. She was drenched. Every hair on her head, every layer on her body. Even the insides of her shoes squelched.

She laughed.

The first few chuckles hurt, like the first breaths after a heavy cough. But the laughter flowed freely, a bird caged too long, finally stretching its wings.

This was ridiculous.

Gentry wiped rain off her face, not that it made a difference. At least she wouldn't need to take a bath now. That made her laugh more.

Pearl's voice barely pierced the din of the rain, calling from the house. Tipping her head back, Gentry opened her mouth, surprised at how quickly the rain filled it. She trudged back to the front door, her shoes squeaking and squashing with each step.

Rooster stood in the doorway. "You're loony," he said. "What are you doing standing—"

Gentry spit the water into his face.

Rooster's eyes bugged. His jaw dropped. Pearl gasped behind him.

His lip quirked. "You're dead."

He rushed her, bending over and grabbing her around the waist. With a grunt, he managed to heave Gentry over his shoulder. Gentry screamed and beat at his back, but Rooster hefted her to a large puddle and dropped her into it. Muddy water splashed in an uneven ring around her.

Gentry spit grit out of her mouth, laughed, and grabbed onto her brother's leg. "Pearl! Help me!"

Pearl hesitated as Rooster struggled in Gentry's grasp, but eventually ran out—leaving the door open—and crashed into Rooster's other leg, landing all three of them in the mud.

The heavy rain washed the dirt from their faces. Pearl splashed Rooster, Gentry splashed Pearl. Their giggles cut through the fog of the storm, and despite the heaviness of her soaking clothes, Gentry felt lighter than she had in a week.

Rooster found his feet and ran toward the stable, Pearl chasing after him. Her skirt was a good three inches longer with all the water weighing it down.

Shielding her eyes, Gentry followed. Rooster grabbed the water pail from outside Bounder's pen and dumped it over his sister's hair. Gentry held her sides and laughed.

Thunder bellowed overhead without lightning, drawing Gentry's attention back heavenward. Her heart skipped a beat as she checked her pocket, but fortunately her ma's necklace still nestled there, safe and sound.

She looked about as she touched the gold and spun slowly

as she searched the valley. Even in the untamed land away from the town, she didn't see a single spirit. Not one eye, blob, or ripple. The absence relieved her, yet a small part of her wanted to see the magic, to reassure herself that what happened in American Fork had, indeed, happened.

Rain trailed hundreds of paths from her hair down her face and neck, and she wondered at it. She didn't know much about this realm hidden within her own, but she wanted to.

What sort of storm scared off even the most terrifying of spirits?

CHAPTER 4

June 7

Dearest Pa,

I hope your travels have been good and that you've been safe on the roads. We've had strange troubles along the paths back home; I pray all has been smooth for you and Rose.

Pearl was humming that song you used to sing to us as children, but for the life of us we can't remember one of the lines. Young ladies in town, and those that live 'round, wear none but your own country linen . . . *and then we cannot recall the third line. Do tell us when you write back. We shall try our hardest to imagine it in your voice.*

We had quite a storm last week. It caused a flash flood in some of the lower points in the valley, but thankfully not in Dry Creek. It did, however, pulverize quite a few plants in the garden. I'm holding my breath, hoping the stalks were sturdy enough for them to come back. Else we'll have to replant and cross our fingers.

And Pa . . . if scary things happen at the mines, you'll come home, won't you?

Rooster passes on his regards. Hoss has been good to us,

increasing his wages and hours. Still, I hope to hear from you soon.

Much Love,
Gentry Sue

"What's that?" Rooster asked, kicking his boots off with more force than usual as he came into the house.

Gentry folded the paper. She used only one sheet, not wanting to waste. Not wanting to purchase more. "A letter to Pa."

"Where will you send it?"

"The Boston Company. He'll get it when he arrives, if he hasn't already. I'm sure he'll send us a better address." She lifted her gaze from the paper and cringed. "Oh Rooster, there's a nasty thing on your shoulder."

Rooster turned his head to his right shoulder, where a dark and rather large grasshopper sat. He swatted it off.

"Not in the house!" Gentry cried.

Rolling his eyes, Rooster brought his socked foot down and crunched the intruder.

Gentry huffed as she stood. "You're in a foul mood. Pattie turn down your advances?"

She meant it in jest, but Rooster didn't smile. He collapsed in one of the threadbare chairs. "Mill isn't hiring. Said they didn't plan to anytime soon."

Gentry drooped. "They already filled Pa's position?"

Rooster shrugged. "Guess so. Didn't seem interested in talking to me."

Gentry frowned. "Rude of them. After Pa worked there and all."

Rooster didn't reply, and silence filled the house for several heartbeats.

Her brother tilted his head. "Pearl?"

"Gone to Ann's."

"Hmm. Storm brought a lot of gulls."

Gentry perked and hurried to the nearest window, peeking outside. The puddles from the storm had sunk into the earth, but a few seagulls flapped about the yard and beyond, never seeming content to stay in one spot. They pecked at the ground and at each other, occasionally taking flight for half a second before resettling somewhere else.

Gentry let out a sigh. "Maybe we can shoot one for supper."

"Pa took the gun."

"He did? Why would he do that?" Gentry's stomach clenched. Not for hunger . . . she'd eaten just an hour ago.

"Indians, I guess." Rooster shrugged and closed his eyes, his head leaning against the back of the chair.

Sighing, Gentry sealed her letter and scrawled the address provided by the mercantile owner. With nothing better to do, Rooster morose, and Pearl gone to play, she might as well make the trek to post it now. She rubbed the folded paper between her thumb and fingers. *Don't forget us,* she thought.

After fixing her hair, Gentry slid her bonnet over her bun and tied it beneath her chin. "I'm heading into town. Do we need anything?"

Rooster, body still and arms folded across his chest, didn't answer. He'd set his hat over his eyes. Tiptoeing past him, she stepped into the too-bright daylight.

Gentry eyed the half-empty stable. It wasn't a terribly long walk to the mercantile, which handled all the mail coming and going on wagon trains. She wanted to stretch her legs, besides. Bounder likely felt the same, so she crossed their yard to her stall, tucking a loose lock of hair under the brim of the bonnet. She checked the mare's feed and water first before opening the pen. Bounder wouldn't wander away, just mosey around the property, chewing on what weeds smelled appetizing.

Bounder cleared the stall door, then hesitated, nickering softly. Her head bounced left and right, her nostrils wide.

"What's wrong?" Gentry asked, running her hand on the velvet of Bounder's nose. She turned about, searching the property and beyond for a coyote. She saw none. Her skin prickled, remembering the earthquake near American Fork.

Bounder blew hard through her nostrils.

One hand still on Bounder's nose, Gentry slipped the other into her pocket, where her ma's necklace lay. Her fingers brushed its chain, and she looked around once more. Palmed the heart pendant. Saw a shadow on her shoulder.

Shrieking, Gentry stumbled back from the mare, both hands brushing her shoulder, her bonnet. Nothing there. Chest light and pulsing, Gentry snatched the necklace out of her pocket, and her eyes cleared. There, on the dirt between her and the horse, bobbed a tar-like thing half made of shadow. It had dark pits for eyes and was shaped like the gummy candy sold in jars at the mercantile.

The "eyes" focused on the necklace in Gentry's hand.

"Go away!" she cried, taking a few steps back. Bounder huffed, but the mare's eyes never focused upon the creature— the *wild magic*. The blob bounced forward, none of the drying dirt of the ground sticking to its smooth, spectral form. It rolled to the right almost playfully, splitting into two smaller versions of itself.

Gentry staggered back.

They won't hurt you, Winn's voice said in her memory.

The twin creatures bobbed toward her, water-like.

"Go away!" She looked around to see if anyone had heard. She was, of course, alone.

The blobs watched her necklace, contorting their strange bodies to follow it when Gentry flailed. What had Winn said about them? They eat gold? *They certainly won't be eating this!*

"Shoo, shoo!" She waved at them, trying to usher them away in the same manner Winn had with the serpent. "You're not wanted."

A shadow fell on her shoulder. Gentry turned to see a third blob of wild magic perched beside her ear. She registered a subtle coolness from its body but no weight before biting down on another shriek and trying to beat it off with her fist. It was, however, the fist that held her ma's necklace, and the blob latched onto it with some unknown appendage, chewing on the fine chain.

"You can't have it!" Gentry shouted, flinging her arm toward the ground and dislodging the creature. The other two blobs watched it right itself. "Go away!"

The third blob, the largest of the three, obediently turned and began bouncing back toward the stable. The other two bobbed toward her in an unsure manner.

For a moment, Gentry's tongue stuck to the roof of her mouth. She swallowed and watched the blob go.

"Stop," she tried, then wondered at herself.

The wild thing stopped and twisted toward her.

Good heavens, it's listening to me. She took a step back. One of the twin blobs followed, and she kicked at it, sending it scurrying back to its mate.

"Do you . . ." She swallowed again. "Do you understand me?"

The blob watched her.

Opening her hand, cupping her palm so the creatures wouldn't see, she checked over her necklace, expecting another broken link. She found none. If this *wild magic* had gotten a taste, it had been a very tiny one.

And now it listened to her?

She thought of Winn's gulls and licked her teeth.

"Shoo," she ordered the twin blobs as she took a few steps toward the listening one, kicking at them with her feet. A few paces from the blob, she said, "Well, then, jump up and down."

The blob jumped.

A smile tempted Gentry's lips. "Do it again."

This time the blob just watched her, disobedient. A strange, almost dizzying sensation flooded her mind, like her thoughts had become slick with oil. She blinked a few times and shook her head, but her mind had gone incoherent, and she couldn't—

Bounder nudged her shoulder, and Gentry came back to herself, eyeing the horse. She rubbed her forehead, then looked back toward the blobs. All three had disappeared, as had the strange sensation in her head.

Shaking herself, she clasped the necklace around her neck and tucked the locket beneath her collar.

"Sorry, girl." She patted Bounder's neck. "They're gone. Be good."

Reaching into her other pocket, Gentry fingered the letter to her father and walked briskly in the direction of the mercantile as her thoughts reordered themselves. Mail the letter, stretch her legs. She started to mull over what chores needed doing upon her return when a seagull standing off the path not far from her let out a weak squawk. She glanced to it, then to another grasshopper near it, similar to the one that had accosted Rooster. The gull eyed her, then seized the insect, crunching it in its beak. Gentry gagged and stepped around it. The bird didn't seem frightened of her at all.

Gentry fingered her necklace through her collar as she walked, wondering at the blobby, candy-like creatures, wondering at wild magic and itching to see Winn one more time, if only to ask him more about it. She walked past the parcel of land her family owned and a little ways down the road before something crunched under her boot, emitting a loud and sickening sound. Pulling back, she saw a grasshopper under her sole, this one larger than the first two. Ahead, another one of the bugs leapt from the road, joining three more on a patch of wild grass.

One of the seagulls cried behind her. She spun and watched it flap into the air, blinding her as it passed in front of the sun. Once she'd blinked the light from her eyes, she noticed a new storm brewing in the distance. Shielding her vision with a hand across her forehead, she squinted at the low, dusty-looking clouds. Queasiness filled her gut. Those weren't clouds rushing toward her. Clouds didn't make buzzing noises like that—low, culminating hums that grew louder with each passing second.

Gentry's stomach dropped to her toes. Swarm.

These weren't grasshoppers. They were *locusts*.

The nastiest curse Gentry's mind could conjure danced on her tongue, but it evaporated from her lips as the buzzing intensified and the black specks grew ever larger. Gripping the letter, she bolted back for the house.

"Rooster!" she shouted, and the front of the swarm hit her, pelting her like dry hail. She shrieked and swatted the insects away. A few landed on her collar, their antennae prodding her necklace. She beat them with her fingers. "Rooster!"

Rooster flung open the door. The nasty things flew and

hopped around them both. He slammed the door shut against their intrusion, then creaked it open and shouted, "Come on!"

Gentry ran in, nearly shoving Rooster to the floor as she barreled into him. Rooster's palms slapped her back, knocking off locusts. Gentry danced up and down to smash them with her boots. She heard Bounder squeal, but the mare was lost among the swarm.

Don't cry, don't cry, don't cry, they're just insects—

The curse reformed and burst from her mouth. She stiffened and cried, "The crops!"

Rooster echoed her profanity and dashed into the bedroom, grabbing the same blankets that had shielded the garden just yesterday. He tossed one to Gentry and sprinted outside. Gentry followed him, sure to shut the door hard behind her.

The things were everywhere, carpeting the ground in patches, clinging to the wood pile, zipping through the air. Pelting her like shot. Gentry kept her forearm in front of her face as she followed Rooster. He jumped the garden fence; Gentry stumbled through the gate.

There were more locusts than leaves.

"Go! Get away!" She grabbed the end of her blanket and swatted at the bugs. "Go, *go!*" Her eyes tried to find Rooster amidst the swarm. What if they hurt him?

The locusts stirred, losing themselves among their endless comrades, only to resettle on different plants. For a moment Gentry saw dancing shadows among them, but the creatures whizzed by each other so swiftly she couldn't be sure. The buzzing surrounded her, drilling into her brain, growing louder when the vermin leapt too close to her ears. Their legs crawled over her, clinging to the cotton of her dress, nibbling at her necklace.

A flash of white slammed into her and knocked her to

the earth. Locusts crunched beneath her. A repetitive, high-pitched cry echoed around her: *aya aya aya!*

Swatting locusts from her vision, Gentry saw one, two, five, *ten* seagulls swooping down from the sky, their beaks stretched wide as they intercepted locusts, chomping down on their crunchy bodies. The *aya aya aya!* multiplied until it became one long, ebbing screech, and with the calls came gull after gull after gull, until the sky was more white and gray than it was blue and black. So many birds swarmed the house, devouring the insects, that for a moment Gentry forgot the locusts all together.

Rooster—whole and well—spat out a storm, using the same obscenities her father favored, and backed up against the house, swatting at bug and bird alike. Gentry scrambled to her feet and rushed to his side, grabbing onto his arm.

"They're eating them!" she shouted over the ceaseless cries. "Look, Rooster!"

Rooster shielded his eyes from wind and wings and spied about, his muscles tense under Gentry's fingers.

Gentry slapped one of the locusts from her collar, then touched her necklace, wondering. Attracted to the gold? Were these locusts like the bizarre spirits? Magically . . . awake? Like Winn's . . .

"Seagulls," she whispered as the gulls feasted. She couldn't see through the cluster of their bodies, nor through the clouds of insects as the locusts fled from the garden, leaping and flying from the crops. Gentry clung to her brother for several more minutes, until the gull cries weakened and seagulls began finding perches wherever they could fit—the roof, the fence, the stables, or the earth itself.

Her gaze lifted and she saw him, the flash of his gold hair through the flock. He looked different in the sunlight, more real and yet more numinous, his hair as golden as the sun, his eyes bright as coins. If his veins glowed, the day shone too brightly for her to see them, or his loose sleeves were too covering, though he'd rolled them up to his elbows.

"Winn," she said, breathless, releasing Rooster and bounding over vegetable beds to the garden fence. He met her with a soft smile. "Winn, thank you."

Rooster eyed the seagulls, grimacing when one emptied its bowels from the eave near him. He inched away, eyeing Gentry, Winn, Gentry. "You know him?"

Winn tipped an invisible hat. "How do you do?"

"Rooster, this is Winn. He helped Pearl and I when we got stuck on our way to American Fork." *And rescued me from magical ghosts. And told me about magic. And he lives in a house made out of birds. I told you about him, didn't I?*

Rooster nodded slowly, making his way to Gentry's side, then up and over the fence. "Pearl talked all about you." He offered his hand, notably looking at the studs in Winn's ears.

"Pearl did, did she?" Winn shook Rooster's hand, but he looked at Gentry. Gentry merely coughed and tried to shake the anxious tremors from her body.

"You have hellish timing," Rooster said as he broke his grip, eyeing the birds. "Where'd they all come from?"

"He, uh," Gentry began, looking back to Winn, who stood straight and dazzling and not at all bothered by . . . anything. "He trains them."

Rooster cocked an eyebrow. "You *train* seagulls?"

"Very smart animals," Winn said.

Rooster turned about and cursed again. "Where's Bounder?"

Gentry's belly sank. "Run off; she wasn't tied up—"

A distant cry reached Gentry's ears—not an equine sound, but a woman's scream. Ducking between fence rails, she escaped the garden and jogged past the men, peering beyond the house toward the rest of Dry Creek. Toward the clouds of black that flitted about homes and farms like chimney smoke.

"Oh no." She exhaled the words. Rooster's footsteps sounded behind her. Spinning on the sole of her foot, she hurried back to Winn.

"They're magic, aren't they," she said out of Rooster's hearing, pinching the chain of her necklace. "The locusts."

Winn nodded—a single bob of his head. "The unrest from the mines riled them. Even all the way out here." He looked over her head, which wasn't hard to do, as he was nearly a full head taller than she. "Poor things."

"I'd hardly call them poor," Gentry said, turning his attention back to her. The mines did this too? Threatened her crops, her horse, her family? And yet she could do nothing to stop it, not like Winn could.

Pushing aside her worthlessness, she asked, "Can't you . . . settle them down?"

He shook his head. "They're too independent, and riled up at that. They won't listen to me like the birds do."

Easing the sharpness from her voice, Gentry asked, "The mines. You mentioned them before."

"I think I mentioned the gold." He absentmindedly brushed a finger over the studs in one of his ears. His left only had three studs again instead of four. "It's their mana, what keeps them awake and astute. What differs them from the dormant."

Rooster eyed them, and Winn dropped his voice. "One of the largest veins of gold is in California, and it's being attacked by zealous miners. It's offsetting the balance, so to speak. We've already felt the repercussions here, and I've seen them farther east too."

"The sulfur ponds, the quakes."

"There was a nasty storm too. Strange, for it to take to the sky." Winn rubbed his chin. "The more gold they pull out, the more everything will forget."

"Forget?" Gentry repeated.

Winn smiled. Gentry's cheeks burned. "Anything of the earth and from the earth has magic. *Had* it—when something becomes too experienced with humans, too domesticated, it forgets the magic it once had—"

"They're everywhere, Gentry." Rooster jogged toward her. One of the locusts fumbled in the soil at Rooster's feet; he lifted his shoe and squashed it. Gentry didn't miss Winn's wince.

"Can you help the others?" Gentry asked, wanting to grab his hands or his shirt or *something,* but she clasped her fingers together instead. "Can I . . . help them?"

Winn frowned at the valley beyond the house. "Magic doesn't like to fight magic. The gulls weren't thrilled with this."

"Huh?" Rooster asked.

Gentry ignored her brother. "Please. They'll destroy everything."

Winn let out a long sigh. Reaching to his right ear, he pulled the highest stud from the cartilage and said, "Turkey!"

One of the larger seagulls, perched on a post, cocked its head before flying over. For the first time, Gentry noticed a pale shimmer around it, almost invisible against the bright light of the sun. *Magically awake.* She touched her necklace.

Winn tossed the stud into the air. Leaping, Turkey swallowed it and took off for the sky—Gentry winced at the loss of at least fifty cents worth of gold. He didn't get far before the other seagulls, somehow sensing his purpose, stirred up dust and took off, soaring deeper into Dry Creek.

Rooster stared. "Did you just . . . ?"

"They're very well trained." Winn's grin returned. "But it's a temporary fix," he added, eyes back to Gentry. "Hopefully the locusts will move on and forget us."

"Someone else's problem." Gentry frowned.

Rooster snorted. "At least not ours." He eyed Winn. "Thanks." He shook Winn's hand again. To Gentry he said, "Let's survey the damage, then look for Bounder," and hopped back over the fence.

Gentry wrung her index finger. "How do they know?"

"Hm?" asked Winn.

"The birds. How do they know what to do?"

"It's bribery and imagination," he said, his words lighter. "They hear your thoughts, when you want them to. Well, these birds do. If you can think it and the birds are willing . . ."

"It happened to me, just before the locusts." Gentry lowered her voice even more. "I saw some of that wild magic. Some little blobs who wanted to snack on this." She looped a finger around the chain of her necklace. "And one of them listened to me. For a moment, anyway."

Winn's brow furrowed. "I . . . wouldn't do that, Gentry. They really are harmless, but wild magic is different from—"

"Gentry," Rooster called over his shoulder, "stop flirting and help me!"

The desert heat soaked deep into Gentry's skin. She whirled on her brother. "I am not—" She couldn't even finish the sentence. She rubbed the heels of both hands into her eyes. "Different from what?"

"From the tame variety," Winn finished, matching Gentry's hushed tone. "Like the seagulls, or other *physical* creatures. Creatures capable of independent thought—"

"You folks all right?"

Gentry spun around at Hoss's voice, her skin still too hot,

and spotted her neighbor sprinting toward them. He passed a narrow glance toward Winn when he arrived.

"Yes, we're fine," Gentry answered, half her thoughts lingering on Winn's unfinished sentence. She rubbed her temples. "We will be."

Hoss looked toward his farm, to the war of bug and bird. "Thought I was done for. Well-timed seagulls. A little far from the lake, but thank the Lord."

Winn cleared his throat.

Gentry said, "Hoss, this is Winn. Winn, this is Hoss Howland, our neighbor."

Hoss, hands on his hips, turned toward Winn and looked him up and down in a manner that seemed almost unfriendly. Very not Hoss. When he did shake Winn's hand, he seemed to be trying to crush it. Gentry felt that itch between her shoulder blades again, but what could she say?

"Winn what?" Hoss asked.

Winn shrugged and withdrew from Hoss's grasp. "Just Winn is fine." He grinned.

"You new in town?"

"More or less."

Hoss raised a brow. "Where'd you settle? You don't look like a farmer."

Gentry murmured, "We're not all farmers, Hoss."

"Just passing through, really. I'm from around." That smile never left his face, yet it wasn't false. Everything about Winn's sunny countenance appeared genuine. Gentry found herself staring and forced her eyes to move away.

"Where's your horse?" Hoss asked, eyeing the stable.

Gentry frowned at Hoss's animosity. "Mr. Howland—"

"Locusts scared it off," replied Winn.

"Aren't you going to look for it?"

Winn shrugged. "I'm not worried."

Hoss somehow managed to both narrow his eyes and raise his brow. He adjusted his hat.

"Winn," Gentry began, "you were saying—"

"Gentry," called Rooster.

She swallowed the question and focused on her brother. "Sorry, sorry." She hurried around to the open gate to let herself into the garden. She didn't need to investigate closely to see the ruined plants, the carnage she'd refused to notice until now. Some of the crops might still come back, but so many were unsalvageable. Just . . . gone.

The elation of the seagulls and Winn's small miracle evaporated from her skin. Her stomach cramped.

This. How was she supposed to fix *this*?

CHAPTER 5

The seagulls drove off the locusts, but no one in Dry Creek survived them unscathed, though Rooster found Bounder roaming near the mercantile. The town was so small it didn't have a governor or even a school, but one of the farmers took leadership upon himself and rallied people at the center of town. Gentry was surprised at the turnout, though the thought that her father should have been there nagged in the back of her mind. Even Winn came, though amid folk who looked common and melancholy, he stood out like a piece of gold in a cart of coal.

But the damage had been done. Half the garden ruined—more if Gentry couldn't coax injured plants back to life. The sight of the beds made Gentry sick, but at least the locusts hadn't eaten it all. She reminded herself of that every time she saw the insects' battlefield from the corner of her eye.

Because the Abrams weren't farmers, their garden was repaired as best as it could be quickly: the beds tidied, the plants watered, some clippings saved and put in water in hopes that they'd grow new roots. Then the townsfolk moved on to help larger families and those with cash crops. Gentry went to Hoss's farm to clear out some of the mess the infestation had left, but Hoss hadn't been struck badly. The seagulls had come just in time.

Rooster helped the other, larger homesteads. Pearl came home, her eyes brimming with tears, but one look at Winn brightened her countenance. Gentry made formal introductions. Pearl didn't bother to ask how Winn knew where they lived, or how he knew Gentry's name. She was young enough to accept it, and for that Gentry was grateful. She couldn't handle the barrage of questions, not right now. No matter how well-intentioned they were.

"Here's what I'm thinking," she said once Pearl ceased her fawning over Winn. She focused on keeping her tone even and her demeanor calm. "Rose won't be back with us for a while yet. We can dismantle part of her stall and use the wood to build planter boxes. We'll keep them inside, away from bugs and direct sunlight." Her stomach eased a little. "Those plants can have the best care, and they can survive frost when it comes, so we can make up a little of what we lost."

Winn said, "Sounds splendid."

The seagull Turkey returned and made himself comfortable on the roof.

Gentry pulled out her father's tools. Handing Winn the hammer, she said, "How did you know they were coming?"

"I sensed a rift in the desert's disposition. Followed it here. Glad I did."

He grinned, and Gentry tried to mirror the expression. "Is there a way for me to know before something happens again? My family, my friends ... I don't want to see them hurt."

The grin faded. "I'm not sure I could teach it, Gentry. It's intuitive. You need to be aware of the world around you and become part of it. Then you'll feel it."

She nodded, though the advice did little to help her.

Winn turned for the stables. She half expected him to magic something or other, but he worked just as any normal man would, yanking bent nails out of the stable wood while Bounder watched nervously. Pearl grabbed planks and heaved until they came free, then held them together while Gentry used the old nails to piece them into planter boxes. Used nails weren't strong, but they would have to do until money arrived from California. Winn sawed down a few of the longer planks and found some chicken wire to refashion into hooks so the boxes hung off the window sills.

Gentry had just started to dig down to moist earth to fill the boxes when Winn's seagulls returned, cawing at random, but something about their sounds drew his attention away, northwest. He pressed his lips together.

Gentry handed her sister the shovel and walked over to Winn. "What's wrong?"

He managed a small smile, but this one wasn't genuine. Already Gentry saw the difference. "Something's amiss over the mountains."

"From . . . the mines?"

Winn sighed. "Maybe. Probably. I'm going to have a look. Will you be all right?"

Gentry nodded. "Almost done, and Rooster will be home soon enough." She touched his elbow, the place ringed with rolled shirtsleeve. "Thank you so much for your help. I don't know what we would have done without you."

Again Winn tipped an invisible hat. "I aim to please, miss."

Gentry smiled. Moving to the garden fence, Winn stooped down and pulled a small groundsel weed out of the ground, plucked the yellow flower from it, and tossed the rest of the plant. He offered the flower to Gentry.

"Until we meet again." The words sounded like a promise.

Without any direction from him that Gentry saw or heard, the seagulls leapt into the air and dived for him, swirling about in a cyclone of feathers, hiding Winn from sight. They rose into the air, then soared with a hawk-like speed west toward the San Pitches. Gentry shielded her eyes and watched him go until the bundle of birds vanished beyond a peak.

Her heart hammered, seeing such a sight. She pinched the groundsel stem in her hands, and it hammered all the more.

"Did you *see* that?" Pearl asked, running to Gentry's side and clinging to her arm. "He just vanished in a bunch of seagulls!"

"Oh no, he rode off."

"What? On what horse?"

"On his." Gentry smiled and pinched Pearl's side, making her sister jump. "We're not done yet, Pearly. Come on."

"You're fibbing," Pearl whined, dragging her feet back to the garden.

"Maybe, maybe not." Gentry shook her head. The planters were a quarter filled with dirt. "Come on, let's get this finished so we can eat." It would be a late supper.

"Is he coming back?"

Gentry met her sister's eyes, brown, like her own, but they looked prettier than Gentry's. More . . . alight. "Do you *want* him to come back?" She winked.

"Gentry, be fair!"

Gentry laughed. "All right, all right. Yes, he'll come back. Now let's shovel."

Pearl grinned and dug the spade into the earth. Gentry,

passing one last glance toward the mountains, tucked the groundsel into one of the button holes on her dress and got to work.

~~~

Gentry walked to the window cut into the side of the mercantile, wringing her finger in her opposite fist. Through it she saw the edge of the counter of the shop as well a small shelf for sorting what mail made it to the small town. An old telegraph sat on a table across from it.

Mr. Olson sorted spices inside, spectacles low on his nose. His white shirt was ironed and crisp, and there was a little oil in his hair. She wondered how much he made and if he'd ever had to go hungry.

He glimpsed her and set the spices down, wiping his hands on his apron before coming to the window. "Ah, Miss Abrams. You're in luck."

Her heart lodged in her throat so tightly she couldn't speak.

"Let's see." He turned to the shelf. Gentry put her hands on the glassless window's sill and leaned forward, watching him search the small cubbies. He pulled a single letter from one of them.

She swallowed her heart down. Finally, a letter! She tried not to dwell on the thinness of it in Mr. Olson's hands. Of course Pa wouldn't have wages to send yet. He probably just started working, and wanted them to know he was all right. Just his handwriting would be enough for Gentry.

"Postage already paid for." Mr. Olson handed the letter to her with a smile.

"Thank you," Gentry breathed, grasping the letter. She scurried away from the mercantile and turned the letter over, but at the sight of the return address, her shoulders—and heart—dropped.

Hannah Hinkle, the neat penmanship read. The name blurred together, and Gentry blinked back tears, taking in deep, raking breaths to calm herself. She silently thanked the breeze that swept by to dry her eyelashes.

Normally she would be jubilant to receive a letter from Hannah, but with time stretching since her father's departure, she was more desperate than ever to hear from him. To know he was all right. To receive some of his wages and get bread on the table, since without the gun, Rooster had a hard time of catching any game.

She opened the letter.

June 4

Dear Gentry, Rooster, and Pearl,

> *Thinking of you. I hope Gentry and Pearl made it back all in one piece. You all are welcome to visit at any time. Please let me know if you need anything. Have you heard from your father?*
>
> *Caleb is running about, encouraged by the other children. He has a sweet, if rambunctious, soul. Getting him to sit through even one hour of church is nigh impossible!*
>
> *Please write back and let me know what's going on in Dry Creek. I'll pay the postage, just get the letter posted.*

Much Love,
Hannah

At least there was Hannah.

Massaging tension from her shoulders, Gentry returned

to the window, handed Mr. Olson the letter to her father, a few precious pennies, and a voiceless prayer that she'd hear from Butch Abrams soon.

~~~

"Math barely makes sense with numbers," Pearl complained from the kitchen table, a small slate before her and a nub of chalk clutched in her fingers. "You can't add letters."

"Pearl." Gentry tried to keep frustration from sharpening her voice as she cleaned the floor. She frowned at a thumb-sized piece of bread left on Ma's old rag rug, now crawling with ants. She picked up the morsel and stomped on the bugs.

"No need to get constipated," Pearl grumbled.

"I—what?" Gentry asked, turning around. She clutched Rooster's drawers and a pair of his work pants under one arm, again in need of patching. "It's not constipated, it's consternated. And I'm not. I explained the letters to you last week."

Ma had always valued education. She'd been a teacher back in Virginia. It wasn't fair to Pearl that their mother's tutoring was cut short.

"I don't remember." Pearl put her head down on the table.

Huffing, Gentry came over and set the mending down on a chair. "The letters stand for something. Don't think of them as letters, but . . . like secrets. You're trying to find out what the secret is."

"It's an X," Pearl said.

Gentry rubbed her forehead. "No, here." She took the slate and rewrote the equation with question marks instead of Xs and Ys. "See? It's a mystery."

"But the answer is right there." She pointed to the four at the other end of the equals sign.

"The four is not the mystery, this is—oh bother!"

The stovetop sizzled as a pot of vegetable broth bubbled over, spilling against the hot surface. Gentry grabbed the handle to move it, then dropped the pan as it burned her palm. More broth sloshed out and steamed, but at least the pan had stayed upright.

Yanking back her sleeve, Gentry dunked her hand into the half-full pail of water on the floor. *Don't cry.*

Pearl, frowning, slid off her chair and grabbed a rag, first wetting it in the same pail and then whisking it over the stove to clean up the hot broth. She peered into the pot. "It's good. It's enough."

"It's not." The now familiar lump reformed in Gentry's throat. She looked at her hand and the red streak crossing her palm, which had only recently lost the marks from her fall in American Fork. No blisters. Not so bad of a burn, but hand injuries were always the worst, especially when there was so much work to be done.

Her mind traveled back to the ledger. When was that next mortgage payment due?

"I'll make tortillas," Pearl said. "Hannah showed me how. They're Mexican."

"I know what tortillas are."

"They'll make up for what you spilled, and we don't have to wait for them to rise, and they won't use much flour."

Gentry pulled her hand from the bucket and gingerly dried it on her skirt. "Thank you, Pearl. That will help."

Pearl beamed and fetched the nearly empty flour sack, her studies blissfully forgotten.

Gentry sat on the floor a long moment, leaning against the wall, staring out over the house. Maybe they could all move to Salt Lake City. There would be more work there, possibly even something for Gentry. Rooster didn't want to be a farmhand forever, after all. The move would be costly . . . but if they found work first, it might be worth it. If.

Gentry frowned. They'd have to say goodbye to this house, the house *they* built when the family was still whole. Before Ma died. And Pa . . . he wouldn't know where to send his letters.

But you'll hear from him before any of this nonsense can happen, she thought, and sighed. Most of the Mormons were poor. Carolyn had said so herself. Who was to say there was even work to be had?

Gentry ached for Virginia. She could get a job teaching if they lived in Virginia. Just like Ma had.

A squishing sound, almost like curds wrung in a cheese-cloth, drew Gentry's attention to the window by the door, its shutters open to encourage the breeze. On the sill bobbed one of the dark, drop-shaped spirits from earlier. The black holes Gentry thought were its eyes rolled about.

Gentry froze and eyed Pearl, who busied herself pressing lard into flour. She touched the gold chain around her neck. "Pearl?"

"Hm?"

"Look at the window. Do you see anything?"

Pearl glanced up from her work, her gaze slowly wandering to the window by the door. It slid passed it to the window at the end of the house, then back. "See what?"

Gentry managed a small smile. "Oh, nothing, it's gone. Just a wasp, I think."

Pearl rolled her eyes and turned back to the dough. Gentry took a step near the window; the blob shivered with . . . delight?

It knows I can see it, she thought, unclasping her necklace and palming it to protect it. But was this the same wild magic that had heeded her earlier, or another one?

She mouthed, "I don't have any gold for you," to it, but of course the small creature didn't understand. She slid the necklace into her pocket. The blob's dark spot-eyes followed the gesture. Seconds later, its body stiffened and it twisted about like taffy. It made that squishing sound again and faded right before Gentry's eyes, as though it was never there at all.

Gentry touched the pane where the creature had sat. She felt nothing, heard nothing. Peered outside so see only desert and dust. She frowned. Had something frightened it, or had it understood her after all?

She looked out over the dusty yard, out toward the mountains. Closed her eyes and took deep, swelling breaths. Tried to feel the earth the way Winn had tried to explain, after the locusts. She'd last seen one of those blob things before the insects attacked. Was something else looming in the future?

Gentry felt nothing, of course.

"When is Pa going to write?" Pearl asked, a smudge of white flour already on her cheek.

Gentry opened her eyes and pulled back from the window. "When he decides to remember us."

Pearl stilled her spoon, expression drawn.

Gentry closed her eyes and shook her head. "No, sorry. I'm sorry. He's probably working very hard to see that we're looked after, and he doesn't have time to write a letter just now. But it will come, and he'll send us enough money to buy a cow and some maple syrup."

Pearl offered a close-lipped smile, and Gentry wondered if, should things get hard enough, Hannah might be willing to take in Pearl too.

Her stomach cramped. It had been doing that a lot lately, and Gentry's fingers tried to knead it loose. She couldn't bear having Pearl live all the way in American Fork. Gentry didn't think she'd be able to sleep without her sister warming the other side of the bed. To have it be just her and Rooster . . .

The door opened almost wide enough to hit the wall behind it. Rooster came in, his shirt damp around his neck, down his chest and back, and under his arms. Dirt dusted him head to toe.

"Speak of the devil," Gentry said.

Rooster merely grunted in reply, kicked off his boots, and slunk down to the floor right there by the door.

Gentry frowned. "Hard day?"

Rooster nodded and wiped the back of his hand over his brow. He pulled off his hat and fanned himself with it.

"Thank you," she murmured.

Another nod.

Today was pay day for Rooster, but Gentry wouldn't ask for the money—she knew it would be one dollar and fifteen cents—right away. Rooster worked harder than any of them, and seeing him beaten down and worn out made the cramping in Gentry's stomach travel up to her chest.

Picking herself up, Gentry fetched a cup and filled it with water, offering it to him. "Supper won't be ready yet, but do you want some oatmeal?"

Rooster merely nodded.

"I'll get a bath ready," she said as the oatmeal set.

"Nah," Rooster replied, half a pant. "I'll do it. I don't want it heated up. I'll be quick."

"I don't mind."

"S'alright."

Forming tortillas, Pearl commented, "You smell like a horse."

Rooster offered a half grin. "Least I have a reason for it. You smell like a hog's backside."

"Hey!"

Gentry laughed. "He's just teasing you."

Her brother stretched his dirty legs out in front of him—she'd sweep the floor after he left for his bath. "Too bad we don't still have that fiddle. I could use a song."

Gentry rubbed her fingertips together, the left ones having already lost their calluses. "Me too." Music always made hardship better, and the walls of this house hadn't heard much of it. The thought made Gentry miss Ma.

"Why aren't you wearing your necklace?" asked Pearl. She set a skillet atop the oven, where the saucepan had been. "You haven't been wearing it much lately. Can I?"

Gentry's hand fell down to her pocket. "No." She retrieved the necklace and fastened it around her neck, careful not to pull on the hairs that had frayed from her bun.

She didn't offer further explanation.

CHAPTER 6

A few days after the arrival of Hannah's letter, Gentry saw a distinct lack of spirits, even when she rode Bounder away from town to exercise her. It put a sick, cold feeling in her belly, one that resurfaced in her bedroom in the middle of the night.

The beds jumped.

"Gentry. Gentry!" Pearl cried, her voice a fishing hook reaching down into Gentry's dreams, snaring her, and reeling her into consciousness. "Gentry, it's happening again!"

The line snagged, the hook dug into her skin, and Gentry shot up in bed, braid whipping as she went. She heard the jostling of the beds against the floor, quaking furniture, and Rooster cursing. Metal clamored and ceramic shattered in the kitchen. Her own body shook.

"God help us," she whispered.

"Get under the bed!" Rooster shouted.

Gentry grabbed Pearl's wrist and dragged her over the side of the bed. They collided with the bucking floorboards. Her arms swept out in a swimmer's stroke to push aside the bags and boxes stored beneath the bed frame. She shoved Pearl under and crawled in after her, though her left shoulder and hip didn't quite clear the shelter.

Something shattered in the kitchen. Gentry held her breath. Beneath her fingers, she felt the cracks between floorboards yawning. The sound of a great crash infiltrated the house. Thunder?

Just as Gentry's lungs were about to explode, the floor relaxed. The clamoring stilled. Cool air kissed her nose.

She waited another minute before crawling out, knees sweeping through dust like snow on the floor. She coughed and fumbled for the dresser, searching for the candle, but it had been knocked off during the quake.

"Candle. Where's the candle?" Her voice shook and somehow sounded too loud in the sudden silence following the shake. "I need light!"

Rooster coughed. "Pearl?"

"She's fine." Gentry's stomach clenched. "Pearl?"

"I'm coming," she whimpered.

"Are you hurt?"

"N-no."

Rooster loomed beside her, his hands sliding over the dresser and then over the floor. "Found it," he said, "but not the matches."

Gentry cursed a dozen times in her head. She crawled on her knees, searching for the small box of matches, tripping over her nightgown. Rooster slid the nightstand out farther from the wall. Pearl crawled out from beneath the bed, coughing.

A sliver caught in Gentry's palm.

Finding her feet, Gentry stood and carefully picked her way toward the kitchen, stepping over the laundry hamper and something else she couldn't see that had fallen out of place. Her foot stepped on something sharp, and she jumped—a jar or glass must have shattered. At least she saw more in the main area. The starlight shone brightly through the—

Gentry stared.

A cool breeze rustled her dress.

"Window," she whispered.

Where a window *had* been, there was now nothing. No planter box, no glass, no *wall*. Gentry stared out onto the ravaged garden, the stable behind it, and the desert landscape beyond. On the floor lay a heap of rubble and splintered wood. The entire wall had fallen in.

Gentry gaped, stiff and cold.

"Got it." Rooster called, and the glow of firelight mixed with the chilly blue of the Utah night sky.

Gentry dropped to her knees, staring. The candlelight grew brighter as Rooster and Pearl stepped out of the bedroom.

"Holy . . ." Rooster began, but he didn't finish.

"It's . . . gone," Gentry whispered. *Don't cry, don't cry, don't cry.*

But the mantra didn't work this time.

Gentry covered her face with her hands and wept.

"Gentry . . ."

Rays of dawn slid over the peaks of the Wasatch Mountains, illuminating the mess of the house.

Pearl prodded her shoulder. "Gentry, it's all right. We'll clean it up."

But there was too much. Shards of dishes littered the kitchen floor, some having flown out into the small living area. Others had caught in Gentry's nightdress. The oven door hung crooked. Pieces of furniture lay on their sides. The few decorations that spotted the walls had fallen. Broken glass from the kitchen window dotted the floor. Splinters and expensive bits of brick lay in an impossible heap. A coat of dust and debris clung to everything, even the window that had survived.

And the damn wall was missing.

Gentry barely had any tears left. Her face felt hot and swollen, her sleeves soaked. Her back hurt, and she was covered in filth, both what had fallen from the ceiling and what had collected under the bed.

How was she supposed to rebuild a wall? How was she supposed to *afford* to rebuild a wall? After the mortgage payment, she would barely *afford* to live inside the three still standing.

Her Pa had built the house too fast. Too many shortcuts. What would he do?

"Gentry, it's not so bad," Pearl murmured, her voice too soft, giving way to the lie in her words. "The stable is still standing. That's good, isn't it?"

Rooster picked his way over the collapsed wall and into the garden, silent.

"Maybe ... maybe Pa will come home and help," Pearl suggested.

Gentry cried anew, burying her face in the crook of her elbow, her knees drawn to her chest.

"Or Hoss," Pearl tried.

"Wonder how he's held up," Rooster said. The concern in his voice wasn't terribly heavy. Hoss could afford some losses. With a sigh, her brother trekked back over the wall pile. "Might as well get dressed before people come and gape."

Gentry lifted her head, her breath hard and sporadic. "C-can't have them g-gaping".

Pearl grabbed her hand and hauled her to her feet. The door to the bedroom didn't close all the way anymore. Gentry leaned against it, forehead to the wood, as Pearl changed. She was so tired. She could have slept right there, standing and all.

Her sister tossed Gentry yesterday's dress. "It's the most clean."

Gentry dressed, numb and slow. She didn't bother putting her hair up. Clasping the pendant of her necklace in her fist, the tip of the heart burrowing into her palm, she offered a weak prayer and ached for her parents.

This had scared the magic away, then. The little blobthing had sensed it. Couldn't it have warned her?

She kneeled at the bed and laid her head on the dusty mattress. She didn't know where to begin. What use was cleaning the house when there wasn't a wall to keep the dirt out? Could she put off the mortgage and use the money on the wall? But how would she pay the mortgage the next month? Then again, Dry Creek was in the middle of nowhere. Surely the debt collectors wouldn't come right away.

She needed a letter from her father now more than ever. She fisted handfuls of blanket.

She'd have to sell Bounder. It was the only way to raise the money . . . but Pearl *loved* that horse, and then they'd have no means of transportation. They'd be trapped in their little hovel in the desert indefinitely.

Gentry's heart hit her navel and cracked open like an egg.

"She's out of sorts," Pearl's voice drifted from the living room, "and she doesn't look very pretty."

Gentry buried her face in dust and blanket. Her leg muscles tensed. She was going to sick up—she felt it. Maybe it would make her feel better, but she hated the idea of wasting food, even if it was only the last undigested dregs from supper.

"I wouldn't look very pretty, either," replied a male voice, and certainly not Rooster's. The shells of Gentry's heart clanked together, and she covered her face with her hands.

Pearl pushed the bedroom door open. "Winn is here."

"I heard," Gentry mumbled, not sure if the words were loud enough to carry.

"Gentry," said Winn, "I'm so sorry. What can I do?"

Lifting her head, Gentry shook it and sat back on her heels. Winn stayed in the doorway, thankfully offering her some space. His face was drawn, his lips tight, his hair swept back unevenly in an almost childish fashion.

Gentry tossed her hands up with feeble effort and let them fall like flapjacks to her lap. "There's nothing to be done." Her voice was airy and raw. "I must have done something very horrible to be punished this way."

Pearl clarified, "She means God."

"Yes, thank you, Pearl," Winn replied. "And I hardly think anyone here has elicited the vengeance of God." To Gentry, he said, "It's the wild—"

"I presumed so," she cut in.

Pearl said, "Rooster is sorting out the split bricks from the whole ones. You can do that."

Winn leaned against the doorframe. "Gentry—"

"I just . . ." Gentry swallowed and clenched her fists together. "I just can't, right now."

Winn sighed. A moment passed—long enough to graze awkwardness—before he said, "Well, I have an idea. Pearl, would you assist me?"

Gentry didn't look over, but she heard Pearl bounce on her feet. "What is it? Ouch!"

Now Gentry lifted her head again. "Pearl, there's glass everywhere—"

"No worries," Winn scooped Pearl up in his arms as though she were a baby. Pearl yelped, and Winn passed a cursory glance over her bare feet. "No harm done. My lady, where are your shoes?"

Pearl's face flushed bright as a trumpet creeper. "By the door." She pointed over his shoulder.

Winn passed a final glance to Gentry, who evaded his eyes, and stepped outside. Glass and ceramic crunched under his boots. Each step made Gentry cringe. Then they were gone, leaving the house silent except for the muted sound of Rooster stacking broken bricks.

Gentry needed to do something. She needed to get up and start sweeping, but to do that would be to see all the brokenness, all the things lost that she couldn't afford to replace. Her body was so tired, and her stomach squeezed and squeezed until her throat burned and her bowels twisted. Her heart had somehow managed to piece itself together. It pulsed with an iron beat inside her head. Her skull ached with every pump.

She should get up. Clean. Make breakfast. Take inventory of what was useless and what was usable. But her limbs were anvils, and the more she thought about it, the higher the bile climbed, and the louder the outhouse called her name.

She studied her hands. Dust had settled in the lines of her palms, tinting them brown.

"Hey." Rooster nudged the bedroom door a little wider. "I'm going to run over to Hoss's and see how he's fared. If he's good, he can help us. Maybe give me an advance to get some lumber."

"We need all your wages for food and the mortgage," Gentry murmured.

"I know. But I'm going to check."

"Fine." The word was dead before it left her mouth.

Rooster left. Another breeze swept through the house.

Holding her stomach with one arm, Gentry leaned on the bed and found her feet. Her headache intensified, and she dropped back to her knees, dry heaving twice. Fortunately, her stomach was as loath to waste food as the rest of her.

She climbed enough to sit on the edge of the bed, cradling her head in her hands. *What would Pa do? Ma?* she thought. She combed through her memories, trying to find an answer, but none came. *I'll tell you what they would do,* came a thought. *Pa would quit his job and sell my fiddle and drag us out west for the sake of a new start and "prosperity," and Ma would agree because she'd slept with another man and didn't want the neighbors to know. That's what they'd do.*

Gentry shuddered and wiped half a tear from her eyelashes. Maybe they could move. Maybe Hannah would take them in until they found work. Gentry cursed her womanhood. She could do so much more if only she could get a real job.

She didn't know exactly how mortgages worked. If they left, she could simply turn over the land and what was left of the house and be all right, yes? Was there interest to pay? Would the bank accept the memories of her mother that lingered in these walls as payment? What would Pa do when he got back and found them mooching off the Mormons *again*?

She needed to go to the mercantile. Maybe he'd finally written. Maybe there was money waiting for them. Maybe this wasn't as bad as it seemed.

Gentry took several deep breaths, coaxing her stomach to settle. She'd been so sick lately, and she wasn't sure why. Once she was steady, she got up, found her hairbrush under Rooster's bed, and combed out her hair before pulling it back. She searched for her ma's compact mirror, finding it near the window. She nearly cried anew when she opened it and saw a crack in the glass.

Gritting her teeth, she checked her face. It wasn't red, but her eyes were still puffy. She dropped the mirror on the mattress and fanned her face, looking toward the ceiling to stall further tears. One thing at a time. There might not be any wagon trains or military troops coming through to carry letters. Did the stage line even pass through Utah?

She had to clean. Throw away all the things the quake had ruined. Rewash all the laundry, the blankets, the pillow cases. Reinventory everything. They would just have to sleep with a gaping hole in the house until Gentry figured out a solution. Maybe they could tack blankets over it, for now. They didn't need blankets—or a wall—until winter.

Winter. Gentry shivered as though it were already here. *Stop it,* she chided herself. *Pa will be back by then.*

Steeling herself, Gentry stepped into the other room, avoiding shards of brokenness despite wearing her shoes. She crept to the fallen wall and the small, unfinished piles Rooster had formed. There were far more broken bricks than whole ones.

In addition to the planter boxes, the rubble had crushed part of the garden row closest to the house. Gentry felt her resolve crumbling.

A seagull squawked from the second garden row. Gentry narrowed her eyes at it. "I see you peck one leaf or swallow a single crumb, and I'll swat you clear to Nebraska, you hear?"

The seagull tilted its head, regarding her.

The wind picked up, blowing dirt into the house and Gentry's eyes. She brought up her arm as a shield and turned away, feeling her chest sink again. The gust settled abruptly, and with it the sound of falling rubble.

Instinct had Gentry fling her arms over her head, but none of the ceiling came down. She turned around and saw a large mound of dirt and some of Bounder's hay atop the broken bricks. Winn and Pearl stood on the other side of it. Gentry saw the glimmer of a vein in Winn's right hand just as it faded, and when he spoke, gold shone in his eyes.

"We're halfway there, Pearl."

"Gentry!" Pearl clapped her hands. "Gentry, Winn's seagulls scooped dirt like a thousand shovels, all the way down to the dark stuff!"

Gentry's gaze darted from Pearl, to the dirt, to Winn, to the dirt. She knew she should say something, but the rawness of her throat presented itself, lump and all. A tremor that started in her belly snaked its way into her shoulders and down her arms until her fingers shook, and her mind couldn't piece any two thoughts together.

"Pearl," said Winn.

"Yes!" Pearl saluted.

Winn began to unroll his sleeves, pulling them down to his wrists. "Water, please. As much as you can carry."

Pearl scrambled up the dirt pile and into the house, leaving dusty tracks in her wake. Gentry spun, watching her, a reprimand somewhere between her lungs and her teeth. But, really, what did it matter?

She turned to Winn. "What is all this?" she asked. Her voice sounded tired and old, like her ma's.

Winn smiled, a soft expression without teeth. A strand of golden hair fell over his eye, the color of which was darkening by the second. He pushed it back. "I'm helping. Isn't it obvious?"

It wasn't, though Gentry didn't say it. She fingered the pendant of her necklace.

Pearl came back, grunting, a pail of water in one hand and a full bowl cradled in her opposite elbow, meaning they'd have to make another trip to the well this morning, if it still stood. Pearl sloshed it onto herself and the worn rug near the stove. Gentry hurried over and took the bowl from her.

"Excellent! Now, dump it on this pile." He gestured to the dirt.

Pearl didn't hesitate.

"Pearl!" Gentry watched the mound of dirt slump into thick mud. Murky water streamed onto the half-ruined rug.

"Trust me," Winn said.

Gentry gawked at him. "But I—"

Pearl grabbed the bowl of water, leaving Gentry alone inside the house. "Please, Gentry. He says he knows what he's doing."

She dumped the remaining water onto the mound, much to Gentry's dismay. She frowned at Winn, her hands still trembling. "I barely know you."

"That can be remedied," Winn said with half a grin. "Stand back, Miss Pearl."

Pearl retreated to Gentry's side.

Winn took off one of his earrings and tossed it into the dirt. It wasn't until that moment that Gentry really *looked* at the earth piled over her broken wall and noticed the shimmer it had, the same worn by the seagulls. She held her breath.

Winn stretched out his arms as though he were about to lift something heavy. If Gentry had not known what to look for, she wouldn't have caught the slight yellowish glow beneath his sleeves. She might not have seen the brightening of his eyes, as though molten gold churned about the dark pupils.

The mud leapt before her eyes, blocking out the sun, growing up like a hundred dark fingers clawing skyward, seeking purchase in the air. It made sounds like popping cartilage, which grew softer but more numerous until the light blacked out completely, and silence filled the newly enclosed space.

Air rushed out of Gentry as her eyes adjusted to the darkness of the house. Stiff, she lifted one hand and took small half steps until it touched the cool, hard wall, solid as stone.

Whole.

Lines of light peeked through the stone. Pearl grabbed Gentry's elbow and yanked her back just before a square fell away—space for a window. Most of the new rock fell into the garden, but some of its dust puffed inside the house.

Gentry stared, her joints as stiff as the wall, her lips parted in a deflated O. A few of her buzzing thoughts collided into coherency.

A wall. The house had a wall. Winn had used his gold to build them a wall.

Beneath the touch of her necklace, Gentry still saw the faint glow of the fresh stone, the one solid brick that comprised the side of their house. How deep had Winn dug to find earth magically alive?

"Magic!" Pearl cried, jumping. She grabbed Gentry's hands and swung her around, breaking her out of her stupor. "Did you see that, Gentry? Look! He's a wizard or something, I know it!"

"Miss Pearl." Winn appeared in the window. He leaned his elbows on the brick sill, his sleeves still loose about his wrists. "Do keep your voice down, or I'll be building houses all over the territory, and I simply can't afford it."

Pearl released Gentry, who steadied herself against one of the chairs. She blinked until the dizziness left her, then stared at Winn, his soft smile and golden countenance, the way the skin around his eyes crinkled as he tried not to laugh at Pearl.

"You . . . did it," Gentry whispered.

Winn's eyes shone with magic. Morning sunlight lapped about his shoulders and highlighted his pale hair. At that moment, Gentry had never seen a more beautiful sight.

She struggled to find her voice. "Thank you." Her hands clutched at her heart, which swelled so much she feared it would burst from her chest. "Oh Winn, you have no idea . . . thank you so much. You've saved us."

His expression softened. No, *this* was the most beautiful sight. Him, leaning on her window, looking at her softly with his dimming eyes and a quirk to his lips. Her swollen heart beat faster, and it hurt.

"You have to stay for supper," Pearl demanded.

His gaze flickered back to Gentry's sister. "Supper is a long way off."

"Then stay all day!"

Winn chuckled. "I will kindly accept your invitation for supper, but until then I must be out and about, checking up on things. Someone's got to keep this place together."

He glanced to Gentry at that last sentence. She nodded, speechless again, numb everywhere except for a slight tingling in her toes.

Winn tipped his invisible hat and vanished from the window. A new breeze swept in, carrying with it the cries of seagulls and the slightest scent of brine, and Gentry knew Winn had gone.

"Oh bother." Pearl tapped her chin. "How do we explain this to Rooster?"

CHAPTER 7

It was indeed difficult to explain to Rooster, who returned an hour after Winn's departure. Pearl gushed at him a thousand words a minute explaining everything in unbelievable, minute detail. But the tale *was* unbelievable, and when Rooster asked Gentry to clarify, she simply said, "It's a miracle, Rooster."

For now, Rooster was content with that.

Hoss, the generous man that he was, gave Rooster a paid day off to help the family while the rest of Dry Creek recovered from the sudden quake. Rooster went to work cleaning up brick and rubble and pushing furniture back where it belonged. Gentry swept broken ceramic and shattered glass, barely noticing the loss now. She gave Pearl a few pennies and the instruction, "Go buy the smallest chicken you can find."

The cast iron pots and pans were unscathed, thankfully, as were the tin pitcher, bowl, and serving tray. The wooden dishes were all right too, save for a cup that had a triangular chip knocked from its lip. Her ma's tea set was in shambles, but the teapot had broken in big enough pieces that Gentry had hope for repairing it. Three teacups and four saucers had survived. The rest were too broken for salvaging and went to the trash. Gentry was thankful they'd sold the china when they did, before it had been scattered in pieces over the floor too.

The glass vase was done in, as well as the small Dutch

shoe Gentry had gotten as a souvenir when she visited Washington as a girl. Pa's beer mug lost its handle—Gentry found it under a chair—and won a chip in its lip as well. Gentry placed it back on its shelf.

Pearl returned with a chicken so small it barely counted as a chicken, which in the end was a job well done. Gentry set her to wiping down every surface while Gentry plucked and prepared the bird. She would make her ma's velvet chicken soup and a jam cake, if she had time. It would be a richer meal than they'd had since before Pa left, but it was the least Gentry could do to thank Winn for the immensity of his help and the loss of his gold earring. She diced, stirred, and seasoned with care, hoping within her still-swollen heart than Winn might be impressed.

Gentry eagle-watched the soup as it cooked—she would hate herself if she burned it and wasted those chicken pennies. She had enough time and jam to put a small cake in the oven. By the time the cry of seagulls announced Winn's return, the house smelled pleasant, the bulk of the grime had been scrubbed away (and the dirty rags added to the ever-growing laundry pile), the bricks had been sorted, and the garden had been tidied. Gentry hadn't counted how many more plants they may have lost, not today. She had already decided to put off further worrying until tomorrow.

Pearl shrieked with pleasure when a knock sounded at the door. Gentry tugged off her apron and checked her hair, tucking a few baby strands behind her ears.

Pearl tore the door open. "Winn! You came!"

"Of course I came. You offered me supper." He grasped her shoulder and squeezed it. He released her and looked into the house. "What a lovely home you have."

Gentry snorted. "As if you haven't seen it." She glanced over the table set for four, like it used to be. "Pearl, spoons."

"Oh." Pearl spun back into the tiny kitchen to retrieve spoons from the dish cloth set by the sink, where the last of the dishes were drying after a thorough scrubbing.

Winn entered the house, and Rooster approached him with extended hand. Winn shook it, firm but brief. Skepticism slanted Rooster's brow. "Thank you for helping us. We couldn't have asked for better."

"Pleasure is mine." He focused on Gentry. "Smells like heaven in here."

Gentry blushed and resisted the urge to wring her hands. "Flattery will get you nowhere, Winn."

"It's actually gotten me plenty of places." He grinned and elbowed Rooster, who chuckled. It warmed Gentry to see her brother laugh.

"Sit down. It's ready." Pearl pulled out a chair at the head of the table. "You get Pa's seat, Winn."

Gentry rolled her lips together, then let herself smile. She set the pot of soup atop a pad on the table and filled everyone's bowls, hers last, just as Ma had done. Rooster offered a quick grace, and they ate.

The first bite drew hot trails through Gentry's mouth. How good it felt, eating something that stuck to the bones. This was turning, oddly, into a very good day.

She glanced at Winn, who caught her eye, and asked, "Winn, I don't think you ever told me your last name."

"It's Maheux," he answered. It sounded familiar.

"Matthew?" Pearl repeated.

"Sort of, but no Ts," Winn said between bites. "It's French."

"You're French?" Rooster asked.

"You don't sound French," Pearl added.

He laughed. "I'm Canadian, actually."

"Really?" Pearl beamed as though she, too, were filled

with magic. Her light faded a bit, and she said, "You don't sound Canadian."

Winn smiled. "And what do Canadians sound like?"

Pearl shrugged and slurped a spoonful of soup.

Gentry studied Winn. He had a few smears of dirt on his white shirt, and she wondered what he'd been up to all day. But if his activities were anything like this morning's, now might not be the best time to ask. He was missing more earrings. She noticed he was already halfway through his bowl, and that made Gentry sit a little straighter. A smile even tickled her lips.

"You're a long way from home," she said.

Winn shrugged, swallowed a spoonful, then leaned his forearms against the table edge. "From Canada, yes, but not from home, not really. I travel a lot," his gaze was knowing, "but I like to stay close to this area, or roundabouts. I actually spent many of my adolescent years with the Hagree."

Pearl asked, "The who?" at the same time Rooster said, "The Indians?"

Gentry looked at Rooster before returning her gaze to Winn.

"They're a small tribe to the west, closer to California," Winn explained. "I, uh," he hesitated, "my father was a scientist. A medicinal scientist, to be specific. He took us all over the continent searching for new remedies for this and cures for that."

As he spoke, his eyes watched the soup bowl, his spoon slowly stirring chunks from the bottom. Gentry sensed a story behind his words.

"The Hagree are friendly," Winn continued, "and he visited them for a while to learn some of their practices."

"That's a long time to stay," Rooster said.

"Oh, I lingered there after he'd gone. I'm actually not sure where he is, now." He smiled, but it wasn't a mirthful gesture. He swept back his hair, revealing two gold studs in each ear.

After supper, as Winn carried dishes to the sink, Gentry asked him, "Where do you get your earrings?"

"Hm?" he asked, but his touching of the studs told her he had heard her. "Oh, a Hagree woman made them for me."

"But how do you afford them?" she asked, quieter. She glanced over her shoulder. Rooster had pulled out their Pa's chess set, and Pearl was bothering him for a game, though Gentry knew Rooster meant to play Winn.

Winn grinned. "When you give gold to the earth, it gives it back, if you stay around long enough." He dropped his hand.

She eyed him, thinking of Turkey. She made a twisted face. "You mean you waited for it to pass through your bird?" A laugh vibrated the last few words.

"I assure you they're sanitized," he replied. "That place, where I first met you. I went back there too. The birds are good at finding them."

"The one in the wall—"

"Consider it a gift."

"Winn—"

He set his hand on her shoulder, but it was distinctly different from how he had touched Pearl earlier. Less playful, more . . . Gentry couldn't really describe it, but the heat of his palm traced heavy lines under her skin, warming her blood. "Do you really want me to chisel around and see if I can find it? The wall would collapse anyway. It's a gift."

Gentry looked down to her hands, the sink. "Thank you." She lifted her eyes. "It means a great deal to me. Us."

He moved his hand, crooking a finger and placing it under Gentry's chin. "Hardly a sacrifice." He dropped his hand to his side. "Now. Dishes."

"You are not doing the dishes."

"Who's going to stop me?"

Rooster said, "I am. You promised me a game, Maheux."

Winn turned, grinning yet again. "That I did. Your sister shall get her way, this time." He offered Gentry a wink that made the heat beneath her skin blaze and walked to the game board, kneeling opposite of Rooster. He took the white pieces. Pearl leaned over the short table with an interest she had never possessed when their father played. Then again, Pa hadn't used his chess board in ... Gentry couldn't remember how long. She wondered how much it would sell for and how angry Pa would be if he came home to discover it missing.

She scrubbed the dishes—it was a quick job—and wordlessly excused herself outside, where the sun had finally fallen behind the mountains, making the sky pink and the earth blue. Folding her arms, she walked to the crops and looked over the gate. If the quake had damaged it, Rooster had already repaired it. A few seagulls rested on the roof. Where the others had gone, Gentry couldn't be sure.

Though her necklace already rested against her collar, Gentry pressed two fingers over the pendant and scanned the area, searching for the dark blobs, but only the seagulls and the new wall whispered of magic tonight. Her gaze fell back upon the garden. Could she magic the plants to maturity the way Winn had magicked the earth into a wall? Somehow multiply the crops and build some stores? But she didn't see that subtle shimmer anywhere in the garden. She let out a sigh. "Couldn't afford it anyway," she mumbled. Even if she *could* do the spells, or whatever they were called, she'd need gold to make them work.

She picked up her necklace, studied it. Winn got his earrings back, didn't he? But what if magic would tear the links apart, or take a bite out of the pendant? Gentry could never reforge it. No, her ma's necklace was too valuable to give up.

She lingered there, leaning on the fence, fingering her necklace. One of the gulls squawked, and Gentry saw a wormy spirit wriggle away from the house, toward Bounder, who also didn't shimmer with magic. The spirits didn't scare her, not anymore. She thought that interesting.

She heard approaching footsteps, but didn't identify them until Winn said, "Are we too dull?"

She smiled. "Hardly. But if I challenge you to a game of chess, Mr. Maheux, I'm certain I'll win."

He smirked. "I believe you. And please, Mr. Maheux is my father. There's a reason I didn't tell you." He leaned on the fence beside her, examining his wall.

Gentry inhaled cool evening air, considering. "Winn."

"That's better."

"Have you ever used magic to find him? Your father?"

He licked his lips. "Yes. I've been searching for him for a while."

The name suddenly clicked in her head, the memory of their meeting outside American Fork coming to the front of her mind. *You don't perchance know an Ira Maheux, do you?*

"The network is so . . . dim," he continued. "Like I said, the magic has receded in so many places. I've tried several times—lost a good few pennies, I'll have you know—but I've never found him. I fear such a feat would take far more gold than I'll ever have."

It was only the surface of the story. Gentry determined it by the sound of his voice and the way his eyes unfocused when he spoke. It was a deep story, a stake driven into the ground until only the hammered surface remained visible. But it was too early to pull up the stake to see what it was made of.

"My father left us six weeks ago to hunt for gold," she said. "He didn't even tell us he was planning it, even considering it. It came out of the blue." She, too, watched the wall. "One day he said he wanted to mine, and the next he was gone. We've been waiting to hear from him. The road he took is a well-traveled one with way stations, but we've not received one letter, and it worries me. He seemed so confident about it . . ."

Winn turned toward her. "I'll help you find him, if you'd like."

She met his gaze. "Why are you so eager to help us? Why do you keep doing us such kindness, without asking anything in return?"

He grinned. "My belly would argue with you."

"I made no promise before you built this wall." She gestured weakly to the solid brick and glassless window. "You're incredibly selfless, Winn. I don't understand you."

"I wasn't always," he countered. Shrugged. "Maybe I'm making up for lost time. Or maybe the earth spirits chose to quake when they did because they thought I should meet you."

He meant their first meeting, not the morning's quake. Gentry stared at him, her pulse speeding through her wrists and neck, her chest flushing beneath her dress.

Winn began to pull away from the fence, but Gentry stopped him with, "The wild magic. I've seen it around here. Even just yesterday."

He relaxed back into the wooden railing. "Oh? Not too frightening, I hope."

She shook her head. "Mostly little blob monsters, shaped like lazy raindrops." She paused. "I think they want my necklace. It's the only gold around here."

"They want your attention."

She nodded. "I noticed. One of them got a little nibble,"

she traced the pad of her thumb down the chain, "and it listened to me for a moment. Just a moment, but it did what I wanted and—"

His fingers touched her wrist, and his voice, soft but firm, broke her words with her name. "Gentry, please never do that again."

She blinked. "What? Why?"

His hand withdrew, and his light eyebrows scrunched together. "I am thrilled you see it—really, I am. It's nice to have someone to relate that world to. But wild magic is wild for a reason."

"But your seagulls—"

"The gulls are different," he continued. "Gulls, the earth, *physical* creatures that are magically awake . . . they're tame. They're," he paused, mulling over his words, "capable of independent thought. Wild magic is made of spirits. They're different from us. Give them a fraction of mental singularity, and they devour it. Steal it from you. Too much, and you won't have a mind left to think for yourself."

Gentry studied Winn's eyes for a moment, processing the information, remembering the blankness of thought she'd had out by the stable. "I didn't know."

Winn rubbed his eyes. "Hardly your fault. Mine, really. They really are harmless. They stay away from cities generally because all the people and thoughts are confusing to them, I suppose. Out here is a little different."

"Perhaps I just think very interesting things," Gentry quipped.

Winn smiled. "Perhaps you do."

He lingered for a moment, leaning against the fence, before a sigh passed his lips. "I suppose it would be decent of me to bid you adieu, hm?"

"You don't have to—"

He gasped, cutting her off. "Gentry Abrams, what would the neighbors think? You shan't coax me into your den of sin."

The flush geysered to her face. She released the fence. "That's not what I meant at all!"

Winn grinned.

She laughed and punched his arm. "You rogue. Your mother would switch your hide."

"I imagine she would."

Gentry took a deep breath and let it all out at once. "You'll be safe out there, wherever you're going, right?" She wondered how many more disasters Winn saw than she did, since he seemed to seek them out. Since he could actually do something to stop them, unlike herself.

"I won't go gallivanting in the mines, if that's what you mean."

She smiled. "You'd best say goodbye to Pearl and Rooster."

"I already have." He tilted his head. "I always save the best for last."

He scooped up her hand and placed a feather-light kiss on the back of it. The moment he released it, the seagulls leapt off the roof. They seemed to multiply as more birds swept out from behind the house or seemingly out of thin air, adding to their numbers.

"Until we meet again," Winn said, and the gulls swept him into the air and over the mountains. Once more, Gentry watched him go until the night swallowed the flock.

She leaned against the fence, rubbing a thumb over the back of her kissed hand. The skin prickled where his lips had been in a most comfortable way.

All good things must come to an end, Gentry thought as she trekked back to her house from the mercantile, lifting her skirt to keep the hem clean. Still no word from Pa. Gentry was almost not surprised. After her chat with Winn, she'd had the thought to write to a way station or some such on the road to California, to ask if a Butch Abrams had passed through. Mr. Olson had helped her find a good address to send the inquiry to. She hated to pay the postage, but a sound mind was worth a couple of pennies.

When she got home, her back hot from the midday sun, she saw Pearl out in the yard atop Bounder, chatting with Hoss. Gentry hurried her pace. When Hoss saw her, he removed his hat. His beard was shorter, she noticed, and cleanly trimmed about his jaw.

"Rooster's all right, isn't he?" Gentry asked, but Pearl's expression was level, so already she had begun to dismiss the idea.

"Glad to tell you he's right as rain," Hoss answered. "Might be my best worker."

Gentry smiled. She'd have to pass the compliment to her brother over supper.

Hoss replaced his hat. "I'm heading to Salt Lake to look at some cows this weekend, and I need a hand or two to come with me. Rooster is an obvious choice, but then I thought, well, my wagon's a wide one. Wouldn't be right if I didn't offer you and Pearl a ride as well, if you'd like to visit town again."

Gentry straightened. "This weekend?"

"I know your last trip wasn't pleasant, but you'd be in good company." He fidgeted with his hat, almost taking it off again, then pressed it down snug, nearly to his brow. "Rooster said you had family up north."

Only Caleb, but Hannah was practically family as well. "We do, in American Fork."

Pearl looped Bounder's reins around her hand. "Oh please, Gentry, let's go. It's so dull here."

Gentry gaped. "Just yesterday our wall . . ." She stopped, not wanting to explain a collapsed wall and its remarkable repair in case Rooster hadn't passed on the story. Instead, she said, "A quake like that, and you think it's dull?"

Pearl shrugged. "Duller than American Fork."

A small voice buried in Gentry's mind said, *Yes, let's go! It'll be grand, and we'll bring the chess set and teach Hannah how to play. She never has, and I'm sure she'd be quite good at it,* but the voice that had become a jumbled mix of her ma, her pa, and an eldest sister said, "We can't all go. Someone has to tend Bounder."

"I can go." Pearl cast a pleading expression at Hoss.

Hoss didn't notice; his dark eyes focused on Gentry. "I could send one of my hands over. It's no problem. Really, I'd like you to come."

Gentry blinked, looking at Hoss anew. His voice sounded younger just then. For a moment she tried to imagine him without the beard and the years of sunbaked skin. Then she noticed his eyes, earnest and deep. Something about them made her think of Winn, and she felt her ears burn beneath her bonnet, though she wasn't sure if it was for thought of Winn or at the knowing she refused to recognize, not now.

"Well." She took a step back. "I suppose I can't argue with that. You're very kind to offer."

Pearl grinned and took Bounder's reins, trotting her in a tight circle of celebration.

Hoss grinned. "I'll plan for you, then. Leaving Friday morning. Should reach American Fork before sunset."

Gentry nodded, and Hoss headed back to the road, walking at first, then jogging.

"We're going to see Hannah and Caleb!" Pearl clapped her hands together.

"Yes." Gentry pulled her gaze away from Hoss and the uncomfortable digging at the center of her chest. "I'd best write her a letter. Bad timing. I just got back from the mercantile."

"Don't be so sour."

Gentry put a hand on her hip. "I have to be, when you're too sweet."

Pearl pulled on the reins, halting the mare. "That's what Ma used to say."

Gentry's hand slid off her hip. *I do sound like her, don't I? When did that happen?* Gentry tried to recall at what moment she morphed from child to adult. When had she started grasping at straws, trying to be a parent?

Instead, she said, "If Rose were here, I'd race you and put you in your place."

Pearl stuck out her tongue. "Bounder is faster, and you know it."

"Rose has better endurance," she countered. That was why Pa took her with him.

Pa. She hoped her letter would come back with good news. She didn't know what they'd do if it didn't.

~~~

The trip to American Fork with Hoss was far more pleasant than it had been when Gentry and Pearl had done it. There were no geysers or sulfur pools eating the road, for starters. No quakes, and very few spirits, though no one else saw them, even when Gentry pointed right at one fluttering near the Wasatch Mountains and asked Pearl if she saw anything. She noticed none of the blob-like creatures that had fed on her necklace and her thoughts, and none of the magic seemed interested in her. They arrived in American Fork in good time.

Rooster slid off the wagon seat, where he had ridden beside Hoss, and helped Pearl, then Gentry, to the ground. He grabbed their bags and slung them over his shoulder, carrying them in. Gentry knew he wanted to see Caleb before heading into Salt Lake City. Caleb was Rooster's only brother, after all.

"Are you sure you won't stop in?" Gentry asked Hoss, coming around to the driver's side of the wagon. "You can't get too much farther tonight, and I'm sure they'd put you up if we asked. They're very nice."

"Sweet of you to offer, Gentry," he replied, "but there's an inn a few miles from here I intend to stay at. Tradition. A friend of mine runs it. We came out here together, from Mississippi."

Gentry nodded. "I suppose I can't argue with that. Do watch after Rooster for me."

She smiled and turned to leave, but Hoss said, "Gentry," with such a weight to it she couldn't take the first step away from the wagon. She turned back to him, wrapping the string of her bonnet around her finger until the knot came loose.

He didn't look at her, but rather down the road. He licked his lips, glanced toward the Hinkle residence, then settled his gaze on his hands. "If you needed . . . what I mean is . . . well, I could take care of you too."

Gentry's stomach tightened, as though a string had fastened to her navel and looped around her highest rib, pulling taut. Her mouth went dry. She didn't need to ask what he meant.

She tried to think of something to say as the silence between them grew the way nothing in the Utah Territory should grow. She tried to swallow and failed.

Rooster came out of the house.

Hoss cleared his throat and met her eyes. "Something to think about, if you would."

She managed a shallow nod, and Hoss turned his attention to Rooster, saying something about making good time. Gentry used the diversion to escape, walking so quickly she practically ran around the back of the wagon. Her chest flushed as she hurried to the house, the heat of it burning up her neck and into her face and ears. She opened the door to Hannah, Pearl, and Hannah's baby, Rachel, stretched out on the floor. Caleb showed Pearl his collection of painted blocks.

"Gentry!" Hannah stood and hurried to her with her arms stretched wide. She embraced Gentry for a moment before pulling back. "Goodness, what's wrong? You look like you've seen a phantom."

"I just need some water," she said. "No, please, I'll get it myself." She offered a smile—at least, she hoped it looked like a smile—and went into the kitchen, filling a cup from a pitcher on the table. She drank it in a few gulps, and the liquid turned to iron in her stomach.

She pulled out one of the chairs around the kitchen table and sat.

She shouldn't be surprised. She knew Hoss liked her, but not . . . enough to make an offer. Not that he had, not *really*. Had he?

She set the cup down and rubbed her eyes. Hoss Howland. The idea had crossed her mind before, but he was . . . Hoss Howland. Her father's friend. Her brother's employer. A man twice her age.

I could take care of you too. And he could, couldn't he? Hoss Howland with his big house and big farm, doing well enough to ride to Salt Lake City and buy cows. Milk, eggs, meat, vegetables. On the table every day, or so Gentry imagined. Shirts and slacks without patches in them. Hired help. He certainly could take care of Gentry. And Rooster. And Pearl. Pa might even come home, and Gentry wouldn't need to worry so much about the mines anymore.

She pressed her fingertips into her eyes, and in the ensuing spots she saw Winn. She lowered her hands and tried to blink them away, but the golden colors held the shape of his face, his tousled hair, his warm eyes.

I always save the best for last.

"Well, isn't this a bother," she whispered, laying her hands on the table, staring down into her empty cup. Since when had she become so likable? She was sour, just as Pearl had said. Sour and bossy and a knot of worry.

Her stomach rumbled in familiar discomfort.

He's just a flirt, Gentry, she told herself. *Who says he's any more interested in you than he is in Pearl? It's just good fun. What benefit could a magic man who flies with birds get from charming a dull desert woman?*

She understood Hoss. Hoss was already in his forties, never married, and didn't have a lot of options. Winn had the world at his fingertips. All it cost was an earring.

"Gentry?" Pearl called from the front room.

"Coming." She filled her cup again and drank the cool water slowly this time. She noticed a crack in the kitchen window and wondered if the earthquake had grazed American Fork too.

When Gentry came into the front room, Hannah said, "Caleb, do you want to show Pearl your books? In your room?"

Caleb nodded but held still.

Pearl looked at Hannah, then at Gentry, before standing and offering her hand to their little brother. "Come on, Cay. Let's go see your books."

Caleb's tan hand grasped Pearl's ring finger, and he allowed her to lead him down the hallway.

Hannah picked up Rachel and crossed the room to the sofa. She sat and patted the cushion next to her.

Pulling off her bonnet, Gentry sat down.

"What's wrong?" she asked.

"Nothing, just a long ride," Gentry said.

"Gentry Sue Abrams, don't you dare lie to me. I'm a Saint; I can tell." She smiled. "Come now," she added, softer, "you don't have a mother to confide in, and I'm sure Pearl is too young to hear your worries. Let me help you. If nothing else, it feels good to let things out, doesn't it?" She paused. "Is it about the quake? Did it hit home?"

Gentry shook her head and leaned back against the couch, staring at the ceiling. "I think Hoss Howland wants to marry me."

"That's great! He's the farmer who dropped you off, isn't he? I didn't get a chance to talk to him."

Gentry nodded.

"Ah," Hannah said.

"He's a lot older than me."

"Willard is sixteen years my senior," she replied.

Still a smaller age gap than me and Hoss, she thought. She shrugged. "I don't know. I didn't think much about it, after we moved out west. There aren't a lot of people around here."

"Not in Dry Creek, I suppose." Hannah had never been to the town, only heard of it from the Abrams. "There are lots of nice young men around here."

"Lots of Mormon men."

"What's wrong with that?"

"Nothing, really."

Hannah quirked a brow. Rachel fussed, so Hannah adjusted her hold and pulled her collar down so the babe could breastfeed. Eyes still on the babe, she said, "Is there someone else?"

Gentry sighed. "Maybe."

Hannah grinned. "There are more men about than you let on."

"Winn doesn't live in Dry Creek, just passes through. On . . . business."

"Oh? He's a businessman?"

"Not exactly." *If not for magic, he might be as poor as I am.*

The smile faded. Hannah looked at Gentry until Gentry met her gaze. "Unrequited?" she asked.

"I don't know."

"Then don't be so down about it."

"It's not just that. I'm not a sappy school girl." Gentry leaned against the backrest. "But we still haven't heard from Pa. He hasn't sent us any wages, and Rooster's pay only goes so far. I wish there was more Pearl and I could do."

"Taking care of the house and the lot is doing something."

"It doesn't make us money," Gentry countered. "I need to buy feed for Bounder if we're going to keep her, and I can't imagine selling her. She came with us from Virginia."

Hannah reached her free hand over and clasped Gentry's. "It will be all right. You'll hear from your father, I'm sure of it. He's a good man."

Is he? Gentry thought, then berated herself. Of course he was.

"We're doing just fine," Hannah said. "And I have a couple dresses I can't fit into anymore, not since Rachel. I'll send them home with you, and some bread and potatoes."

"Hannah, we don't need—"

"I've plenty to spare."

"No. It's fine."

"Gentry Sue Abrams," Hannah said, and Gentry winced at the second use of her full name. At her ma's name within her own, *Sue Abrams.* "You need to humble yourself."

Gentry scoffed. "You say that like I'm prideful. I don't have anything to take pride in."

"You are prideful!" Hannah spoke a little too loudly. She must have heard it too, for she flushed rather prettily. Lowering her voice, she continued, "Everyone has hard times. I've had hard times, Carolyn has had hard times. Your folks have had hard times."

Gentry thought of Caleb.

"But the reason God put more than one person on the earth is so we'd help each other."

Don't cry. Don't cry.

"And I am going to help you because He has given me the means to do so. You hear me? Don't pretend like you wouldn't do just the same, if not more, were our positions switched."

Gentry shook her head and looked upward, blinking to prevent tears.

Hannah squeezed Gentry's hand.

"Thank you," Gentry whispered.

CHAPTER 8

Hannah didn't mention their conversation the next day, for which Gentry was grateful. All carried on as normal. Pearl and Gentry fit right in with the Hinkle household, and Hannah and Carolyn filled their bellies with food and their ears with conversation and local gossip. Gentry had only gotten a glimpse of Willard Hinkle, as he was still back and forth to Salt Lake City, trying to deal with territorial business licenses and the like for his potential printing company.

The Hinkles had a large yard, and Carolyn had recently acquired a dog as well. Gentry spent long hours out there with the children, taking turns carrying the smaller ones on her shoulders as they ran back and forth, the mutt licking their ankles as they went. After Caleb had his nap, Gentry rehearsed colors and numbers with him—at least, for as long as his attention held. It was good to be away from Dry Creek and her life in general. She could ignore it for a little while, and hopefully, when she returned, there would be a letter waiting for her.

A knock came at the door as Gentry helped dice garlic cloves in the kitchen for supper, Hannah at her side. Carolyn answered it, and when she returned she said, "That was the Johnson boy, running about inviting everyone to a bonfire."

"Louie?" asked Hannah.

"Albert," Carolyn corrected.

"Bonfire?" Gentry asked.

Hannah straightened, a fiendish smile growing on her lips. "Yes, of course! We should all go."

Carolyn snorted and returned to her biscuit dough. "And leave the kids here to tend themselves?"

"Well, *you* should go, Gentry. And Pearl," Hannah amended. "There will be music and dancing, and you can meet some of the young folk around here." She added a wink for emphasis.

Gentry peeled another clove of garlic. "I haven't been to a bonfire since we left Virginia."

"So long?" Hannah asked, sounding offended. "Well, you must go. And I'll come with you. That's all right, isn't it Carolyn?"

"What use have I for dancing like a heathen around a fire?" Carolyn retorted, but there was the sound of humor in it. "Yes, go, but I'm not washing the smoke out of your clothes. It's toward the lake, is all he told me. Sunset, like I couldn't figure that out myself."

A warm shiver coursed through Gentry's middle. She'd loved summer bonfires back home. Sometimes they'd get meat to roast over the flames before the music began. Gentry would take Rooster's hands and swing him around until he got sick and she got yelled at.

Hannah would be there. Maybe Gentry didn't have to play mother tonight.

"I see you." Hannah handed Gentry a lamb's-quarter to chop. She nudged her with her elbow. "I'm going to tell Pearl."

She grinned like a little girl and hurried out of the kitchen.

Gentry heard Pearl's gasp of excitement a few minutes later.

~~~

By the time Gentry walked to the bonfire, the sun was a quarter set, and the sound of tuning fiddles and banjos pecked the air. She walked hand in hand with Pearl, Hannah striding beside her with Rachel in her arms. Necklace resting soundly against her neck, she looked around for spirits, then searched the passing flora for the shimmer of magic. No shimmer, but she thought she saw a streak of something ethereal in the darkening sky.

Gentry, Pearl, and Hannah weren't alone on the path; a few children raced ahead of their parents, and a number of adolescents half skipped their way to the growing fire. There weren't many older persons in attendance, save for some of the musicians.

Hannah found a slice of log to perch on, and Gentry walked Pearl around the circumference of the fire, which steadily grew until it was well taller than she. Even at a distance, the heat pricked her cheeks and made her green dress appear brown. It colored Pearl's dark blonde hair ginger.

When the sun reached half set, someone pulled out a goat-skin drum and began beating a steady rhythm. Pearl jumped in place, pulling Gentry toward the fire. Gentry angled them closer to Hannah, trying to ignore the glances from strangers. Soon, however, it would be dark enough that no one would be recognizable, and in that sort of darkness, Gentry could be anyone she wanted.

An older gentleman on a banjo began plucking chords. Several of the adolescents left their seats on wood and earth. When the fiddle began, Gentry's soul came alive.

She grabbed Pearl's hands in her own and splayed their arms out to their sides, then tugged her into the bodies that began to churn counterclockwise around the fire. Pearl easily remembered the steps of the dance from Virginia: two skips with arms out, two skips with arms in. Gentry laughed, and at the other side of the fire, with their arms in, she spun Pearl, switching places with her, nearly bumping into a gal and her beau, but Gentry didn't care. The fire blazed hot, the music loud, and those not dancing clapped to the beat, creating a vibration that thrummed through Gentry's ribs.

"I know this song!" Gentry shouted over music and talk and cries of glee as more and more people filed around the bonfire. "'Leather Breeches'—the Virginia reel!"

"Virginia is here!" Pearl yelled back.

The words filled her chest to bursting, and Gentry tugged Pearl around the fire a second time, laughing again when Pearl tripped and nearly knocked both of them over.

Pearl pulled Gentry around again, releasing one of her hands to form a new dance, something like the jig Ma used to do with them. They faced forward and skipped holding one hand, then turned toward each other and skipped again. Over and over, the pattern easy and alluring, stealing Gentry's breath and turning Pearl's cheeks pink.

The song calmed, and Gentry stumbled, fingers still laced with her sister's, toward Hannah, who was barely visible among all the new arrivals. Dozens of people swarmed around the fire, maybe a hundred. Several danced, others kept time as a new song started, others chatted or simply watched.

Gentry collapsed at the foot of the log Hannah perched upon, her skirt billowing around her legs. Her cheeks ached from smiling.

"You look thirteen out there!" Hannah laughed.

"I do?" Pearl asked, not realizing Hannah had addressed Gentry.

Hannah went with the mistake and answered, "One year older and wiser too."

Gentry turned around so she faced the fire, planting her palms on the dry, packed earth and leaning back, her chest heaving. She was glad she'd worn her lighter dress today. The sun had nearly set, but she was baking.

Then, just below the glow of the fire on the lake side, she spotted a seagull.

She touched her necklace, ensuring it was still there. "I'll be right back." She picked herself up and dusted off her hands. She gave the dancers a wide berth, returning a few nods from the men nearby. She blinked the burning colors of yellow and orange from her eyes and studied the seagull. It flapped its wings once, but didn't fly away.

Yes, there it was. The subtle shimmer around its body, almost like a halo. She crouched a few paces away, not wanting to scare it.

"If you're one of Winn's," she said, "tell him to get over here. I want to see him dance."

The gull cocked its head to one side, examining her for a moment, before flying off toward the lake.

Gentry watched it go for a moment, but she didn't linger long. She didn't want to miss anything.

As she returned, two boys rushed by her, taking turns with a hoop and stick. Another kicked a ball, and a woman, Gentry assumed his mother, yelled after him. Up ahead, a boy about Pearl's age with dark, curly hair and suspenders squatted near Pearl and Hannah, saying something Gentry couldn't hear over all the blissful noise. She could, however, see the pinking of Pearl's cheeks and the nod of her head. The boy offered his hand, Pearl took it, and they danced toward the fire.

The next song began, another Gentry knew—"Robison County," though with a few chord variations from the one she'd learned. Kneeling beside Hannah, she said, "Who is that?"

"Huh?"

"That boy?" Gentry said, a little louder.

Hannah grinned. "That's Albert Ryerson. Second oldest of five boys. Nice chap."

Gentry nodded and scanned the people prancing around the fire, their forms half silhouette. After a moment, Pearl and Albert popped out from behind the fire, skipping together, Albert occasionally twirling her under his arm. Their movements were awkward, but judging by their countenances, neither of them noticed.

"We'll have to move to American Fork if this keeps up," Gentry jested.

"Yes. Do!" Hannah laughed.

Gentry turned, casting her shadow over Hannah and Rachel. "Do you want me to hold her? You can have a turn."

Hannah looked aghast. "I'm not dancing by myself."

"Then give her to someone and I'll dance with you."

Hannah shook her head no, but stopped halfway through the action. Biting her lip, she looked around, face to face, and finally called, "Abiline!"

The woman who had been yelling after the boy with the ball earlier turned about, scanning until she met Hannah's eyes. She came over without hesitation.

Hannah stood and asked, "Would you hold her for one song? I need to show my friend here how to dance." She winked.

Gentry rolled her eyes.

"Of course." Abiline took Rachel with gentle hands.

With a sudden burst of energy, Hannah grabbed Gentry's wrist and dragged her toward the fire, slipping into a space between children brave enough to skip about solo. Despite her words about teaching Gentry to dance, she used the same steps Gentry and Pearl had used, arms wide and then drawn in, each with two skips to the beat of the drum. The song ended a few seconds later, but when the next started, Gentry adjusted their rhythm. They circled the fire another two times, their steps uneven as they avoided stepping on each other's toes and the feet of the dancers swirling around them.

A second hand caught one of Gentry's wrists, as well as one of Hannah's, and spun them away from the fire. Hannah laughed and tripped into Gentry, but stayed upright.

Gentry looked over, her fast-beating heart lurching. "Winn!"

He grinned, his teeth bright in the flickering light. Hannah's eyes went wide at the name.

"I beg your utmost pardon," Winn said to Hannah with a British sort of bow, "but I must insist I take this young lady for a spin, if you'd be so kind."

Hannah easily relented. "By all means; I was just warming her up for you." Hannah passed a knowing glance Gentry's way—one Gentry prayed Winn didn't see—and hurried back to Abiline. Gentry's eyes followed her, noticing Rooster on the edge of the shadows, making his way to the festivities. He and the others had returned, then.

"So it *was* one of your birds." Gentry had to nearly shout to be heard. She grabbed Winn's arms and moved him back before Pearl and Albert crashed into them, though neither child seemed to notice.

The clappers picked up their pace, or maybe Gentry just imagined they did, but it and the disappeared sun gave her courage. She grabbed both of Winn's hands, the faint roughness of his palms sending a thrill through her arms. "I want to see you dance!"

"You Americans are loony." His grin was as wide as she'd ever seen it. "As you please, mademoiselle."

He pulled her toward the fire, through the dancers, until Gentry felt the heat of it winding into her hair and pressing against her back. Winn dropped one of her hands and looped his arm under her shoulder and around her back, pulling her close. Her body burned where she touched him and burned where the fire touched her. Through the scent of smoke, she smelled clean earth and butternut.

Winn pulled her around the fire in a soft but brisk skip, lacing his fingers with hers, guiding them with his out-stretched arm. On their second loop, he pulled their arms in and spun Gentry around, lifting all but her toes from the ground. Gentry shrieked, which elicited a laugh from Winn. The sound of it was musical, flowing in perfect harmony with the fiddle and banjo.

Winn was a brave dancer, holding onto Gentry for the next song, weaving their bodies in and out of the other dancers, twirling them about this couple or that one, never quite running into them. Gentry's fingers clutched at his shirt behind his shoulder, feeling the shifting muscle beneath his skin. She looked into his gold-flecked eyes and tripped, but Winn tightened his hold around her, and she regained her footing. By the time that second song ended, her feet were nearly numb.

Winn readied to pull her into another song, but she gasped, laughing, and said, "No, no, stop! My legs will fall off!"

"Then I'll carry you!"

"That won't be fun for either of us." She panted, laughed, then grabbed one of his hands, tugging him through the dancers as they slowed and waited for the next melody. Dust clouded around her shoes. She found Hannah on her same log, swaying as the new song began, Rachel's head on her shoulder. Hannah kept time patting her hand against the babe's back.

"Hannah!" Gentry called, the spot between her lungs burning in a pleasant way. "Hannah, where's Rooster?"

"Somewhere around here. He didn't hesitate finding a nice lady to dance with." She eyed Winn. "You must be Winn."

She spoke as though she'd heard all about him, not as though Gentry had simply said his name in passing. Gentry's cheeks were already flushed beneath the layer of night.

Winn extended his left hand—his right still held Gentry's—and awkwardly shook Hannah's.

"And you are Hannah, if I heard correctly."

"You are correct. We're good friends of the Abrams. And I'm happy to be a good friend of yours too."

Winn grinned.

A new voice said, "I don't believe we've had the pleasure."

At first Gentry didn't recognize the newcomer; his hat shadowed his face. But he moved closer, hand extended, and the cords at the back of Gentry's neck tightened.

"Hoss!" Of course Hoss would be here with Rooster. All the farmhands probably were.

Winn's gaze moved from Hoss's arm to his face, perhaps recognizing him from before. This time he released Gentry's fingers to shake Hoss's hand properly. "We have, my good man. In Dry Creek."

"Ah, yes. Well." Hoss hefted a long, smooth stick that looked like it'd been screwed off a broom. "Care for a challenge?"

Winn blinked. "I'm not familiar."

Hoss jerked his thumb to the side, near where Abiline had retaken her spot. There, in the space outside the dancers, men were doing stick pulls. Gentry knew the game. Two men sat facing each other, the soles of their feet pressed together, and held the stick horizontally between them. They pulled, and the stronger man would lift the weaker to his feet. It was like an absurd sort of arm wrestle.

"Hoss—" Gentry began.

Winn interrupted, "Sure," as though Hoss had offered him a stick of candy and not a feat of strength.

Hannah's lips formed a tight O, and she looked at Gentry. The men walked toward the space and Gentry sighed. "This will be fun."

"Indeed. I don't even care if I lose my seat." Hannah stood and followed Gentry's path. "Is he . . . where is he from?"

"Canada."

"Oh. I didn't think men pierced their ears in Canada." She pursed her lips, thoughtful.

Gentry and Hannah squeezed in among onlookers as a stick-pull match between two men Gentry didn't recognize ended. Hoss raised his staff to draw attention to himself, opening the space for him and Winn. Gentry folded her arms, unsure what to think. She glanced over her shoulder to search for Rooster—she thought she found him, but it was too dark to tell, and he wasn't angled toward the light. When she looked back, Winn and Hoss had taken their positions sole-to-sole. Winn had taken the easier inside grip on the stick, while Hoss's thick hands took the outside.

A seagull landed on a nearby rock, unnoticed by the bystanders.

"Go!" shouted a man off to the side, and the men's arms pulled taut, their shoulders quivering ever so slightly. Winn's back was to Gentry, and his hair covered most of his face and neck. Hoss faced her, his lip pulling back slightly, his teeth clenched together.

Winn's rump began to lift off the ground. A glimmer of victory shone in Hoss's eyes, and he heaved back with a grunt, nearly throwing Winn over his head. Winn stumbled, nearly falling over. The men watching laughed.

Gentry took a step forward, but she relaxed when Winn turned around, chuckling as well. His smile was sincere, and he offered a hand to Hoss to help him to his feet.

"Can't beat a farmer," he said.

Hoss responded in turn, but Gentry didn't hear it. A new pair scrambled out to the arena, and a few men came up to Winn and Hoss, chatting.

Gentry noticed the music again and turned away from the game, toward the musicians, her fingers itching. She knew this song—"Briar Picker Brown." It was nearly at an end. Memories of Virginia strummed through her blood, and she wondered . . .

"I'll be right back," she told Hannah, and she jogged to the bonfire crowd, picking her way around it just as "Briar Picker Brown" ended. She touched the arm of the fiddle player, an older man whose hair was half gray.

"Request?" he asked, eyes bright.

"Yes. Is there a chance . . ." The musicians were away from the light. She was out of practice, but the darkness hid her, didn't it? "Would you like a break? I would love a turn at the fiddle."

He looked surprised. "You play?"

"I used to." She had played often, before Pa sold the fiddle to help pay for the trip out west. "If it's a bother—"

"By all means, young lady." He handed her the fiddle and the bow. A few loose horse hairs danced at the end of it. "My arm is tired," he joked.

The banjo player looked over, as did a few bystanders, probably wondering why the music hadn't restarted.

Swallowing, pulse beating hard, Gentry leaned toward the others in the tiny band. "Do you know 'Turkey in the Straw'?"

"It's a requirement to know 'Turkey in the Straw,'" said the fiddler behind her.

"It's my favorite."

The banjo player smiled. The drummer began a quick beat on his drum, and the banjo player began plucking familiar chords, repeating them, waiting for Gentry to jump in.

Gentry raised the fiddle to her shoulder and sat her chin on its edge. The body was a little wider than she was used to, but the familiar weight on her shoulder stirred a pleasant nostalgia. She found her fingers, and placed the bow on two of the strings, pulling it back slowly for the first chord, then the second.

The third clashed against the banjo. She winced, cold lancing down her back.

It's fine. You're rusty. She closed her eyes, the banjo player plucking his notes on repeat again, waiting for her. The dancers didn't seem to notice. *Play by heart.*

She kept her eyes closed and repeated the first chord, the second, the third, sliding the pads of her fingers up and down the strings to give them that sour flavor that opened the song. She repeated them, pulled out a long drawl, then plucked an E.

There it was. She remembered and opened her eyes.

Her arm came to life as the quick notes of the song rushed through her, the bow pulling back and forth in an almost mad dance, the fingers of her left hand lifting up and down, finding their keys by memory against the strings. She began pumping her heel in beat with the rhythm, drew the bow out long again, and dived back into the quick arpeggios. She moved with the music, strands of hair falling free from her bun and dancing around her cheeks.

She heard the banjo move into its final measures, and she drew her last few chords. The nearby listeners who had heard the exchange between herself and the fiddler clapped their hands, and Gentry lowered the instrument, again breathless.

"Thank you," she said.

"Thank *you.*" The fiddler gestured to his fiddle. "You want to go again?"

Gentry grinned and shook her head. "I'm out of practice. My arm already hurts."

She handed back the instrument, feeling revitalized, as though all the energy she'd danced out near the fire had flooded back into her. She wondered if this was what the seagulls felt like when they swallowed gold.

As she walked away, she heard one set of clapping that didn't match the rhythm of the others, and she noticed Winn, looking golden himself in the glow on the bonfire, applauding her.

"You're amazing." His voice was more awed than amused, and the sound of it drilled down to Gentry's core. "I didn't know you could do that. You've never played for me."

Gentry shrugged, tucking hair behind her ears to give her hands something to do. "My pa taught me, but we sold the fiddle."

"A shame. You're remarkable."

She stood a pace from him, the bonfire burning far to her left. It made one of Winn's eyes gold, while the one in shadow looked brown. It did that to all of him, painting one side bright and splendid, the other calm and cool. On one side Winn was a wizard, a magician, whatever she could call it. On the other, he was a normal man, someone who might live next door. Someone she might have said goodbye to back home.

His different-colored eyes watched her, free of mirth. His lips relaxed, free of smile. He just watched her, and Gentry couldn't pull her eyes away.

She swallowed. "Where do you go? When I don't see you, I mean."

He tilted his head to one side, much like a seagull, and his countenance changed as the magical half of his lips quirked upward. "Wherever the earth calls me. I'm trying to keep it as tame as possible. Waga once said it was my calling."

"Who?"

"I'll introduce you someday."

He truly lived on the breeze, then, in that house of birds. Gentry couldn't fathom such an existence. "Will you come back to Dry Creek? If Hoss is here, we'll head back tomorrow morning."

"I'd take you myself, but then we'd have to explain things, and I don't want to explain magic to those who can't see it. Such a shame."

He reached forward and tucked a strand of hair Gentry had missed behind her ear, his touch cooler than her blazing skin.

"Gentry!"

Gentry turned, breaking the spell. It took a moment for her mind to pull away from Winn and focus her eyes, but when she did, she saw Rooster waving for her to come down to the fire. He shouted something else, but the music muffled it.

It was still dark, and Gentry had a little courage left.

She took Winn's hand. "Come on." She let her lips pull into a smile. "I've had a long enough rest, and the fire won't burn forever."

Though, as they stumbled toward the flames and Winn pulled her close for another song, Gentry wished it would.

CHAPTER 9

Gentry woke early the next morning to depart for Dry Creek. The ride home was slow, as they had to walk two cows with them. The wagon jostled just enough to make sleeping on the way difficult. She brought with her two new dresses, one for herself and one she would hem for Pearl, some stock groceries from Hannah's kitchen, and a few extra dollars in her pocket. Hannah threatened to make a scene when Gentry tried to refuse them, but ultimately, she was grateful for the money. She was getting quite skilled at stretching pennies. It would help immensely.

Gentry noted that Hoss was particularly quiet on this trip, only occasionally chatting to whichever farmhand sat next to him on the driver's seat. It made Gentry uneasy, and she tried to remember what sort of volume Hoss had had on the way *to* American Fork. She couldn't remember. Perhaps he'd been just as quiet and she only noticed it now because of the unspoken words between them. Because of Winn.

She turned her head to where no one would see her smile save one of the cows and a bell-shaped spirit that crept in the ruts the wheels left behind, sensing her gold, or perhaps

Hoss's. She still felt Winn's arm around her, his hand pressed against her back. Last night had been the best night she'd had since leaving Virginia.

The bell spirit followed them for nearly an hour before losing interest and fading into the air, which made the remainder of the journey rather tedious. They reached Dry Creek at sunset, all of them tired and sore. Hoss drove by the Abrams's home so they could unload Hannah's charity. Gentry thanked him profusely, and he left with a smile on his face. That was good, at least. She hated the idea of Hoss being angry with her.

Unfortunately, Dry Creek was too quick to remind her of her responsibilities. Weeds had taken the opportunity of her leave to sprout in the garden, something had spoiled in the kitchen, making the whole house smell bad, and Gentry hadn't done laundry while in American Fork, so once she and her siblings unloaded their bags, there would be a fresh load.

She sighed, opened the windows to air the place out, and went to bed, sleeping with a fist around her ma's locket in case any wild magic snuck into the house for a late-night snack. They, and the laundry, would have to wait until morning.

~~~

Gentry took the long way to the mercantile atop Bounder's back, Pearl snug on the saddle behind her, letting the horse trot out and get some exercise. Hoss had done as he promised and sent a farmhand to care for her, but Gentry doubted she'd been let out of the stall save to graze. The saddle had been left crookedly on its hooks, just as Gentry had left it.

Gentry slid off the saddle when they arrived, careful to keep her skirt over her legs. Pearl scooted up on the saddle and took the reins as Gentry jogged to the window.

"Anything for the Abrams?"

Mr. Olson, already back at the cubbies, started. "Oh, Gentry. Hello, and yes, I do have something. From that way station we found."

Gentry's lungs filled to bursting.

He clasped the envelope and handed it to her. "Here you are. Good luck."

She nodded her thanks and took the letter, walking around to the other side of the mercantile, where she leaned against its shaded wall. Pearl trotted Bounder over as well.

"Is it from Pa?"

Gentry didn't answer, merely tore the paper open and read. She sighed in relief. "No, but it's from the way station on the California border. They say Butch Abrams passed through on June 14. Which means he made it safely."

She lowered the letter, pinching her lips together. That was a month ago. Surely he would have sent a letter by now if the way station responded so quickly. What was keeping him? Perhaps the mining companies paid their workers only once a month. In that case, they would hear from him soon.

She passed the sentiment on to her sister.

Pearl frowned. "I hope so. I miss him. He'll come home in the fall, right?"

"I don't know," Gentry replied. "I'm waiting for him to tell us." She didn't think California wintered the way Utah did. The miners would likely work year-round.

They returned home, and Pearl took charge of preparing supper while Gentry cleaned out the oven. It was dirty business, and her apron only protected her so much. She'd probably have black fingernails for a week.

Rooster came home sweaty and weary. Hanging his hat, he said, "You wouldn't believe it."

Gentry slipped a quarter log into the oven and wiped her brow. "Believe what? One of the cows turn out to be a bull?"

"Is Hoss sweet on you?"

Gentry paused, staring into the oven for a long moment before turning toward her brother. She felt Pearl's eyes on the back of her head. "What do you mean?"

Rooster frowned. "You know what I mean."

"Yes, but what makes you ask it?"

Rooster shook his head. "You'll see soon enough. Pretty sure he's heading over."

"Now?" Gentry moved to stand and smacked her head on the oven lip. She bit down a curse and resisted rubbing the spot with her grubby fingers. Wincing, she stood and added, "Did you invite him?"

Rooster shook his head in the negative, his lip twisted down.

"Rooster, tell me."

"I don't even know what to say," he responded, more confused than anything else. "At the bonfire, I thought Winn—"

A firm knock sounded at the door.

"Bother," Gentry mumbled, finding a half-clean rag, wetting it, and scrubbing it over her fingers.

Rooster opened the door. "I didn't break something, did I?"

Hoss laughed at the other side of it. "If you had, I would have knocked harder. Your sister here?"

"Which one?" Rooster asked, but he opened the door the rest of the way.

Gentry brushed loose hair back with her one clean hand. "Hoss! We weren't expecting you." She cast a quick, hard look at Rooster.

"I know I'm interrupting, and I apologize." He held a box about the length of Gentry's arm in his hands. "I only mean to be a minute."

Gentry wiped off her other hand and gestured to him.

"Please, come in. You'll have to excuse me, I was cleaning out the oven."

"You look just fine," Hoss said with a half smile. He came in, and Rooster shut the door behind him.

Pearl, eyeing the box, asked, "What's that?"

"This is a gift." He set the box on the table. "A family gift. For Butch too, when he gets back."

He added the last sentence hastily, almost as though he were guilty of something.

Gentry glanced to Rooster, hoping to read something on his face, but he wasn't looking at her. "Hoss, you give us so much already—"

"I wanted to. You're good folk, and you should have one."

The words confused her. She waited for Pearl, ever the excited one, to move forward and open the box, but she stayed planted by the oven, and Rooster was no help, so Gentry approached it, hoping Hoss wouldn't notice her nails.

Swallowing, she pulled back the thin wooden panel and gasped.

There, on a bed of paper, lay a fiddle and bow.

Her eyes went wide, her mouth dry. She reached forward to touch the instrument, then drew her hand back. "Hoss, where . . . ?"

"Saw you playing last night," he said, suddenly sheepish, which was an odd manner for such a large man. "I know Butch played too. Didn't realize how much you loved it. I bartered with the fiddle player. Turns out he had more than one; this was his son's before he quit."

The light gleamed off the fiddle's gloss. Gentry gave in to temptation and grasped its neck, pulling it from the box. She cradled the familiar weight of its hollow body. How much would this have cost?

"It's too much." She choked the words out. "Rooster and Pearl, they don't play—"

"We can listen, though," Rooster murmured. "Was saying just the other day I missed music."

Pearl danced. "We can write to Pa and tell him!"

Gentry's gaze fluttered down the length of the fiddle, her heart doing somersaults. She knew what this was. She knew why Rooster had asked if Hoss was sweet on her. She had ridden right next to this box on the wagon and never known . . .

"I—*we*—can't accept this. It's too grand a gift, Hoss." Despite her words, she couldn't peel her fingers from the instrument.

"If you don't, it'll sit unused in my attic," Hoss insisted. "I don't ask anything in return, Gentry. Only that you take it."

The gloss of the instrument shone in the light coming through the windows. "Thank you," she whispered, holding the fiddle to her chest. "This means . . . so much. Thank you, truly."

Hoss grinned and nodded. It made her skin feel too thick. How could she manage such a debt to him? He claimed not to want anything in return, but how could an unmarried man like himself offer such a heartfelt, *expensive* gift and not expect anything in return? Yet already Gentry knew she would cry if he *did* take it back. Part of her spirit had already tied itself to the fiddle's strings.

She forced herself to relinquish the fiddle, setting it gently on the table. "You must stay for supper. We'll have enough. I insist, if you haven't already . . ."

"I would love to," he said. "Very kind of you."

"Don't speak of kindness to me, Hoss Howland." She eyed her brother. "Rooster, would you put this somewhere safe?"

"You have to play!" Hoss chuckled.

"I will. I will, after we eat." She chewed her lip, trying to think of something to do. Light the fire. She could do that. But as she knelt back to the small pile of wood, Hoss insisted he do it, so she merely stood back and watched, picking soot from under her nails, her fingers cold.

"When is Butch heading back?" he asked once he finished, wiping his hands on his trousers.

"I . . . we haven't heard from him," she answered.

"Yeah," Pearl chimed.

Hoss's brow lowered. "Still no word? That's odd."

It relieved Gentry to have someone else think so.

Hoss's gaze settled heavily on her. "If you folks need help . . ."

"Oh, no, we're fine," Gentry lied. "Pa made sure we'd be all right before he left."

The fib tasted bitter on her tongue. She pointedly did not look at the ledger behind her, the one with all the numbers for their declining household. She heard it whisper the digits to her if she held her breath.

"All right," Hoss said, "but let me know if I can help. I'm happy to."

"I know." Gentry swallowed a sigh and nodded to cover it up. "You give Rooster work, and that's help enough."

"That's not help, that's paying for a job well done." Hoss lifted a hand as though to touch Gentry's arm, maybe her shoulder, but switched direction suddenly and instead ran over his beard. "So," he said, "what's on the menu?"

∼∼∼

Gentry woke a little early the next morning, dressed, and got the oven heated for the day's meals. She heard Rooster get up, caught the sound of his suspenders snapping. Pearl would probably be squirming under the covers, trying to get as many extra minutes of slumber as she could.

Gentry set the box on the kitchen table with care and reverently slid its lid away. She had tuned the fiddle last night and even found rosin at the bottom of the case, but she plucked each string again, turning the pegs in tiny increments until she heard the clear notes: G, D, A, E. After applying a little of the rosin to her bow, she played a slow version of "My Love Is But a Lassie."

Rooster came out of the bedroom, and Gentry expected him to comment on the hour, but he only smiled at her.

There was music in the house again.

Though Gentry had lost her fiddle calluses and her fingers were still sore from the bonfire, she played one more song before hurrying to breakfast, ensuring Rooster had something to eat before heading to work. Pearl poked her head out just as Rooster left, rubbing sleep from her eyes. She frowned at the smell of oatmeal, *again*, and ducked back inside to dress. Sighing, Gentry returned to her fiddle and played "Come Thou Fount of Every Blessing." Oatmeal was cheap, though they only had salt and a little butter to season it. No cinnamon and sugar like Ma used to make.

An off-beat percussion interrupted the second verse. Gentry stilled the bow, realizing it had been a knock on the door. She looked out the window—the one that still had glass in it—and wondered at the hour. Had Rooster forgotten something and locked himself out?

She hurried to the door and opened it. Her heart plummeted to her feet and bounced back again.

"Winn!" A dozen birds pecked about the property behind him.

Winn smiled, elbow leaning on the door frame. "A lovely tune beckoned me. Didn't you say you sold yours?"

"I, uh, someone gave this to me." She stepped aside to let him in, relieved that the house was tidy. Winn raised a brow and eyed the fiddle on the table. Smoothing her skirt, Gentry asked, "What brings you here?"

"A trip," he answered vaguely. He studied his magic-built wall for two seconds before saying, "You're so talented, Gentry. I can't even read music."

She flushed. "It's not hard; I could teach you."

"Maybe not. I'm more of an appreciator than a creator. Who is the benefactor?"

Gentry glanced at the fiddle neck still clutched in her hand. She suddenly felt like she sat in a confessional, with no screen to separate her from the priest. "I . . . our neighbor, Hoss, gave it to me. The one Rooster works for."

"Stick pull."

She nodded.

Winn ran his hand down his chin and neck. "Nice enough fellow." A frown tugged on his mouth.

Gentry set the fiddle inside its box, casting Winn a sidelong look. Was he angry? Then again, he might not care what gifts other unmarried men may have given to her. Would Hoss be upset to know Winn was here? That Gentry would rather talk to *him* than play the music Hoss had given her?

Winn's frown morphed into a smile.

"What?" Gentry dared to ask.

"We're going on a trip today," he said. "Please," he added.

Her skin tingled from neck to navel. "What?"

"I'm going somewhere, and I want you to come with me." He strode to the table with a Pearl-like excitement. "You'll like it. I think."

Pearl, fully dressed, stumbled out of the bedroom. "Winn! Are you staying for breakfast?"

"I already ate, but thank you."

"I can't." The tingling turned cold. She wrung her fist around her index finger. "I mean, just *us*? Alone?" She paused. "Where would we go?"

"Do you trust me?" he asked.

Gentry swallowed, moths fluttering under her ribs. "I can't just leave Pearl here alone." There was laundry to fold, and Bounder needed exercise, and the bread wasn't started—

"I want to come!" Pearl chimed.

Grasping the back of a chair, Winn turned his head toward Pearl. "Now Pearl, I can't court a woman if her sister is tagging along, now can I?"

A wave of heat scorched the moths and turned Gentry red down to her toes. Her tongue tied in knots. Did he really just say . . . ? Gentry backed away, pressing her fingers to her neck to try and cool herself, but her hands were just as hot as the rest of her.

Pearl frowned, but she didn't seem to notice the forward proclamation or the tomato hue of Gentry's countenance. "I suppose not."

"You're eleven, right?"

"Twelve."

"That's right, twelve." Winn grinned. "Practically an adult. Perfectly capable of taking care of yourself and being queen of the house for a while."

Gentry grabbed the front of her dress and shook it, trying to cool off. Her thoughts were a racing jumble, and something round and popping—perhaps a mad giggle—bounced beneath her ribs.

Pearl folded her arms, but her frown lifted. "Yes, I am." She pointedly gazed at Gentry. "I can even make supper."

Gentry's mouth parted. Yes, Pearl *did* know how to cook . . . but Gentry couldn't possibly go anywhere with *only* Winn, regardless of Pearl's age. What would Pa think?

Then again, Pa wasn't here. Neither was Rooster. Nor Hoss.

Good heavens, am I considering this?

"Perfect." Winn pushed off the chair, clapped his hands, and turned toward Gentry. The twist in his lips told Gentry that neither her color nor her countenance had returned to normal, and that made her fidget. He placed his hands on his hips—Gentry tried very hard not to look at his hips—and said, "Now I just need consent and we'll be off." He smirked. "I'll be a gentleman, Gentry."

Knowing he added that last part in reply to her flush only made her skin burn more. Gentry's eyes moved from Winn to Pearl and back again. This wasn't really happening, was it? Her mind flipped and stretched, thoughts tilting back and forth like the pans on a scale.

She found herself nodding.

Winn gave her a full, genuine smile. Grasping her hand, he said, "Bye, Pearl!" and swung the door open, pulling Gentry into the morning sunlight.

"You're a rogue," she croaked.

"You make it sound like such a bad thing." He pulled her toward the stable. Bounder, uninterested, chomped at weeds encroaching her gate.

Winn led Gentry behind the stable, the back of which faced the untamed territory, as the Abrams lived on the southwest edge of Dry Creek. No one would see them here, and Gentry's pulse turned wild.

"Heavens, Gentry, I'm not going to bite you." Winn released her hand.

She shook her head. "It's not that, just . . ." She fumbled over words, but all of them sounded positively stupid in her head, so instead she asked, "Where are we going?"

"A little north, a lot west." The seagulls began to pour

around the sides of the stable as though Winn merely thought them there, and he probably did. "We're going to visit the Hagree."

Gentry stiffened. "The Indians?"

"They're not Indians," Winn chided as the seagulls swirled about him, forming a white chimney and a gray door with two steps leading up to it. "India is quite a ways from here, though I admit I've never been."

"Well, what am I supposed to call them?"

"The Hagree," he suggested, mirth dancing on his lips. Gentry tried not to look at his lips, but she was doing a poor job of it. "They won't hurt you, and neither will I. Don't you trust me?"

He extended his hand, and Gentry took it, the feel of his skin sending rows of gooseflesh up her arms.

The house of birds looked just as it had the first time she'd stepped into it—a marblesque room with blocky shelves and furniture, a golden, mystical light glowing in the corners. This time, however, as Winn stepped in behind her, the door broke into two dozen flapping wings, the entrance sealing completely. The floor seemed to shoot upward, forcing Gentry's stomach toward her pelvis. She stumbled, and Winn caught her by the forearms.

"Sorry, sorry, should have warned you." He led her to a wall so she could steady herself. "I don't have company often."

He rapped two knuckles on the wall, and the magicked gulls reorganized themselves, expanding the wall ever so slightly as they made room for a window.

Wind gushed up and over Gentry, blowing through her hair and reminding her that she hadn't grabbed her bonnet before leaving the house. She blinked against the rushing air and gripped the sill, peering out.

Her breath rushed into the wind as the mountains fell

away from the house, as the sky grew larger and larger over-head. The house of birds moved diagonally into the very sky itself at an impressive speed. She saw every speck of sagebrush, every trail and road leading into and away from Dry Creek, even a few spirits on the mountains.

She jumped as a carmine-colored being swept by the window, pausing on its three wings to study her in a very catlike fashion before flying away again. Gentry stuck her head out the window and watched it soar away, the gold pendant of her necklace rattling against her collar.

The house neared the clouds and slowed, floating a little more smoothly as it continued west.

"This is astounding." Gentry's words were more air than voice. Winn watched her as he leaned against the wall, arms folded across his chest. "This is how you see the world every day? You act like it's so commonplace."

He stepped forward and glanced out the window, the air tousling his golden hair. "I suppose it seems that way, after so long." His lips turned up ever so slightly. "But I'm glad you like it."

"How do you *do* all this?" She studied the faraway world. "Aren't you afraid they'll see you?"

He shook his head. "The birds know how to hide us."

Gentry leaned out the window a little farther, fingers clutching the sill. Westward. This could take them all the way to California, couldn't it? Winn had offered, once. How would she explain to her father, were they to find him?

"The Hagree are the reason I know anything of this world," Winn said, a little softer.

"They're magicians?"

Winn shrugged. "There are few people who can see the world the way you and I can; a few of them live with this tribe."

She glanced to him, but his gaze had settled beyond the window. Instead of prodding, she asked, "How often do you see them?"

Again, a twitch of a smile. "Not often enough."

The house jolted. Shrieking, Gentry grasped the sill with hands *and* arms. Winn did the same, one protective arm around her. The touch spurred the most pleasant buzzing sensation in her torso until the house dropped and Gentry's stomach lurched.

Winn cursed under his breath. He released her and lifted himself onto the sill, leaning out too far to be safe, peering into the sky. "It's a hawk. Come on, friends! You're bigger than it is!"

The house lurched again.

Winn tugged an earring from his right lobe—it looked painful—and held it out in his palm, turned toward the current so the wind wouldn't blow it away. Gentry's heart raced. Winn just kept his arm outstretched.

"What are you doing?" she cried.

"Gathering air," he said, not nearly as alarmed as he should be, especially as the house shifted once more and he nearly fell out a window. Gentry grabbed a fistful of his pant leg in a white-knuckled grip.

"Takes a minute to get the kind that listens," he added.

His earring disappeared.

"Here we go." He let go of the sill and leaned out, his knees barely gripping the house. Gentry yelped and grabbed his other pant leg.

Winn pulled his right hand back—the one that had borne the earring—and then threw it forward as though throwing a heavy ball. He waited, looking up, and finally reached back for the sill, his hair windblown as he slid into the house.

"All better." He grinned.

Gentry released him and stepped back as the house steadied. "What was *that*?"

"I told you, a hawk. It's gone now."

Gentry gaped at him, her pulse hammering down her arms and at the back of her neck. "Winn Henry *Maheux*!"

He cocked an eyebrow and laughed. "I don't have a middle name."

"It sounds more serious if I use one," she countered. She pressed a hand to her breast to still her frantic heart. "If this is your idea of courting me, you're out of your mind!"

Winn burst into laughter far more emphatic than Gentry had ever heard. Boisterous enough that, despite herself, she smiled too.

He sat down on a seagull-bench, holding his side. With his other hand he wiped at a tear. "Oh, Gentry," he said between chuckles, "you and I are going to get along swimmingly."

~~~

Gentry leaned into a wall when the house began to descend. She peered out the window and didn't recognize a thing—even the Wasatch Mountains had vanished from sight. There was a stretch of desert and sagebrush behind them and a patch of green ahead, though nothing out west would ever be as green as Virginia. Still, it was beautiful.

Winn gently grasped her forearm for support as the house landed. Two heartbeats after it did, the marble-like structure fractured and flew apart, the seagulls becoming seagulls once more. They took off into the green in two massive flocks, only a few cries among them.

Winn put his hands on his hips. "They need a rest." He looked around for a moment before extending his hand to Gentry. "This way."

Gentry slipped her hand into his, shivering at the sensation of his skin against hers. He smiled and pulled her just a little north of the seagulls' flight.

Rocky patches cut through the green, a lot of which was comprised of shrubs and short trees. There were a few shallow creeks, which surprised Gentry, given the dry summer heat. There must have been a lake or river nearby. In the distance sat mountains half the size of the Wasatch, with softer peaks and duller coloring, almost like they were giant mounds of sand. Gentry fanned herself with her free hand as they walked; the house of birds had kept them cool during the trip, and now she had to readjust to the heat.

Winn helped her over a rocky creek bed and paused, listening, eyes focused on some stubby trees at the top of an incline. His gold-flecked eyes searched for a long moment.

Gentry swallowed. "Is something there?"

"Nothing that will hurt us." His gaze landed on a particular copse of trees. He waved his arm back and forth before continuing on. Gentry studied the area as they passed, but she couldn't tell what had caught Winn's attention. An Indian? Surely Winn wouldn't be waving to a mountain lion.

They climbed a hill, and when they crested it, Gentry looked down onto a village of Indian huts—Winn called them *wickiups.* They weren't the teepees Gentry always saw in pictures and heard described in stories. These dwellings were wide and round on top, assembled from branches and animal hides and all things earthy. They were comparable in size to Gentry's home in Dry Creek.

A few Indians—Hagree—noticed her and Winn as they neared. Her skin seemed to tighten. While the caravan Gentry had crossed the plains with had no violent run-ins with natives, stories of bloodshed and rape circulated through the settlements she'd passed through. She urged her speeding heart to calm. Winn had said this tribe was friendly. They were his *friends*. Didn't it mean something if Winn trusted her enough to bring her here? She took deep breath after deep breath, trying to quench a strange thirst in her lungs.

As they neared, a few of the Hagree noticed and stared. Gentry squeezed Winn's hand harder. Other Hagree jumped like startled deer and ran farther into the camp, shouting something in a hard, foreign language Gentry's tongue could never hope to imitate.

Perhaps they were just as scared of her as she was of them.

Stepping close enough to Winn to walk on his heels, she said, "Are you sure—"

"You're safe," he murmured. "Trust me."

Gentry's grip didn't relax.

An older Hagree man jogged down the center of the village—there were no roads—his face sun-wrinkled and dark, his chest uncovered. He wore a sort of short skirt made of two thin hides stitched together—rabbit?—and had two raccoon tails tacked to one hip. His dark, gray-streaked hair was held back by a rust-red band of cloth. He wore western-style boots. At his side trotted a small fox, of all things, its coat orange and thin.

He shouted something at Winn in that same hard tongue and smiled, stopping only two paces away. Gentry hid half herself behind Winn as the Hagree man continued talking, but this time it sounded like . . . French?

Winn laughed and replied in kind. He released Gentry and placed his hand on the man's shoulder, touching his forehead to the man's. Turning back to Gentry, he said something else in French and gestured to her.

The man uttered a few words and nodded, his grin widening. The smile helped her relax. She noticed he had two gold studs identical to Winn's in each ear. Did this man know about magic too?

Gentry glanced to the fox and back again. "English, please?"

Winn grinned. "This is Waga. He was one of my caretakers when I lived with the Hagree. I just introduced you."

Gentry nodded and met Waga's dark eyes. "Hello." She tried not to sound as small as she felt.

"Hello," he repeated with a smile and a thick accent. "Hello."

He spouted a jumble of words to Winn—only a few were French, Gentry thought—and waved for them to follow. Much to Gentry's relief, Winn took her hand again, rooting her in the one familiar thing she had in this place: himself.

"That's Awenasa." He pointed to a woman grinding something in a bowl, a babe tied to her back. "She had another! Goodness, that woman must have thirteen or fourteen children by now."

Winn's casual manner put Gentry further at ease. "So many?" Even the Mormons would be impressed.

"That's called lacrosse," he continued, pointing to some young boys carrying around large sticks with spoon-shaped nets at their ends. A few noticed Winn and Gentry and stopped to stare. Winn gestured beyond them. "That's Kanagotta—he's an ornery fellow."

Gentry locked eyes with a middle-aged Indian sitting cross-legged outside a wickiup. He scowled at her, and she quickly averted her eyes.

They walked a little farther before Winn turned, angling his body against Gentry's. "Focus on Waga."

Gentry stared at the old man's back, which looked something like a raisin. Her gaze dropped to the fox heeling him. She caught that faint shimmer around its tail identical to the one Winn's seagulls sported. "Why?"

"Unless you want to see a pronghorn being gutted."

She was no stranger to cutting into animals for meat, but the largest creature she'd ever carved was a duck, and she never enjoyed it. She focused on the stitching of Waga's skirt. "No, thank you."

Waga quickened his pace and veered right, calling out in his hard Hagree tongue. A moment later an equally wrinkled woman came out and rushed to Winn, giving him the same forehead-touching gesture as Waga had before. She prattled at him in all hard syllables for a long minute before noticing Gentry and prattling more.

Waga answered.

"How much of this do you understand?" Gentry whispered to Winn, who leaned down to hear her better.

He shrugged. "About half. Saleli," he gestured to the woman conversing with Waga, "is very traditional and has no desire to learn any white-man languages, but she expects you to understand everything she says." A nostalgic smile touched his lips. "Saleli is Waga's wife, more or less."

Gentry felt herself blush. "More or less?"

Winn left it at that, for Saleli returned to him and jabbered more. Winn gave a few one-word responses in what Gentry assumed was Hagree by the sound. His accent softened the words. Then Saleli turned to Gentry with a cross expression and spoke to her. Gentry stiffened.

Winn whispered, "Just nod."

Gentry nodded. Saleli quieted and folded her arms, seeming somewhat appeased, and stepped inside her wickiup.

"Winn?" Gentry asked. "What did I just agree to?"

Winn shrugged. "I have no idea."

Saleli returned, grabbed Winn's wrist, and slapped her

hand against his. Winn closed his fist and said a single Hagree word with a low bow of his head.

Waga claimed his attention then, exchanging a few words in broken French, though Gentry thought she heard one or two words in English, before guiding Winn to a few more people, one of whom Winn identified as the chief, who had also been one of his caretakers. Winn exchanged a few words with Chief Sequah—again in a mix of Hagree and French—before leading Gentry toward the edge of the little village, toward a copse of rough-barked trees. Gentry found a seat on a splintering log and stared at the sky. A little past noon. She wondered how Pearl was faring without her.

"I thought you could use a break." Winn perched beside her. "That was mostly greetings and the equivalent of small talk. And asking who you were." He nudged her.

Gentry smiled. "It's all very . . . different."

"I should have given you better warning. I forget that this is bizarre to other people."

Shaking her head, Gentry said, "Not bizarre, just different. I've never been somewhere where no one speaks English."

"The younger kids do, but we're not well acquainted."

Gentry rubbed her hands together, checking for splinters, before folding them in her lap. She glanced back toward the village. A few Hagree girls clustered behind a hanging pronghorn hide, peering out at her and giggling.

She turned her attention to Winn before the giggles made her self-conscious. "How long has it been since you lived here?"

"I left the first time when I was nearly sixteen." He looked at her hands, then his. "Not this spot exactly; they move around a bit."

Gentry studied his face, the line of his jaw and the shape

of his nose. One of his studs had returned to his right ear. She recalled Saleli taking his hand. Had she given the stud to him? "The first time?"

He smiled, but there wasn't much brightness to it.

Gentry touched her necklace. "When I first met you—well, the second time—you told me there was a long story about all of this."

"Mm," he agreed, setting his hands on the log behind him and leaning back. "I mentioned my father was a medicinal scientist, yes?"

Gentry nodded.

Winn stared out into the trees. "We found this tribe when I was Pearl's age. My father wanted to learn about the plants around here and the medical practices of the Hagree, see if he could find anything useful for his research, something to study further in a lab. But my mother," he paused for a moment, swallowed. "She got sick while we were out here. Even now I still don't know exactly what ailed her, but she passed away."

"Oh Winn," Gentry murmured, "I'm so sorry."

A sad smile graced his lips. "We're similar, there. Though you never told me what happened to yours."

"Childbirth."

"Pearl?"

"No." Gentry wrung her index finger in her fist. "Caleb. He's ... my half brother. Hannah, in American Fork, took him in."

Winn nodded. They sat in silence for a moment before he continued his story.

"My father ... I don't know what went through his mind, but I guess he turned his grief into work. Cadavers are hard to come by, and he thought he might learn something before we buried her."

Gentry's face chilled as blood drained from it. She pressed a hand to her mouth.

Winn leaned forward, resting his elbows on his knees. "I was *so* angry with him. We had something of a shouting match, and I ran off. Let me tell you, the desert is not kind to the unprepared."

Gentry felt she should say something, but words died on her tongue.

"The Hagree found me after a while, brought me back. By then my dad had left for 'civilization,' and I didn't feel like following him. So I stayed. First with Chief Sequah, then with Waga and Saleli." His face brightened a little. A warm breeze tousled his golden hair. "They're the ones who taught me about the earth and the gold."

"Magic," Gentry whispered.

"I was mesmerized, and I got greedy. It's all a balance, Gentry, but I didn't understand that, not really. So I left like the buffoon I was and got into trouble. A lot of trouble. When I wasn't abusing the earth, making trees and elk and gulls do my bidding, I was pickpocketing in cities and sneaking around trying to get my hands on more gold so I could have *more* power." He sighed. "Nearly got myself killed by angry bankers and bears—"

"Bears?"

"Oh, believe me," he watched her eyes, "bankers are much worse."

"Winn—"

He shrugged. "Eventually I came back and got thoroughly scolded by about every Hagree man and woman I knew, and some who I didn't know." He chuckled and his eyes unfocused, lost in memory. "They taught me, and this time I listened. Moderation, heart, responsibility. All that good stuff you don't learn in school."

Gentry scoffed.

"I went out to forage one day after that—after I finally understood—and he showed up." Winn tilted his head toward a seagull—Turkey—perched on one of the thicker tree branches ahead of them. The bird cocked his pale head and watched them through that faint, magical shimmer. "He took an unnatural liking to me, followed me around like a dog. Eventually the others joined him.

"I'd once abused them," he continued, "but once I learned to listen to them, we understood one another."

Gentry took a moment to process the information. "Is that why they follow you around, even without gold?"

"Or maybe I follow them around." His eyes crinkled. "The ability to truly *listen* creates a bond stronger than gold." He looked at her, and Gentry became aware of how close they sat, of how many breaths lay between them, of the beautiful patterns of gold and brown in his eyes.

She knitted and reknitted her fingers together. "That is an amazing story. Thank you, for telling me." She hesitated before adding, "Your father . . ."

"I've been searching for him for a while," he said. "He's my only family by blood. He travels for work; he could be anywhere."

"I hope you find him."

Reaching over, Winn took Gentry's hand in his. "I hope I do too."

CHAPTER 10

The small fox that had trailed Waga around the little village jumped over Gentry's side of the log, startling her. It landed on noiseless paws and regarded Winn with amber eyes. Yes—there was definitely a shimmer to the creature.

"Seems like Waga wants us," Winn said.

"Is that his . . . Turkey?" Gentry asked. "He knows about magic too?"

Winn stood and pulled Gentry with him. "They all know about magic, Gentry. It's no secret, here." He offered her a lopsided smile. "Few partake in it, though."

"Only a few?" Gentry asked as the fox skittered away. Winn didn't seem bothered by its departure, so Gentry wasn't either. "If I had magic—"

"Anyone can use magic," Winn interrupted softly, "just like anyone can learn to ride a horse or, I don't know, milk a cow. Hmmm," he paused, "let's go with the horse analogy. Anyone can learn to ride a horse, so say everyone does. They all go out and find horses and break them and ride them, and then there are no horses left in the wild. The environment suffers and the animals forget what it was ever like to be free."

Gentry mulled the idea for a moment. "You make me feel guilty about Bounder."

"Don't be." He smiled. "That mare was born broken from

her magical ties. I've never seen a domesticated animal that wasn't."

"But we're born with them? Magical ties, I mean."

Winn mulled for a moment; Gentry watched his tongue move behind his lips. "Magic exists in and of itself. But when we—humans—try to control it, we become a medium. Like a pump to water. It flows through us the same way it flows through the earth."

Gentry nodded. *Thus the glowing veins.*

Tilting his head toward the small village, he asked, "Ready for more?"

She squeezed his hand. "Yes."

Winn pulled her back over the log and guided her between the wickiups. She spied the fox ahead before it turned a corner. It had waited for them.

Two Hagree women watched Gentry as she passed by and whispered to one another. Gentry tried not to notice.

"Just speak to them in English," Winn said as they approached Waga and Saleli's home. "I can always translate."

Saleli came out of the house and went straight to Winn, speaking to him in quick Hagree before gesturing for them to follow her inside. Gentry let Winn lead the way.

The wickiup was larger inside than Gentry had assumed, about twice the size of the bedroom of her house. There were a few slits to let in light. The walls were brown and stitched together between long, bent branches. Bedrolls lay against the walls, along with sacks, chests, pans, and other knickknacks. One large pole stood in the middle of the space, supporting the wickiup's center. The space smelled like old sweat and leather and something floral.

Saleli talked for a good long time, Winn responding in turn. She sat at a small stool and took a hammer from her dress pocket to work on something small that Gentry couldn't make out. At one point the conversation lulled, and Gentry tried, "You have a very nice home," in a voice far too mousy for her liking. Saleli looked at Winn, who translated. The older woman merely nodded as though the compliment was obvious and got back to work.

A few more Hagree came into the wickiup—Winn made sure to name each of them, though many of their names were long and strange, and each time Gentry heard one she forgot the last. Each wanted to see Winn, to exchange a few words, or to show off a new rifle, or to make broad gestures about something Gentry couldn't piece together. She tried to stand to the side so as not to interrupt the foreignness of it all. Winn's eyes always found her, however, so she knew she wasn't forgotten.

Gentry's attention returned to the new stud in Winn's ear, wondering where the gold had come from. A coin, maybe? Or a filling? She'd heard rumors about Indians raiding graves, but quickly dismissed the idea. She'd get nowhere fast thinking ill of strangers. Her ma used to tell her that.

She wondered what Winn's mother used to tell him.

Waga entered with a long pipe and spoke to Winn in French, gesturing toward the door. Winn glanced to Gentry and shook his head. Waga argued with him for a minute before leaving with a grunt.

Winn pushed the flap to the wickiup open. "Let's get some air." The fluid English sounded wonderful to Gentry's ears.

They stepped outside, the air feeling cooler than it had in the wickiup. Women built fires outside their dwellings, many of which had spits and pots over them. Gentry peered to the sky. The sun's descent marked the start of evening. Had so much time passed?

"I should get back soon." She noticed a seagull hopping around the back of a wickiup.

"Not yet," Winn replied, though the words sounded like a plea. He pressed his hand to Gentry's back, right between her shoulder blades, and Gentry felt the heat of his touch rise into her cheeks. She looked at the ground in hopes that he didn't notice, wishing she had remembered her bonnet. Winn continued, "After their smoking ring there'll be supper, and I want to show you something later."

Supper . . . Rooster would be back by then. What would he think of Gentry's absence?

Would it be so bad to not be the parent just for one night?

Giving into her curiosity, Gentry asked, "What?"

He grinned so easily. Gentry's stomach fluttered—it was such a strange, relieving feeling to have after so many days of cramping. "It's a secret."

Gentry's mouth copied the smile—she couldn't help it—and noticed the magical shimmer around a few sun-dried shrubs. She could explain everything once she got home. Rooster knew her too well to think she was doing anything disgraceful. "Smoking ring. Is that what Waga was talking to you about?"

Winn nodded. "It's a men-only venture, however."

"You should go."

"And what, leave you to Saleli's devices?" He snorted. "Hardly. I want to stretch my legs. We've been sitting around all day."

Sitting around all day. While Pearl did all the housework. Was it foolish of Gentry to be here? Would she come home to find Pearl in tears and Rooster fuming the way her Pa surely would have if he hadn't left?

Winn's hand on her shoulder brought her back to the present. "I know that look," he said.

"What look?"

"That look you get when you're worried," he answered.

"I have a look?"

"Relax, Gentry." He slipped his hand from her back. He offered the crook of his elbow and she looped her arm through it, energized by the gesture. "Everyone needs a day off."

"I just had a day off. In American Fork."

"That doesn't count."

"Oh?" She cocked an eyebrow and looked at him. "And why not?"

He chuckled. "I'll think of a reason. Give me a few minutes."

Gentry managed a smile. They walked in a comfortable silence, tracing the circumference of the little Hagree village. Gentry estimated there were about thirty wickiups in it, perhaps ninety to one hundred people total.

"Winn," Gentry said when he didn't come up with his reason, "How do you . . . get by? You travel so easily, but what about everything else?"

He slipped his free hand into his trouser pocket. "A little of everything, I suppose. The Hagree taught me how to live off the earth, even in a place like this," he tilted his chin toward some sagebrush, "and the seagulls make it easier. The rest is just temporary work."

Gentry tried to imagine such a life, spiriting from place to place, sending out bird-servants to find . . . what? Grubs? Tubers? Seagulls didn't hunt, except for fish. "Like what?"

"Hmmm." He paused, thinking. "The last job I had was on a dairy farm in Missouri, mucking stalls and cleaning up after the animals. I did that for a few weeks."

Gentry's stomach began to tighten again. "Before that?"

"A lot of dirty jobs people are willing to hire out to

strangers." He laughed. "I worked on a fishing boat in Maryland once, farmhand a couple of times. Never stayed longer than a month or so."

Gentry's steps slowed a little. "Why not?"

He looked at her. A few strands of golden hair dangling before his forehead shadowed his eyes. Gentry had the urge to smooth them back, but she kept her hand at her side.

"I don't know," he finally answered. "I've been lots of places. Guess I didn't feel like I belonged in any of them."

The distance between them and the wickiups gradually increased. "Where *do* you belong?"

"I wish I could tell you," he said. "Maybe Dry Creek."

Gentry stumbled, and Winn tightened his arm around hers to keep her upright. "Whoa there." He laughed. "That flat ground will get you every time."

"Oh hush." Gentry touched one of her cheeks to cool it. "There was a rock," she lied.

Her eyes did spy a large, black cricket underfoot—a locust—and with a garbled shriek she brought the sole of her shoe down hard on its body, crunching it flat.

"*Wiki taimo!*" sounded harsh Hagree words.

Releasing Winn, Gentry turned and saw a Hagree woman of perhaps thirty walking nearby, toward the village, with a dead grouse dangling from her hands. She eyed Gentry, her clothes, and said, "Kind. *Kind.*"

Gentry tried not to cower. "Excuse me?" Her fingers clutched her necklace.

The woman pointed to Gentry's feet. "Be *kind* to it." Her English carried a heavy accent. She glanced to Winn, then back to Gentry. "It is *earth.* Be kind to it."

"I-I'm sorry," Gentry said, and it was enough. The Hagree woman turned away, her expression unreadable, and trekked back to the village. Gentry pressed the pads of her fingers to her heart, willing it to slow. That woman had just killed that grouse, hadn't she?

But she plans to eat it, Gentry thought. Lifting her shoe, she examined the split pieces of the locust underfoot. Had it had a shimmer, like the ones that had attacked Dry Creek? Gentry hadn't noticed. If it had, the glow was gone now.

Winn's hand rested on her shoulder. "It's all right."

"No, I . . . suppose she's right." Gentry sighed. "I've never considered bugs anything more than . . . bugs."

"Most people don't." Winn offered the crook of his arm once more. "Supper?"

～～～

Winn taught Gentry how to say *thank you* in Hagree, so with a broken accent and flushed cheeks, she thanked Waga and Saleli as the sun began to set. Many of the Hagree began to gather toward the center of the village, where several youth began building the skeleton for a bonfire. Gentry wondered at it, as well as at the drums being pulled from wickiups, but she imagined the Hagree's festivities would be much different than those had in American Fork. Still, part of Gentry wished to hide in the shadows of night and dance with Winn again.

Looking at the darkening sky, Gentry's mind flew back to Dry Creek. Pearl and Rooster would have eaten by now. Were they waiting up for her? Were they worried, or did they trust Winn enough to bring her home all in one piece?

Had the post arrived today with news from California?

"That look, Gentry."

Gentry tried to smooth her expression over with a smile. "Sorry. I should probably be getting back home."

"Not yet," he whispered, a sly, almost feline grin dancing

across his mouth. He clasped both of her hands. "Not until I show you the stars."

Gentry tilted her head to one side. "Mr. Maheux, I'm well aware of what the stars look like." That was the one bonus of living out west. The stars somehow seemed brighter here.

"Please," he whispered, drawing his head closer to hers so their foreheads almost touched. Gentry's ears burned as she gazed into his eyes, which grew more golden even as she watched. "Just for a moment."

She let out a long, shaky breath, hoping Winn didn't hear the tremble in it, and nodded.

Winn pulled Gentry away from the Hagree village—if he had made any goodbyes, he must have done so following supper, for he made no effort to bid anyone farewell now. One white bird, then another, sprung up over the nearest hill. They multiplied like popping corn and rushed toward them. Gentry's body grew light in anticipation of them. Just before they surrounded her, Winn squeezed her hand and pulled her close, wrapped one arm around her waist, and lifted her just in time for the seagulls to slip underfoot and harden into the floor of the mystical bird house. Gentry laughed, and her stomach lurched as the still-forming house hoisted her skyward. Wings pieced together into a semblance of marble until the deep blue of the sky vanished overhead, and the west-facing window glowed with the blushing horizon of twilight.

Her gaze went back to Winn, who still held her close. She fit against him so nicely. She only imagined what her ma would say, were she still around. Then again, maybe she wouldn't mind. In the end, her mother hadn't cared much for propriety.

"Gentry," he murmured, his voice husky, his breath warm.

She could kiss him, she realized, and a cool tingling

encircled her crown and dripped down her neck. All it would take was lifting herself onto her toes and turning her head ever so slightly to the left. Would Winn close that lingering space between them? Did he really think of her the way she thought of him?

She pressed her fingers to his chest, trying to feel his heartbeat, desperate to know if it beat as quickly as hers. But Winn misread the gesture, perhaps thinking she wanted to push him away, and his arm slackened its hold on her. He stepped back, close but not close enough, an easy smile finding its way to his lips. It shocked Gentry how cold she felt with that bit of distance between them. She couldn't think of a way to close it. She swallowed hard and eased her heart back down.

Winn glanced out the window. "We're almost there."

Gentry blinked into awareness. She didn't see the San Pitches or the Wasatch out the window, just the last tendrils of the sun on the desert horizon. "Already?"

"Mount Moriah." He stepped toward the window and put his hand on the wall beside it. Perhaps sensing the intent beneath his touch, the house rotated slowly until the window faced eastward, toward a tall, gray mountain ahead. "It's not as majestic as the Wasatch range, but its peak will be a little warmer."

Gentry marveled at the mountain, at the house growing level with it. Winn offered his hand, and Gentry took it without prompting. A moment later, the house bumped and shook, and the seagulls became seagulls once more, dissipating into the desert night like a thousand dandelion seeds.

The top of the mountain was wide and smooth, almost free of loose soil. A little farther down the slope the ever-thriving sagebrush grew, and even farther down grew clusters of pine trees. Gentry thought it would be very pretty in the snow, if it snowed here at all. The air smelled like cooling earth and that subtle sweetness desert nights always carried with them.

"Look." Winn pointed upward, and Gentry tilted her head back to see.

Stars. They came alive as she watched, winking into existence, filling the bright streak that cut through the center of the sky and speckling the indigo beyond. Letting go of Winn's hand, Gentry turned slowly, taking in the great expanse of the sky. Yes, the stars were visible from her home in Dry Creek, but when was the last time she had really *looked* at them?

"They're beautiful." She stopped to stare eastward, where the edges of night had begun to turn black and the stars were especially bright. She reached beside her, found Winn's arm, and traced it up to his shoulder. Leaning her head back against it, she watched the stars twinkle. After a few minutes, she saw one streak across the sky.

"Did you see that?" She straightened. "It's good luck to see a shooting star."

"Did you make a wish?"

Gentry licked her lips and peered back toward the sky, where the streak had been. "I wouldn't know where to start."

Winn's countenance drooped. "Gentry—"

"I'm looking for my father too." She met his eyes for a moment. "We haven't had word of him since he left, though I know he made it to California safely. I contacted a post there. I know he's in California, but he hasn't written. And surely . . . *surely* he's received his wages by now."

She folded her arms, suddenly cold. "We've been waiting all summer for him. For anything, but he's silent. Why is he silent, Winn? Why hasn't he tried to help us?"

Winn frowned. "I meant what I said. I can take you there. It's not much farther than the Hagree."

Her arms slackened. "All the way to California? To the Boston Company?"

He nodded.

"Oh Winn." She let her hands drop. "That would be . . . so helpful. I need to know. I just . . ." her stomach cramped, and she pressed a few fingers into it. Perhaps her supper wasn't settling as well as she had hoped.

"I could take you in the morning."

She shook her head. "I need a few days to get things in order. But yes, please. Winn, it would mean so much to me."

His smile returned and was contagious. "Anything for you, Gentry," he said, and her stomach loosened. "Shall we—"

He paused, turning suddenly toward the north, squinting through the darkness. His shoulders tensed, and nearby the seagulls grew restless, rustling their feathers and squawking deep in their gullets.

Gentry searched the sky, the horizon, but saw—and felt—nothing. "What is it?"

Winn's jaw clenched. "Something's wrong again."

"Wrong?" she asked, then realization struck. "The mines?"

He nodded.

"Is it bad?"

He didn't answer, but his silence was answer enough. Shoulders still tense, he said, "I'll take you home, then—"

"I'm coming with you."

He turned toward her, his brow raised and creasing his forehead.

"It will be faster, won't it? You'll get there sooner?" she asked. "I want to help. I mean, I won't be very useful, but—"

He grabbed her hands. "Yes. Thank you, Gentry." Releasing her, he put his middle finger and thumb to his lips and whistled, then waved his other arm, stirring the seagulls to life. They flew into the air with the speed of falcons and began to spiral around Gentry and Winn in a way much different than when they flew to form the house.

"Hold on." Winn offered his arm. Gentry slipped hers around the crook of his elbow.

He chuckled. "No, really. *Hold on.*"

He embraced her, eliciting a small squeak from Gentry. The wind around them sped, a bird-made torrent that tugged pieces of hair out of Gentry's bun and stung her eyes. She squeezed her eyelids shut and clutched Winn's shirt in her fists. Her feet lifted off the ground without any floor to support them, and she soared blindly into the sky, skirt whipping as they raced across the desert.

CHAPTER 11

The wind shrieked in Gentry's ears, whistling and screeching an untamed melody. Winn's chest was the only solid thing around her, and weightlessness engulfed her. She tried to peek, but the gusts drew tears from her eyes. She saw only snippets of blurring birds: white and gray, white and gray.

When her feet found ground, it jarred her. The wind lessened, but her head still spun in tight circles. Her body trembled. Her knuckles ached from her fingers' death grip on Winn's shirt.

The gusts finally settled, allowing new sound into her ears—rumbling, like a belch deep in the belly but so much *bigger*. And the trembling—that wasn't her. That was the ground, just like when she and Pearl led Bounder off the road to American Fork.

She opened her eyes to the darkness. A three-quarter moon illuminated the night, along with so many stars. The ground quivered and opened onto more stars—no, those were ponds reflecting the sky. A whole network of them, like pockets in a slice of bread. The air had a musty, earthy smell, but there was something wrong underneath it. Something Gentry couldn't describe. Something she had to stop before it reached home.

"Winn," she whispered.

"This is big." His face pointed toward the ponds. He cursed under his breath. "I shouldn't have brought—"

A gull cried and flew down to him, tossing him a bunch of long sticks and grass. He grabbed them, clamping them in his fist as his other hand dug into his trouser pockets until he found a match. He struck it on one of the branches twice to get it to light, then lit the end of the branches. Gentry's eyes caught a faint shimmer that was more than mere heat.

Winn palmed an earring and waved his hand over the fire, and it burst, growing exponentially, so hot and bright that Gentry staggered back and shielded her eyes, blinking spots. When she looked again, the sticks stood upright in the ground of their own accord, the bright firelight crackling and reaching outward, shaking as the earth quaked with renewed vigor.

"The mines did this?" Gentry asked, but Winn didn't answer. He might not have heard her—she could barely hear herself. The reflected stars rippled and shuddered in the pools. Gentry gasped as a geyser shot up from one of the larger ponds. It sputtered into the sky far higher than the one on the road to American Fork had, and it stretched four times as wide. A brilliant shimmer surrounded it. Water droplets fell like stardust over the broken earth. The pungent smell of sulfur assaulted her nose.

She didn't see Winn reach for her, only felt the tug as he jerked her behind him. Gold shimmered beneath his shirtsleeves, and when she saw his face, the veins in his neck and cheeks glowed a brilliant yellow. His other hand stretched toward the geyser, fingers crooked, tendons hard and straight.

She gawked at him, at the fire, at the raging geyser that

continued to feed from the ponds. It pumped foul steam into the air and fought against the magicked fire.

"Winn—"

"Stay at my back." His voice strained, and he released her, using the same hand to pluck two earrings from his ears. He threw the earrings into the air, and two bold seagulls swept in and caught them in their mouths. Instead of eating the gold, however, they soared past the smoke and steam toward the geyser, dropping the precious metal into it.

"Be calm!" Winn shouted. It was the first time Gentry had ever heard him give voice to his strange magic. The first time she'd ever heard him raise his voice, period. An unseen force pushed him backward; his shoes scuffed the earth, marking where he had once stood. Pulse pounding in her ears, Gentry braced herself against him, surprised when his body pushed back. Peeking over his shoulder, she saw the familiar shimmer the gulls always wore dancing in the space between Winn and the geyser.

The boiling geyser grew taller. Steam surrounded them and began eating at the edges of the fire. A force of invisible heat slammed into Winn and Gentry, making them both skid back a pace. Gentry bit down on a scream and threw her weight into her shoulder. Every muscle in Winn's back had gone taut. It, too, began to glow in zigzagging shapes muted by the linen of his shirt.

Winn reached for his last earrings—a wave of wet heat collided into him and Gentry as he did. Gentry didn't see where he threw the gold studs or if a gull gobbled them up. The birds seemed to have vanished. Gentry's dress stuck to her skin with the steam, and a dull ache radiated from her shoulder and neck from where she supported Winn.

"Calm yourself! There's none to hurt you here!" Winn bellowed something in the hard tones of the Hagree. Gentry nearly tripped as the earth buckled in response. Her foot slid in mud—water began to seep up from beneath the soil.

She turned, pressing both her hands into Winn's shoulder blades, which heaved with his breaths. Both his arms stretched forward with crooked stiffness, and his veins glowed so brightly Gentry couldn't look at them directly. *Please help him, please help him,* she prayed, for Gentry could do nothing but steady him against the onslaught of magic her natural eyes were blind to.

Winn's left hand swung back to her, his gold-lit fingers clasping her ma's necklace and pulling the chain taught against her neck. Gentry gasped, slipping momentarily. *No, not that,* she pleaded. *Please don't use that.*

But Winn was out of gold, and the geyser—

The quaking settled to a shiver. Gentry dared to peer over Winn's shoulder at the geyser, which slowly, *so* slowly, began to slim and shrink, its fetid waters fountaining with less and less gusto, until the water settled into a pond of a thousand ripples and the earth quieted to such an extreme that even silence sounded loud.

Winn released her necklace and dropped to one knee, the gold gone out of him.

"Winn." Gentry's voice rattled up her throat. She forced her wobbly legs forward and knelt in front of him. Sweat slicked his hair, and his face looked older. His shoulders slumped. Panic pulsed strength into Gentry's limbs. "Winn, are you hurt? Winn?"

"I'm all right," he said between breaths, and Gentry swallowed her relief. He tried to smile, but it slipped off his mouth. "One . . . moment."

Gentry smoothed back locks of his hair and, not knowing what else to do, straightened his collar. No gold adorned his ears. A single gull cawed far to the right.

Moving away from the fallen geyser, Gentry hurried to the closest pond, knelt at its bank, and dipped her hand into its water. She smelled the bit pooling in her palm and tasted it with a flick of her tongue. Untainted. Scooping as much as two hands could hold, she walked it back to Winn.

"Is this safe to drink?" She knelt before him once more.

Winn didn't answer; he cupped her hands in his and dropped his face into the water. Seconds later he pulled back and ran his forearm over his wet face. His movements were heavy, weary. *Oh, Winn.*

"Thank you," she whispered. "For stopping that thing. No one else would have."

He managed a single dry chuckle and swallowed. "One of my few talents." His eyes swirled with a few remnants of gold. "Thank you."

"I didn't do anything."

He touched her chin, but the effort seemed to tire him, and his arm dropped to his knee. "I need to take you home."

"You don't have to—"

"Your brother isn't a small man." He tried that smile again. "I'd hate to see what your father looks like." He paused. "Don't tell Hoss."

A weak laugh struggled through the tight walls of her throat. "I won't. I promise. I'm so sorry."

"For what?"

Gentry didn't answer. Instead she stood and looped one of Winn's arms over her neck, helping him to his feet. He was surprisingly heavy. Gentry imagined how much taming a wild, magicked geyser took out of a man.

He leaned on her, and she said, "If you can't—"

"Ssshhh." He raised a weak hand. The seagulls reappeared as if from the air itself. The last of the fire winked out, and moonlit feathers surrounded them, forming the familiar house of gray and white with its sourceless pale light. The moment it was finished, Winn collapsed on the bench.

Gentry hurried to a blocky shelf. "Turkey."

Nothing happened.

"Turkey," Winn groaned.

The "stone" changed to feathers that pulled apart like the bellows of an accordion and spit out Winn's bag. Gentry grabbed it and dug through it until she found a half-filled waterskin. Praising the Lord for the discovery, she hurried back to Winn and offered it.

"You're an angel," he mumbled, popping the cork and guzzling from the container. He paused halfway through and looked at her.

"I'm fine, you drink it," she said, and he did.

After draining the waterskin, Winn set it on the bench next to him. Wringing her hands, Gentry sat on his other side. "Is there anything else I can do?"

He smiled, tired but genuine. "You've done more than enough, Gentry. I'll be fine in a bit."

"Someone should really pay you for this."

He laughed and rubbed his eyes. "That would be nice, eh?" His countenance grew serious. "It's all the mining. It's too much."

"There are mines in Utah," Gentry said. "Lots of places."

"I know," he sighed. "Small mines don't matter. They have repercussions the rest of us see as regular anomalies. How do you think all that mess on the Yellowstone River happened?"

"That's in the northern territories?"

Winn nodded. "But California . . . veins of gold in the earth are similar to the veins in our own body. Instead of blood, however, they funnel magic throughout the world. Mining veins like the ones in California is like cutting open an artery. The earth . . . she's retaliating." He rubbed a thumb over pale stubble on his jaw. "It's only going to get worse. That mess by the Egret—I've never seen it so bad."

Gentry assumed the Egret was where Winn had just fought the massive geyser.

He continued, "I'll poke around a bit, maybe, when we go there."

Gentry straightened. That was right—Winn was taking her to California. To find Pa. To get answers. It would be good to see Pa again, to see how he fared. If things were going well. If not, maybe he would come home. Maybe the mill would rehire him. If it was doing well, he could pay the next mortgage bill . . . which was, Gentry realized, overdue.

She chewed on her lip. If Pa's mining efforts *were* going well, then he was part of the problem. She touched her necklace, wondering if she could show him the truth somehow.

The house began its slow descent. Gentry carefully made her way to the window and looked over the shadows of Dry Creek. She blinked against the darkness and eventually made out the stable as well as a millipede-like creature scurrying a ways behind it, its body glowing with magic. It dug down into the ground without really digging at all and disappeared.

The house settled and the birds broke apart, keeping their flock behind the stable. Gentry stepped off the enchantment without any problem—she was getting used to it, it seemed.

Winn offered her his elbow. His skin was pleasantly warm beneath the cotton sleeve, though the small thrill it sent up her arm felt cool. He escorted her to the house, his steps slow. Then again, maybe it was Gentry's pace that held him back. She'd spent a full and rather adventurous day with him, yet she didn't want it to end.

"It's a good thing," she said, "that I don't have any close

neighbors. In a town as dull as this one, I'm sure the sight of us would make for gossip." Or worse.

Winn grinned. "She's worried about the impropriety, not the birds."

"You've never worried about the birds. Why should I?"

He glanced at her, his eyes brown and glimmering with only moonlight now, which Gentry found far more beautiful than gold. "Touché."

She avoided looking at the crops as they passed—she didn't need the reminder of how poorly they coped. The door to her small home loomed ahead, and her pulse quickened, remembering Mount Moriah. Any weariness worming through her body flitted away, lightening and loosening her limbs.

Winn stopped just beyond where her doorstep would be, had they built one. "Three days, then, if that's what you want."

Until California, he meant. She nodded. That would be enough time to get the house and her thoughts in order and to see that Pearl and Rooster were taken care of. With the speed Winn traveled, they could probably make it to California and back in a day. *A day.* The thought made her bones light, like they could float right out of her skin.

His lip quirked and he took her hand, kissing it as he was wont to do. "I look forward to it. Until then."

He stepped back, but Gentry held fast, interlocking her fingers with his. He paused and gazed at her. Gentry's heart beat in her throat. Rooster and Pearl were only a wall away. But . . .

But.

She pulled on his hand ever so gently, but it was enough for him to take a step forward. Her pulse hammered in her ears, and she stood on her toes.

Winn smiled. His hand slipped behind her head, just

below her bun. Gentry managed one quick intake of breath before his lips covered hers, warm and sweet, filling her with the scent of earth and butternut. Gooseflesh prickled her arms.

Winn's thumb traced the nape of her neck. He pulled back and looked into her eyes. Gentry felt warm and cold all at once. She exhaled, slow and steady.

"Until then," he whispered, and he kissed her forehead. He released her fingers one by one. Gentry watched him retreat until the birds took him away into the night.

CHAPTER 12

Gentry's thoughts buzzed as she slipped into the dark house and pressed the door shut behind her. She couldn't stop smiling. Her skin tingled, and she was *happy*.

"Waiting up for you is going to leave me real tired tomorrow."

Gentry jumped at her brother's voice and turned around. She was just able to make Rooster out in one of the chairs in the front room. She let out a breath. At least he hadn't wasted a candle. "I know. I'm sorry. Something unexpected came up."

"Mmhm."

Gentry folded her arms. "My virtue is intact, if that's what you're worried about."

Rooster snorted. Paused. "Anyone else see you two together?"

She shook her head, but in the darkness, she wasn't sure he saw it.

Rooster walked to the window, the one that had cracked panes from the quake, and peered outside. After a moment, he said, "Winn's not normal, is he?"

Gentry's arms slipped to her sides. "No. He's not."

"I kept thinking Pearl was too old for all these fanciful stories she's been weaving about him." He watched the stars, or perhaps the San Pitches. "But ... that wall. Those birds." He ran a hand through his hair.

"It's a good different, Rooster." Gentry walked to his side.

"I know. He fixed our wall and saved the crops. What's left of them, anyway." He rubbed his neck. "Just be smart about him, Gentry. There ain't much of a rumor mill in these parts, but," he sighed, "be smart."

Gentry bit her lip. He didn't say anything for a long moment, so she filled the silence with, "He's taking me to California."

Rooster spun from the window. "What?"

"He can travel faster than a train, Rooster. It's ... magic." She watched his shadowed features, trying to gauge his reaction. "I could get there and back in a day—"

"Find Pa," he interjected, his voice soft.

She nodded. "Find Pa. We know he's in California. I'm sure he made it to the company."

Rooster slid his hands into his trouser pockets, and Gentry noticed that he still wore his day clothes. The crinkle of paper alerted her to what appeared to be a folded letter slipping behind the fabric. Who was he writing to?

"I've been thinking about that, Gen." He glanced back to the cracked window. "The way Pa's been since we got here, maybe—"

"Don't worry about it." She spoke a little too quickly. "Winn's coming in three days. I'll go, find Pa, and come back. Maybe with him—who knows?" She tried to smile. "A little impropriety is worth that, I think."

Rooster paused, then nodded. "Might be better if *I* went. In case it takes more than a day."

"That's more than a day of no wages." A frown touched her lips. "Even if we came up with a great excuse for you to miss work."

"I'm looking around for something else. Not much in

Dry Creek, but places like American Fork aren't too far. I could come home on the weekends. Willard Hinkle's got prospects for that printing press."

Gentry smiled. "I'm grateful that you try. Truly."

Rooster was quiet for a moment. "Be careful."

"I always am."

He put a hand on her shoulder. "I know you are." Took his hand away. "I know."

The first yawn of the night pressed against Gentry's lips, and she stifled it with the back of her hand. "Let's get some sleep, or we'll both be useless in the morning."

~~~

Gentry carried a large cotton bag in the crook of her elbow—it had an orange patch on one of the bottom corners—and tread carefully around the displays in the mercantile. A long counter stretched across its far side, behind which stood Mr. Olson, who helped another customer with the purchase catalog. Luxurious things like maple syrup or women's shoes had to be special ordered.

Fortunately for Gentry, she had no need for fancy supplies, just the run-of-the-mill groceries and items needed to run a half-efficient household. She picked up a small bar of lavender soap and turned it over, wincing at the number penned on the back of its simple label. Placing it back, she grabbed the unscented variety and stuck it in her bag before checking her list again: flour, soap, candles and matches, sewing needle, dark thread, salt, butter or lard (whichever was cheapest), preserves, and hay for Bounder.

Gentry stared at the word *preserves*. Strawberry preserves would be so nice to have, but her pocket felt so light . . .

"Oh, Gentry," said Pearl, who had accompanied her on the trip, "imagine a dress made out of this." She stood by a bolt of fabric on a shelf against the wall—cotton dyed dark blue with a few white flowers printed on it.

"It would be too warm in the summer, I'm sure," Gentry said, and Pearl frowned, reevaluating the cloth. *And it would be,* Gentry thought, *even if it didn't cost this entire list's worth for a yard.*

"Miss Abrams?" Mr. Olson looked up as his previous customer exited the store. "Can I help you?"

"Yes." Gentry scuffled to the front of the store. Over her shoulder, she said, "Pearl, grab three candles and a box of matches, would you?"

Her sister dropped the fabric and walked to the other end of the store to investigate the candles.

Gentry readied her list. "Salt and flour, please—your smallest bags, if you would."

Mr. Olson nodded and stepped into a back room, returning seconds later with two too-small bags. He set them on the counter.

"I didn't see the sewing supplies by the fabric," Gentry continued.

Mr. Olson raised his brows, then rolled his eyes. "That no-good son of mine is behind on his chores, again. Was supposed to stock them after closing last night. What can I get you?"

"A needle and thread, if you would."

He departed for a little longer this time. Pearl brought the candle and matches to the counter, and Mr. Olson returned with a wooden box of spools and a red cloth stuck full of needles. Gentry took the cloth first and found a needle of medium thickness, then browsed the thread and selected a brown spool.

"Ugly," Pearl murmured, but Gentry didn't reply. "Salt, eggs," she hated ordering eggs, but their last chicken had stopped laying and been slaughtered before Pa left. "And a bit of, um, lard, if you would."

Pearl frowned.

"And Mr. Olson? Do you have any preserves in?"

Her sister's countenance immediately brightened.

"That I do. Raspberry and huckleberry. What will you have?"

"What's the price?"

"Let's see." He squatted to the shelves beneath the counter. "Raspberry is twenty cents, and huckleberry is twenty-five."

Gentry pressed her lips together, avoiding her sister's gaze. She pulled her small wallet from her pocket and counted out the bills and coins in it. Her mouth went a little dry. Swallowing against it, she said, "Not today, then. But if I could order four bales of hay for my horse, that would be wonderful."

Mr. Olson nodded. "It's out in the back; I'll have it loaded up if you bring your wagon around. Let's see," he counted the things on the counter—Gentry quickly added the soap in her bag—and said, "one dollar and forty-one cents."

Gentry quickly focused her eyes on her coin pouch to hide the flush that crept into her face. She busied herself counting out the money, all of which totaled one dollar and thirty cents. She suppressed a sigh. "Everything but one of the candles, then, if you would."

"We have to have light," Pearl murmured beside her.

"I can't make a dime magically appear, Pearl," Gentry whispered back.

Regardless of whether or not Mr. Olson heard the

exchange, he selected one candle and slipped it under the countertop. Gentry paid him, placing a single penny back into her pouch. She pressed her shoulders back and kept her chin high—some semblance of the confidence she didn't feel.

"Do you need help out?" Mr. Olson asked.

"Oh no." Gentry slipped the smaller items into her bag. "This is fine for us. But I will bring the wagon around. Thank you, Mr. Olson."

He smiled. "Anytime."

Gentry and her sister collected their groceries and stepped back out into the hot summer sun. Bounder lifted her head for a second before turning her attention to some shepherd's purse she'd already gnawed down to the roots. Gentry's back prickled, waiting for Pearl to say something about the preserves or the candle, but her sister remained quiet, and Gentry offered silent thanks to the Lord. They got into the wagon seat and drove to the back of the store, where Mr. Olson's "lazy son," a few years Gentry's junior, loaded the hay bales with a cross expression. Gentry thanked him and hurried Bounder home, eager to be within her own walls once more. At least there were beans and carrots that survived the desert heat, flash flood, and locusts. At least they had those, however far Gentry could stretch them.

Gentry pulled the canvas bag over her shoulder after setting the brake for the wagon—they'd leave the hay for Rooster to move when he got home. Sliding to the ground, she said, "Pearl, I need you to dig up the potato bed and see if anything's salvageable, then replant half of what is."

Pearl hopped down from her seat and wiped her brow. "Can I do it tonight? It's so hot, Gentry."

"Please, Pearl."

Pearl sighed. "Fine, but I'm wearing your sun hat to do it."

Gentry didn't protest. Patting Bounder's nose—she'd unhitch the horse and let her graze what she could after putting the groceries away—she hurried into the house, out of the hot sun. She'd only just unloaded the bag when she heard the distinct sound of vomiting behind her.

Turning around, Gentry said, "Pearl?" But her sister was just coming through the door, right as rain.

Gentry set down the brown thread and hurried into the bedroom. The smell of vomit pierced her nostrils. Rooster lay on his belly across Pa's old bed, his head and shoulders off the mattress. A bowl quarter-filled with bile rested on the floor.

"Oh Rooster." Gentry hurried to his side. He still had his work pants on, and his shirt was unbuttoned. Sweat slicked back his dark hair, and his skin was white and clammy. "When did you get home?"

Rooster groaned and rested his head on the edge of the thin mattress. "I don't know. An hour . . ."

He jerked back to the bowl and dry heaved twice before sour-smelling bile dripped from his lips. Gentry hurried back to the kitchen, passing Pearl, who stood in the doorway, and filled a cup with water. She offered it to Rooster, who managed a sip.

"Is he all right?" Pearl asked.

Gentry put her hand on his forehead. Clammy, but too warm. "It's not something you ate," she murmured, "or we'd all be sick. Oh Rooster." She felt the lightness of the wallet still in her pocket. Her stomach tightened. They had nothing in the house to help him. "Pearl, can you take the thread back to Mr. Olson and get some peppermint water?"

Rooster blinked heavy lids for a moment before grumbling, "I don't need it." He dry heaved again, nearly spilling the cup of water in his hands.

Gentry frowned and tried to rub smooth the tense

muscles in her brother's back. "I can pull threads from old clothes. Pearl?"

Pearl nodded and hurried back through the house. Moments later, Gentry heard Bounder take off in the direction of the mercantile.

"I'm sorry," Rooster grumbled, planting his face into the mattress. "I tried to—"

"You can't do anything when you're sick like this," she said. "Try to sip some water." Gentry gingerly picked up the bowl of vomit and walked it outside to the outhouse, dumping its contents down the deep hole there. Rooster was heaving again when she got back, and she barely got the bowl under him in time to save the floor from his retching.

"Do you want some broth?" she offered.

Rooster groaned.

She unclipped his suspenders from the back of his trousers. Rooster slapped her hands away.

"I'm too old to be undressed by my sister." Half of his words gurgled. "I'll . . . survive."

Gentry stood and put her hands on her hips. "You'd survive better if it weren't so damned hot." She moved to the window and coaxed the pane open, hoping to get something of a breeze passing through the house. She wet a rag and set it on her brother's head, then placed a pot of water on the stove for vegetable broth, just in case. The beans and carrots would be just right for that.

Less than an hour later, Pearl rode to the house and, cheeks flushed, delivered the bottle of peppermint water. Gentry handed her a spoon and the broth and left her tending Rooster. Gnawing on a piece of bread, Gentry tidied the house and went through the mending pile, trying to find something not worth salvaging that she might harvest for thread. She ultimately decided on her old dress—Hannah had just given her a new one, besides. The threads were thin and short, but they would do.

When Pearl emerged from the room with the pepper-mint water and half a bowl of broth, Gentry said, "Let's get the bales moved."

Pearl nodded without comment.

The work wasn't too bad with both of them heaving. Bounder grazed what she could before Gentry got her back in the shade of her stable. She unhitched the small tub from its hook on the wall and brought it inside. She and Pearl took turns fetching water until the thing was filled enough for baths.

With Rooster occupying the bedroom, Gentry strung two blankets around a corner of the house for privacy. She let Pearl bathe first so she could get supper started. A little early in the day for a bath, but they were both hot and sweaty, and the cool water would do Rooster good when he woke. Gentry set to making the vegetable broth into a heartier soup. When Pearl was dry and dressed, Gentry took her turn in the cool water. Her body ached for her to just sit in it, maybe even sleep in it, but she scrubbed quickly with the new, unscented soap and got out, putting on her other dress so she could wash the first. The table was set by the time Rooster woke. He managed to walk to the tub without emptying the meager contents of his stomach, which Gentry took for a good sign. Uninterested in supper, he went back to bed with a cup of water.

Gentry stayed up late, wanting to get a start on the laundry since they had the tub ready. The night was warm, so she left the windows open, though the one Winn had made couldn't close anyway. She thought of him, wondering where he was now. Did he go back to visit the Hagree? Did another earthly ailment demand his attention? He had little to no gold left, unless he returned to the fallen geyser in hopes of retrieving it. Gentry wondered if his seagulls simply scouted for gold and brought it to him, but then he wouldn't need the odd jobs he'd spoken of. As far as she knew, all his earrings came from the generosity of his foster family—the Indians dwelling to the west.

Leaving her laundry to soak and her candle to flicker, Gentry crossed the small living space and rested her elbows on the rock wall of her father's house, looking into the indigo sky. Crickets amid the crops sang to the warm air. The breeze smelled clean. Not rain clean like Virginia, but clean in the way only wide open spaces untouched by people could smell.

Closing her eyes, Gentry let herself dream. Let herself reminisce on the touch of Winn's warm hand against her neck and the taste of his lips. Let her body shiver. Let her heart thrill without berating it.

For the first time since leaving Virginia, Gentry felt true hope. Hope that things might come around, that her family could be happy and whole, that her future might be bright. Bright as the veins that lit up Winn's hands. She opened her eyes and let out a breath, wishing on a shooting star she couldn't see. One of the mountains far off shimmered, and as Gentry's eyes adjusted, she saw movement above them— shapeless beings dancing and swirling around one another, celebrating the quiet of the night and the music of the insects. She watched them, mesmerized. She didn't hear Rooster approach until he spoke.

"Late nights are normal for you," he said.

Gentry turned, studying her brother against the single lit candle within their home. "How are you feeling?"

"Better. Not great, but better."

She smiled, then had a thought. "Come here, to the window."

He did. "Something out there?"

"Look there." Gentry pointed to the enlivened peak in the San Pitches. She unclasped the necklace from her neck and pooled its chain into her brother's palm. She held onto the locket. "Keep watching."

Rooster blinked, searching. After a moment he said, "What is that?"

"Do you see it?"

"Not birds," he said. "And the moon is reflecting off the mountain."

"It's magic," she whispered.

Rooster chuckled.

"Watch." She pulled the necklace away.

Rooster blinked again. "Where did it—"

She pressed the locket against his fingers. He turned his head toward her, slowly pulling his gaze from the mountains. Looked down at the necklace. A question wrote itself in the lines of his forehead.

"It's magic," she repeated. "This is what Winn sees. It's all around us."

Rooster swallowed. Moved his fingers from the locket. Touched it again. "What kind of magic?"

"The kind that lives," she said. "Unseen, like the wind."

Rooster's stomach grumbled. He pulled away from the necklace. "This place is bizarre, Gentry. Magic?"

"The quake, the rain. It's all part of it. It's the part we don't see," she whispered.

He nodded, accepting it in silence. Winn's presence and Pearl's stories readied him for it, Gentry supposed.

She pocketed the necklace. "Let's go to sleep." She walked toward the tub of soaking laundry and blew out the candle.

In her bed, Pearl slumbering beside her, Gentry planned for California.

CHAPTER 13

Rooster stayed home from work again the next day, but the lost wages didn't bother Gentry as much as they normally would have. She'd be seeing Pa soon and setting things straight. She'd imagined all sorts of scenarios. What if he'd sent wages only to have them stolen or lost in the mail? What if he'd been saving them up to send all at once, not realizing how destitute his children had become? Perhaps he had miscalculated Rooster's pay. Perhaps he wasn't making enough money to send more than pennies, in which case Gentry hoped he'd simply come home.

The third day Gentry woke before the sun poked its head over the Wasatch Mountains. She dressed quickly and braided her hair before coiling it at the back of her head—something that would look a little fancier without getting in the way. She washed her face and hurried to the kitchen to start water boiling for oatmeal. She'd cleaned everything the day before, making the house nearly spotless for Pearl and Rooster to enjoy in her absence. She'd even plucked enough thread from her old dress to patch one of her brother's pockets and stitch a hole in the armpit of Pearl's favorite blouse.

Her locket bounced at her collar as she set bowls out for herself and her siblings—would Winn need breakfast?—and noted the fiddle case resting on a shelf in the corner. She hadn't played yesterday, wanting to get as much work done as possible. Nor the day before that. Her fingers suddenly ached for the pressure of the strings, but music could wait until tomorrow. Tomorrow would be a bright day; Gentry felt sure.

Rooster was up first, his coloring back to normal. He pulled on a suspender strap and collapsed into a chair at the table. "Any mail come in while I was out?"

"I didn't check. Who are you expecting to hear from?"

Her brother merely shook his head. "Nothing to get excited about. I'm starving."

"You've eaten like a bird for two days, so I'm not surprised," Gentry replied, picking up his bowl and heaping a large serving of oatmeal in it. She stirred some flour into it to bulk it up and topped it with a little butter. Rooster dug in. If he noticed the flour substitution or the plain taste, he didn't remark on it.

Pearl moseyed out of the bedroom, rubbing her eyes. Gentry served her, then scooped some oatmeal for herself. It was especially bland, but she resisted using more butter. She would work things out with their Pa today, yes, but the sensible part of her warned to keep rationing until answers were had.

A seagull appeared on the sill of the glassless window at the other end of the house. Gentry shoveled the rest of breakfast down as an ensuing burst of wind rustled through the room, shaking one of the pans hanging by a nail on the kitchen wall.

Gentry dumped her bowl into the small washbasin and wiped her mouth on her sleeve before hurrying to the door, Pearl on her heels. The sun had brightened already, and a breeze that smelled like the sea wafted over her. Winn walked through a flock of seagulls from the direction of the stables, where Bounder shook her head in obvious dismay at his arrival.

Pearl darted past Gentry, her oatmeal bowl still in hand. "How long are you going to stay? Is it true your ma's an Indian? Do you want some oatmeal? But I don't think Gentry made enough—"

Gentry flushed and, smoothing her skirt, walked a few steps to meet him. He wore only one earring in each ear. "Are you hungry?" she asked.

Winn flashed her a smile that nearly liquefied her knees. "I already ate, but thank you for offering. Both of you." He put his hand on Pearl's head and ruffled the hair pulled back into a sloppy bun. "And I'm afraid I'm not staying long. This trip will take us a full day, give or take."

Pearl frowned. "Why does only Gentry get to go?"

Gentry frowned. "Do you really want to pick through all the miners in California yourself?"

"Yes."

"Unfortunately"—a seagull pecked at one of his boot-laces—"I don't have the strongest arms in the territory and fear I can't carry two women at once. This does involve a bit of carrying." He winked at her, and Gentry looked away in hopes that neither he nor Pearl would see her ears turn red.

"But," Winn continued, "I promise you and I will have an adventure all our own soon enough. A very socially acceptable and appropriate one." He glanced back to Gentry at the last sentence. "Shall we?"

"One moment." Gentry hurried back into the house, where Rooster was putting his bowl in the sink. She pulled on her bonnet and gathered her small bag of things—just in case—and turned back for the door.

"Sure this is safe?" Rooster asked.

She smiled, and it felt as genuine as one of Winn's. "I promise I'll be safe."

Rooster dug into his pocket and pulled out a folded paper. Gentry didn't recognize it—it must have been from Hoss's home. "Give Pa this letter from me, if you would."

Gentry took the letter and nodded. "I will."

Rooster nodded, and Gentry hurried back outside. Winn bent over and whispered something to Pearl, who widened her eyes. "Really?" she asked, but Winn didn't answer, only straightened and looked at Gentry.

To Pearl, Gentry said, "Make sure Bounder gets some exercise today."

Pearl nodded, hesitated, and walked back to the house, glancing over her shoulder almost every other step.

Winn offered his elbow, which Gentry took, and he led her to the stables, the seagulls waddling after, a few taking flight to catch up. Before reaching Bounder, Winn dropped his elbow and let his hand slide down Gentry's arm until his fingers entwined with hers. Shivers like dulled needles buzzed up her arm, and she bit down on a girlish grin.

He pulled her behind the stable. "The especially windy way will get us there faster," he explained. "I'm afraid that's the only way to make it there and back before the neighbors can gossip."

Gentry's heart quickened, remembering their journey to the Egret, the ear-splitting tornado of birds, the protective and almost intimate way Winn had held her to keep her from falling. Taking a deep breath, she nodded. "That will be fine. I'm ready. Thank you, so much, for this. Do you think . . . do you think we'll find him?"

Winn's countenance fell a fraction. "I'm sure we will." His change of expression, albeit slight, nagged at the back of Gentry's thoughts, but she dismissed it.

Releasing her hand, Winn turned toward her and took her bonnet strings in hand, tying a second knot in the bow under her chin. The action warmed her under the morning sun.

"Don't want it falling off." His voice had gone soft.

Her eyes dropped to his lips, remembering their kiss. Wondering if he would kiss her again. Clearing her throat, trying to think of something to say. "You would look good in spectacles."

Winn blinked and laughed. "Spectacles?"

Gentry shrugged. "Not many people do, but . . ."

"Hopefully I'll never need them. Ready?"

Gentry nodded. Winn led her away from the stable. Without a verbal command, the gulls took to the air and flew toward them, circling them in a cyclone of pale feathers. Their wind pulled on Gentry's skirt. Winn pulled her close. She put her arms around him, looping them under his arms with her hands on his shoulders. His encircled her waist. The gusts grew stronger, and the birds blurred. Gentry shut her eyes, and as her feet lifted from the earth, she felt Winn's lips against the skin below her ear.

"Trust me," he whispered, and they rose into the morning together.

~~~

The flight was longer than it had been when Winn and Gentry went to the Egret. Such a thing was to be expected, but by the time Winn's birds set them down, Gentry's arms, neck, and back cramped something fierce, and her head spun like she'd been twirling all morning. She sank to the earth on her knees, eyes shut, and took deep, slow breaths. *Don't throw up in front of Winn. Not in front of Winn. Oh God, please help me not to lose my breakfast.*

"Sorry," he said after a long minute. "I forget it takes getting used to. I usually go slower for these distances, but—"

"It's all right." She opened her eyes and blinked. The ground was dry and dusty. Had she left the desert at all? "Just . . . one moment."

She pulled her bonnet off—it had protected her hair, at least—and leaned over, inhaling, exhaling. She stretched her neck and rolled her shoulders. She was supposed to repeat this again tonight?

Gentry took in her surroundings. Lots of hills. Green hills, brown hills. No giant peaks like in Utah Territory. Were they really in California?

Winn helped Gentry stand. "Don't want to plop down in the middle of San Francisco." He wore a sheepish grin. Sheepish didn't look natural on him, yet Gentry found the expression endearing. "It's a bit of a walk."

"I could use a walk." She followed him down the hill and around another. The exercise loosened her muscles, and as they crested yet another hill, she caught the familiar scent of the ocean. Grabbing her skirt in two handfuls, Gentry jogged up the subtle path on the hill, passing Winn. Something deep in her gut fueled her limbs, and she reached the peak quickly.

San Francisco.

It stretched before her, hugging a wide bay that opened into the endless ocean. How Gentry had missed the ocean. Buildings of all sorts speckled the earth—houses and mills and shops and others she couldn't identify, not from so far. Men on horseback trotted through the streets. Wagons full of barrels and slides, women holding children's hands. Tents had been pitched even between houses or near the river. The city had the messy terrain of Utah and the crowds of Virginia, like the two had mixed and tumbled to the edge of the ocean. The air was a little cooler here, and while the air itself smelled earthy, the early afternoon breeze carried a salty freshness that made Gentry ache for Virginia.

There were so many people. Gentry squinted and peered toward the river, where the bulk of the crowds congregated. Wasn't gold first found in those waters?

Winn caught up to her and held out his hand as though presenting the prize hog at the fair. "Abracadabra. California."

A laugh escaped Gentry's throat—an airy, crackling sound, like it had been sitting on her diaphragm all morning, waiting for a crack to release. "You're amazing, Winn." She couldn't catch her breath, taking in all of this. Pa was down there, somewhere. "Imagine what people would say, knowing they could fly across the states and territories as you do."

"Better they don't know." His hand touched the back of her neck and pulled on the chain of her necklace. "Look."

Gentry touched the pendant, then scanned the city once more, taking in the buildings, the people, the hills, the bay. Nothing. No shimmers, no wild magic. It was positively normal.

"They've run from this place," Winn said. "The ones that can."

"That can?"

"We'd be in a mite of trouble if entire hills tried to up and leave, hm?" he asked, but there was sadness in his eyes.

Gentry nodded and released her necklace. They took in the view a moment longer, but Gentry hadn't come to marvel at the gold rush. "Where should I start? Looking for my father?"

"The Boston Company is northwest of here." The slightest frown pulled on his lips. "Not far. You did say Boston Company, right?"

Gentry nodded. Moths began to flutter between her ribs, but they didn't keep her from noticing the droop in Winn's expression. So subtle. Had she not seen him so often, she wouldn't have noticed it.

She swallowed and gripped the strap of her small bag. She started down the path leading into the city, Winn following.

There were more tents Gentry hadn't seen from up on the hill and several stores selling shovels and pans and slacks, all for prices that made Gentry's eyes bug. Winn directed her down one street and then another. They passed a hotel new enough that it had no chipped paint or weathering on its sign, and the smell of bread and frying oil wafted through the window. Gentry's stomach gurgled—it would be about lunchtime, but she had a biscuit and some carrots in her bag. She'd eat them soon enough.

The trek was a long one, but Gentry didn't complain. Didn't talk much, either, not knowing what to talk about. Not wanting to gush the whirlwind of thoughts in her skull at Winn. Where was Pa? Would he look different? Would he be happy to see her? Why wouldn't he be happy to see her? How would she explain coming to San Francisco? What did Rooster's note say? Did Pa stay in a hotel or in one of those tents? Had he found gold?

Why hadn't he written?

The city changed where it met the river. Log houses half the size of Gentry's bedroom scattered the banks. There was one mill and another structure that appeared to be some sort of fort. Everywhere in between was spotted with tents. Small manmade canals looped off the river, directing water away. A few men used long rakes to stir the river bottom and bring it close to shore, as though they were afraid of getting their feet wet. Others stood shoulder to shoulder around long troughs, shaking pans of mud. Others stood in the shallows of the river, walking along or filling buckets, turning over the soaked earth with shovels.

So many people. Was there so much gold to be had?

Winn gestured ahead, to the fort. Troughs surrounded it, connected to make a great angled slide for sifting gold. Men in work clothes—some in just their long johns—surrounded the thing, barely making space for a woman to walk. There weren't many women, but there were some, likely attending their husbands. Gentry didn't see anyone wading into the river itself.

A ways behind the fort, people had built some sort of mining shaft into one of the hills.

Straightening her back, Gentry searched the crowd for her father, but she didn't recognize anyone. Instead she found someone sitting on a rock with a pan and marched to him.

"Excuse me. I'm looking for Butch Abrams. Do you know him?"

The man lifted his eyes. He looked to be about Pa's age. His skin was darkly suntanned, and he was missing one of his front teeth. He glimpsed her up and down before answering, "Can't say I do."

"Do you have a foreman? Someone in charge?"

The man lowered his pan and looked over the other workers. "Methinks you want Mr. Webber, but God knows where he is. Might try the doctor. He knows most everybody with our folk."

Gentry nodded. "Where might I find him?"

"Charlie's probably in there." He tilted his head toward the fort. "What did you say your name was?"

Gentry merely replied "Thank you," and went on her way. Winn met up with her halfway to the fort.

"I need a Mr. Webber or a man named Charlie, the doctor," she said.

Winn nodded. "Are you sure it was Boston Company?"

She paused. "I'm certain. Why?"

Winn shook his head. "No reason." He offered his hand to help Gentry over one of the shallow canals. They approached the side of the fort—there were hooks and nails all over the wall, likely for hanging things at the end of the day. A ladder and a trowel remained.

"Can I help you?"

Gentry turned at the voice, spying a man coming down a set of stairs that ran up the outside of the building. He was dressed far more sharply than any of the workers, with a well-trimmed, salt-and-pepper beard and bowler hat. His inquiry stiffened the air between them, but it wasn't entirely unfriendly.

Gentry turned toward him. "Yes, please. I'm looking for a foreman or perhaps the doctor."

"Mmhm." The man adjusted his hat and glanced to Winn. He looked a little too long—Gentry wondered if Winn's eyes had flashed gold or if, perhaps, he looked familiar. "And why would you be needing either of them? Mr. Webber is busy and off-site, and the good doctor only sees to the Boston Company. He doesn't do house calls."

Gentry straightened and squared her shoulders. "I'm searching for one of the employees—Butch Abrams. Is he here?"

"Butch Abrams," the man repeated. He frowned, eyed Winn again, and said, "This way."

He opened one of two doors on the ground floor of the building. Gentry followed, Winn behind her. The room within was wide and sparsely furnished. It had windows, but Gentry still had to blink several times before her eyes adjusted to the dimmer light. The man—after checking his pocket watch—crossed the room to a long, narrow table pushed against the wall. Books and ledgers littered it. He sifted through the clutter until he found a particularly large ledger. He flipped through it, read a few pages, flipped back.

"There's no Butch Abrams working here, miss." He still scanned one of the pages.

Gentry's heart sank. She clutched her hands together, forcing herself not to wring her fingers. "I'm sorry, you must be mistaken. Butch Abrams is my father. He set out to work for the Boston Company in May. He made it to California."

The man turned to the back of the ledger and read for a long minute. Swallowing against a tight throat, Gentry glanced at Winn, who looked back with an unsure expression. Gentry pressed her hands to her breast and stared at the ledger in the man's hands, offering a silent prayer.

"We've never hired a Butch or an Abrams," he finally said. The words floated in the air for several seconds before registering in Gentry's ears. "Though I think we've gotten a letter or two addressed to an Abrams, if I recall." He closed the ledger and shrugged. "Threw them away."

Gentry's body went cold. The chill started at her crown and flowed like molasses down her neck, chest, arms, stomach, and legs. Her stomach shrunk to the size of a pinhead. Her joints rippled into gelatin.

Her mind couldn't register how long she stood there, staring at this stranger. He said, "Miss?" and she didn't think it was the first time.

"Thank you," Winn answered for her, his hand at the center of Gentry's back. "We'll be on our way."

The man nodded, and suddenly Gentry faced the other way. The door, the bright afternoon. The sound of panning and picking fuzzed in her ears. Her legs were numb, yet somehow Winn directed her away.

And then Gentry was sitting on a boulder, with no recollection as to how she got there.

Winn crouched in front of her. "Gentry."

She tried to swallow, but her mouth had gone dry.

Winn sighed. "I came here, the day after I last saw you," he explained. "I spoke to a few people at the company. None of them had ever heard the name Butch Abrams. I checked with the post office—they keep records, and sometimes people leave notes—but I didn't find his name there, either. I thought ... I thought I must have had some information wrong. The company, the name. Maybe he used a false one. I thought maybe you'd notice something I didn't." He sighed. "I should have mentioned it, but you were so hopeful. I wanted to be wrong."

Her ears were ringing. Her fingers were ice beneath the hot summer sun.

"But I didn't look everywhere," he hastily added. "Boston may have been full. There are other companies here we could ask—you'd know his thinking better than anyone. Maybe he set off on his own, farther up the river—"

"He's gone," she whispered. The words sounded to her like they'd been carried on the wind, but she recognized her own voice. Her bones sank against her flesh as they registered. "He's gone."

"We can ask the—"

"He's gone," she repeated, peering out past the river, where the ocean would be, had a hill not been in the way. "I know he is."

"Gentry—"

"He was never the same after Ma ..." she paused, her throat constricting, and forced a deep breath. "I knew it too. He never ... talked about gold. Mining. Never before, even to Rooster. Just all of a sudden, and he left ..."

Her voice trickled to muteness, but the unspoken words radiated inside her mind: *He left us.*

204

He left us.

He left us.

And Gentry knew. She'd known it all along. Their ma had died. Been unfaithful. If Caleb wasn't Pa's, who was to say Gentry was? Rooster? Pearl? They were barely getting by. The West wasn't what her pa thought it would be. Too hot, too hard. They were too poor. Three children to care for by himself. He never smiled. Never laughed. He was there, but he wasn't there.

No letters. No wages. But Gentry knew. She knew he hadn't been attacked by Indians or fallen from his horse or some other horrid thing. He left. Because he didn't want to stay.

He left us.

She couldn't look at Winn. Didn't know if he heard her thoughts. He said her name, but she didn't answer. Couldn't. She could barely breathe.

There were no wages coming. No hope at the end of the road.

Her father was never coming home.

CHAPTER 14

"Gentry!" Rooster stood from his chair as she walked through the door. A candle flickered from the center of the kitchen table, its light bouncing off Pearl's tired and worried features. "Do you know what time it is? What happened? He didn't get rough with you, did—"

Gentry knew the moment Winn stepped into the house after her—the moment her brother's angry words cut short and his eyes looked past her. He had their Pa in his eyes. They all did.

Gentry pushed past her brother and trudged to the dark bedroom. Behind her, Winn said, "I need to speak with you." A moment later, the front door closed.

"Gentry?" Pearl asked, but Gentry disappeared into the shadows of their shared room and shut that door as well.

"Gentry," Winn said, crouching before her seat on the marble-esque bench. The house floated somewhere above central California. "Gentry," he repeated, taking her face in his hands. "I'm so sorry. I thought . . . I had to be wrong. I thought you should check for yourself. Was I wrong? Did I hurt you?"

She didn't answer. Her body lulled with the gentle movements of the bird-made house.

"It will be all right," he whispered, dropping his hands to

hers. "I'll take care of you. And Rooster and Pearl. See? We'll be fine. Trust me."

But he couldn't take care of them. Winn was just as poor as they were. He didn't know the month's mortgage payment was late and Gentry expected a notice any week now. He didn't know there wasn't enough food to last the week—that they'd have to skip lunch until Rooster's next check. And Rooster was in bad need of new trousers. He couldn't go to work without trousers, could he?

"Please," she begged, "just take me home."

She dropped onto her mattress—the old, thin mattress that hurt her back and was filled with holes. She pressed a knuckle into her belly, trying to relieve the tightness there. She hadn't eaten, had she? But thoughts of the carrots and biscuit made her nauseous. Her body was too tight to fit food.

She would have to sell Bounder. The mare cost too much to keep, and they could get good money for her in Salt Lake City. How Gentry would get home after the sale, she didn't know. She could have taken Rose, had Pa not claimed her first.

He'd taken Rose. He'd taken their savings. He'd left them with *nothing.*

Gentry leapt from the bed and snatched the empty candleholder off the nightstand, throwing it with all her strength into the opposite wall. It hit the wood with a *thud* and dropped to Rooster's bed.

"You *abandoned* us," she whispered, hot tears stinging her eyes and blurring the shadows. She grabbed her ma's locket and jerked the chain from her neck, throwing it as well. "You *both* did!"

Sobbing, Gentry dropped to her knees and cradled her face in her hands. Maybe if she had worked harder, Pa wouldn't have left. Maybe if she had been a boy, he would have loved her more. Maybe she should have tried harder to keep the family in Virginia. Maybe if her ma had been faithful, she wouldn't have died, and Pa wouldn't have left. *Maybe, maybe, maybe.* Gentry shuddered and gasped for air, tears leaking through her fingers.

She didn't hear the door creak, only saw the light of the candle press against her eyelids. "Gentry?" Pearl asked.

"Blow it out!" she cried. "We can't afford to waste a-another candle!"

The candle extinguished. Holding her aching middle, Gentry bent over and wept, her tears pattering against the uneven floorboards.

Pearl's arms circled her. *Not in front of Pearl,* she thought, but it was too late for that, wasn't it? It was too late for everything.

Gentry leaned into her sister's shoulder, soaking her blouse, crying against the relentless twisting and burning of her gut. Hadn't she been punished enough?

Pearl whispered, "He's not coming home . . . is he?"

Gentry didn't answer, and Pearl wept with her.

$\sim\!\sim$

Gentry woke pressed against her sister in the center of their mattress, the blanket down around her hips. The sun had already risen, yet Gentry stared over the mop of Pearl's blonde hair for a long moment, unable to stir herself to readiness. She heard Rooster behind her, fumbling for some article of clothing or another, shutting a drawer. Leaving the room. Gentry studied the wall, searching for patterns in the rough grain of the wood and not finding any. When Pearl moved and began to rub her eyes, Gentry rolled over to the edge of the mattress. It creaked a familiar song under her weight.

Her body ached, though she couldn't decipher why. She hadn't done anything particularly strenuous yesterday, had she? But there were the gulls and the flight. That could make anyone stiff, she supposed.

She thought about Winn, her mind full of dreamy, almost incoherent flashes of memory and questions. She couldn't piece together anything complex. So she merely thought about him, and that was that.

She hadn't bothered to change into nightcap and gown, so she peeled off her dress and changed her underclothes. Her hairbrush had a surprising weight this morning; it strained her shoulders to run it through her locks. She examined the ends of her hair. She needed a trim. She stared at the hairbrush and noted the missing bristles without counting them. She couldn't count this morning, either.

Hair twisted and tucked, she stepped into the rest of the house. It felt overly spacious, for once. Empty. Missing something. The bare walls hurt her eyes. Rooster opened and closed cupboard doors.

"I can make flapjacks." The hoarseness of her voice surprised her. "If you can wait."

Rooster pressed his lips together and looked out the window—the one with the cracked glass, near the door. He nodded and sat down.

The kitchen was very far away. Gentry's legs hurt by the time she reached it. Flour, eggs, a little sugar. When Ma was alive, they had preserves to go on their flapjacks. In Virginia, they'd had maple syrup sometimes.

Gentry made the simplest batter she could, in the smallest proportions—enough to feed Rooster and Pearl. Her stomach didn't want food, not yet. She supposed that was a blessing.

As the first cake sizzled in the pan, Gentry asked, "Where's Winn?"

"I asked him to go home," Rooster replied. His voice sounded different too. Not hoarse, but lower and softer. Older. "So we could sort things out."

Gentry flipped the cake. Set it on a plate. Started another. Flipped it. "He told you."

A pause. "Yeah. I shouldn't be ... I don't know. Surprised, but it still ..."

He didn't finish the sentence. Gentry plated the second flapjack and started a third. If she scraped the bowl, she could get a small fourth.

Pearl came out of the room. She said nothing. Sat by Rooster.

Breakfast cooked, Gentry set the plate on the table. Rooster took the small cake off the top, blew on it, and chewed slowly. "We should write to Hannah."

"I don't want to burden her." A little more of her mind woke up—the part that could count. They had seven eggs left, one pound of flour. Too many days until Rooster's next payment.

"They always welcome us," he offered, his voice still hushed and low and old.

Gentry turned from the stove and leaned against the cupboard, letting the coals warm her back. "For visits, yes. And I think they would take us in, but we have nothing to offer them. Nothing but hungry bellies and crowded beds. We have nothing to offer anyone."

That's not true, whispered another part of her thoughts as they groggily stirred into awareness. *You have something to offer.*

The memory played out. The Hinkles' house, the setting sun against its eaves, the wagon and the farmhands beside her. Hoss leaning down to make his offer.

She glanced to the fiddle, stowed away in its box of pine. Hoss.

She rubbed her temples, his name thick as marmalade as it churned in her mind. Hoss. Hoss could take care of them. Hoss had already offered.

She blinked, and in the darkness behind her eyelids, she saw Winn outlined in gold.

Turning around, Gentry fumbled for a cup and filled it with the last water from the bucket from their last draw. She sipped it slowly, its coolness sloshing against the sides of her stomach, making her shiver.

Rooster stood. He'd eaten two flapjacks. Was two flapjacks enough? Gentry didn't think so, but she didn't say anything.

Her brother didn't move until both her eyes locked with his. "Eat," he said, and he shuffled for the door, taking his hat off the hook there and planting it on his head.

Gentry swallowed. "Don't tell—"

"I'm not telling anyone." Rooster's hand lingered on the doorknob. His shoulders slumped. "Besides, maybe we're wrong."

He left, closing the door too firmly behind him.

Gentry looked at the plate. One cake left. Pearl still nibbled on hers, her bites dainty and rabbitlike. Gentry sat across from her and, hesitant, tore the cake into uneven halves, leaving the bigger for Pearl. She took a bite. The bread tasted bland and a little gummy. She chewed and swallowed, feeling when the bit of food hit the bottom of her stomach.

Hoss.

Hoss had been one of the first people to visit the Abrams family after they built their house, though he'd never met her ma. Few had, before Caleb was born. He'd always been friendly when he came by. Made decent friends with Pa.

Gentry wasn't sure when he'd noticed her. When she discerned that his friendliness might be a little more than the goodwill of a neighbor. Maybe around the time he hired Rooster on. He'd offered her brother that job—Rooster hadn't asked for it.

If you needed... what I mean is... well, I could take care of you too.

"Gentry?"

Gentry started, nearly choking on a half-chewed piece of flapjack on her tongue. She looked at Pearl, noticing for the first time the thickness around her eyes from crying. Gentry lifted a hand and felt her own face. She likely didn't look much better.

Pearl fiddled with her flapjack—her appetite must not have been much bigger than Gentry's. A few long seconds passed. "We'll have to sell Bounder, won't we?"

Hoss.

Her heart constricted at the thought, tighter than her stomach had ever been. She took a deep breath, hoping the air would inflate her and smooth out all the wrinkles inside. It didn't. "I don't know, Pearl. Maybe not. I need to think on it a bit."

Pearl nodded and cast her gaze to the tabletop.

"When you're done, could you fetch some water?"

She nodded and set down her unfinished breakfast, heading straight to the empty pail and out the door. Gentry frowned as she went. Leaving her breakfast too, Gentry retreated into the bedroom, wringing her hands the whole way.

Hoss, she thought, and her heart beat back, *Winn.*

Winn.

Oh, Winn.

Gentry shut the bedroom door and leaned her forehead against it. Trying not to think of the man who magically appeared in her life, yet her thoughts were veined with gold. His voice echoed in her ears, and his smile carved itself across her breast. She licked her lips, thinking of the taste of butternut, but her tongue found only the saltiness of her own tears.

It's all right. We'll be fine.

Do you trust me?

Trust me?

Trust me.

"But I can't," she whispered. Straightening, she wiped her sleeve across her eyes.

Oh yes, she could run off with him, if he asked. She could let him sweep her up into his house of birds and travel all of the States and beyond with him, visiting Indians and fighting off mad magic and staying in hotels while he worked odd jobs here and there, never settling in any one place for long. But Rooster and Pearl—they couldn't live like that. There would never be enough for them. Winn provided only for himself, not a whole family. And why should he?

He hadn't *asked* her, either. And what if he never did? What if Winn swept through women the same way he swept through territories and jobs? Gentry didn't really know, did she?

Hoss. Hoss had a successful farm. Hoss had employees. Hoss had stability. He had never made Gentry's heart flutter, but perhaps she might learn to love him. How could she not love a man who put a stable, stationary roof over her head and food in her siblings' stomachs? And he wasn't a bad-looking fellow, either.

Yes, Gentry had one thing to offer: herself. Her hands in the kitchen, her energy to keep the house clean, her virtue. It was not such a hard thing to give to another, to make her family happy.

But she wanted Winn.

More tears came, and she wiped each of them away before they fell. How much crying could she do? None of these tears would pay the mortgage or mend her clothes. Yet despite how she reasoned, she couldn't hold them back, so she sank onto the edge of her bed and let them flow—as many as her dehydrated body could spare.

Last night, she mourned her father.

Today, she mourned Winn.

~~~

Gentry heated the iron in the dying coals of their small oven and used it to smooth out the skirt of her green dress. Then she unbound her hair and brushed it, taking more care to pin it this time, smoothing the locks into place. She splashed her face with cold water and patted it dry. Had she perfume, she would have dabbed it on as well, but today the natural scents of the desert would have to do.

"Where are you going?" Pearl asked. She'd watched Gentry's preparations in silence—she hadn't come into the bedroom since fetching the water, which meant Gentry's tears hadn't been as quiet as she hoped—until now. "To that little church? It's not Sunday."

"No." Gentry shook her hands to keep her palms from sweating. She walked to the far side of the house, trying not to notice the magic-made wall that still contained Winn's earring at its core, and back again. Trying to work out the muscles that had tied themselves in knots as she readied herself. The exercise did little to help.

"My bonnet," she began, and Pearl pointed to the table where it lay. Gentry picked it up and shook it out before carefully tying it onto her head. She felt like she should bring something with her—a loaf of bread, a basket of apples—but, of course, she didn't have anything of the sort, unless Hoss had a fancy for old hay.

She waved her hands back and forth again, urging them dry.

"I'm going to the Howland farm," she finally said. She didn't like the mousy pitch of her voice.

Pearl rested her chin on the broom. "Why? Did Rooster forget something?"

"Something . . . or something." She smoothed out her skirt again. "Well, I'll let you know after what it's all for."

"After?"

Gentry nodded.

"You're acting funny. Kind of like Pa did when—"

"No." The word pricked her tongue, and Pearl closed her mouth with an audible clink of her teeth. "I mean, no, I'm not . . . please don't compare me to Pa. Or Ma. Or anyone." She pressed her fingers below her ribs, trying to ease a new cramp. "I promise I'll make more sense as soon as I'm back. Good sense. This is a good thing."

Pearl nodded, slowly, and Gentry's tongue felt too big for her mouth. *A good thing,* she repeated to herself, smoothing her skirt and wiping her hands clean at the same time. *A good thing. A good thing.*

"Well." She eyed the door. Pushed herself toward it. "I'll be back. Take care."

Pearl merely watched with a skewed eyebrow. Gentry bit down on the nonsensical words dancing between her teeth and stepped out into the bright afternoon. Judging by the too-hot sun, it was just a little past noon. Gentry had thought it later. *At least the heat will give me a healthy flush,* she thought, then sighed. Those were her ma's words.

At the thought of her mother, Gentry scanned the floor until she saw the glimmer of the gold locket by the leg of her bed. She picked it up and examined the chain. It had broken at the link Agnes had put into the chain at American Fork. Pinching the link in her fingers, Gentry looped it back through the chain and cinched it closed with her teeth. She clasped it around her neck, letting it rest on the collar of her dress instead of being hidden by it.

To get from her small homestead to Hoss's farm, she took the subtle road, which was little more than two wagon tracks denting the desert soil. She was nearly to the halfway point when she saw a figure coming toward her. Her first thought was that Rooster was coming home sick again, or perhaps there wasn't enough work to keep him on today, and her stomach twisted. However, as she neared, she recognized Hoss Howland himself, and her stomach twisted in the other direction.

He tilted his hat when they were still several paces apart and called, "Afternoon to you, Miss Gentry. Odd seeing you out here. I was just on my way to invite you and Miss Pearl for lunch."

Gentry swallowed. The air sweltered around her. "I-is that so?" she asked. "Without a horse?"

Hoss paused about two paces from her. "Indeed— thought my legs could use the stretch. But what are you doing out and about?"

Of course, the only thing in this direction was Hoss's farm, and he knew that. Gentry felt dizzy a moment, her core cold and her skin burning, her insides a swirl. Lord help her, what was she supposed to say? Was this too forward? But Hoss had mentioned it first . . . but that was a while ago, wasn't it? But she couldn't wait. She'd been waiting since Pa left, and they'd run out of time.

"I w-was meaning to talk to you." She cleared her throat in as ladylike a manner as she could manage.

"Oh?" He adjusted the brim of his hat to see her better. His brows were raised in expectation.

Gentry began to wring her finger in her fist, then noticed and dropped her hands to her sides. She smoothed her skirt, but that took only a moment, and her hands were free again. She clasped them behind her back.

"I did want to thank you for the fiddle." She cursed her tongue.

Hoss laughed. "You already have. But I'm glad you're enjoying it. Sure would love to hear you play."

"You will." She studied the ground between them. No, *look at his face.* She lifted her gaze. Hoss's eyes had a bit of green to them. His beard was a little rough and in need of a trim—it hid half of his lips. Gentry tried to imagine kissing those lips. She could do it, couldn't she? The beard would just—

"I've been thinking about American Fork," she blurted before her thoughts ran rampant. "About our last trip there. What you said before you and Rooster went into Salt Lake."

She readied to explain further, but the crease in Hoss's forehead and the stiffening of his posture told her he remembered quite well the brief words he'd uttered to her that evening.

Gentry waited for him to say something, but he didn't. Had she stunned him? Silence began to swelter beneath the blistering sun. A drop of sweat traced the curve of her spine. It reminded her of holding a chicken in her hands during the seconds before she had to snap its neck.

"I mean," she blundered, unable to bear the quiet, "if I understood you correctly. If you meant . . . that is, if you still mean—"

"I do." His voice was quiet yet penetrating. Those two

simple words sliced through Gentry's, and the hot and cold warring inside her thundered.

"Then," she swallowed, and her gut sank, "I would accept you."

The new silence that fell seemed to last eternity, though Gentry counted three and a half heartbeats before Hoss blinked and a smile pulled on his lips. He pulled his hat off. "You really mean it?"

Gritting her teeth against the spike of pain in her chest, Gentry nodded.

"I'll be!" In a blur, Hoss scooped her up and swung her around, eliciting a shriek from her. He set her down and laughed. "You really mean it?"

Gentry smiled at his happiness. "I said I did, didn't I?"

Hoss stepped back. "This is . . . I'm surprised, is all. This is wonderful. Come, come for lunch! Let's talk. Let's celebrate!"

Gentry managed a laugh—a quiet, strained one, but she thought it sounded genuine enough. "Pearl is—"

"Pearl. Yes, let's get Pearl." He grabbed her hand and grinned wider than she'd ever seen him grin. "Let's get Pearl!"

And they did.

CHAPTER 15

Hoss's farmhouse was several times the size of Gentry's—about the same size as the Hinkles'—and painted blue with white trim. He had painted it last spring, when Gentry had mentioned the colors would look fine on it. Perhaps that was when this all started.

Acres of corn and pumpkin stretched behind the home, but Hoss ushered Gentry and Pearl inside too quickly for Gentry to try and spot her brother in the rows between crops. In the kitchen, Hoss had laid out a finer feast than Gentry had seen in months—cheese and bread with jam and milk and chicken and raspberries. Her eyes marveled. Did Hoss merely want a nice meal to share today, or did he eat like this regularly? It crossed Gentry's mind all the meals she could make in his home—rich stews and cornbread and pies. So many pies. Then she saw Hoss's beaming face and averted her gaze in shame.

"Don't hesitate." He pulled out Gentry's chair for her. "I'll shout for Rooster—he should join us."

Gentry sat, and Pearl took the chair behind her, eyes wide as she took in the jam and cheese. Hoss hurried out the back door, which connected with his large kitchen. Gentry always thought it odd for him to have such a large kitchen when he barely used it. Then again, he'd likely built this house intending to have a wife.

Gentry's stomach shriveled to the size of a marble, but she loaded up a plate of food anyway. She'd force every bite down, if she had to. She wouldn't forgive herself for wasting such a meal—and such generosity—because she felt a little sick.

"What's all this about?" Pearl asked when Gentry handed her a plate. "Why is Hoss so happy?"

"He invited us for lunch." She busied herself filling Pearl's cup with milk.

"But he's so happy about it."

Gentry sat down, staring at the raspberries in front of her. She loved raspberries. Her mouth usually watered at the sight of raspberries.

Gentry folded her hands in her lap, squeezing her fingers until they hurt. "Pearl, you know Hoss is fond of us."

Her sister eyed her with a crooked brow.

"He is. And he's in need of a wife. He asked me a little while ago, and today I said yes."

The door opened, and Hoss bounded in, Rooster behind him.

Pearl's chin dropped. "But what about Winn?"

Gentry stiffened with alarm, but Hoss didn't seem to have heard. He was chuckling over something, and as Rooster stepped into the kitchen, his clothes already stained from the morning's work, Hoss said, "We're going to be brothers, you and I."

Rooster slipped off his hat. "Brothers?" he asked, noticing Gentry and Pearl. His eyes narrowed at Gentry.

Hoss's face fell. "It's not so bad."

Pulling his attention from his sisters, Rooster shook his

head. "Oh, no, I'm just surprised. Gentry never said anything to me."

Gentry picked up her fork. "And why should I gush about such things to my little brother?"

Rooster watched her a moment more before tugging his gaze away and taking Hoss's hand. "Congratulations," he said, and Hoss's good humor seemed to return.

He pushed Rooster toward the table. "Go on, eat," he said to Gentry and Pearl. "I put the food out for it, no need to wait."

His eyes met Gentry's, and he flashed a grin. Gentry tried to mirror it before popping a raspberry in her mouth.

It wasn't as sweet as she remembered.

~~~

Gentry expected a barrage of tactless questions from her sister as they trekked back to their home, but Pearl was unusually silent. She walked with her hands shoved into the pockets of her skirt and her heels scraping the dirt road with every step. Nearly a quarter hour passed before Gentry realized she was doing the same.

"Pearl."

Pearl didn't say anything.

Gentry sighed. "Are you upset with me? Sick?"

Pearl shrugged.

With a groan, Gentry ripped her hands from her pockets and flung them into the air. "Can you at least talk to me?" *Do I really have to do this all by myself?* "You like Hoss."

Pearl glanced at her under the rim of her bonnet. "Hoss is old."

"So is Willard."

"Who? Oh." She remembered Hannah's husband. "I just . . . I don't understand."

Gentry folded her arms, but the heat made it uncomfortable, and they fell back to her sides. "There's nothing to understand. Pa isn't coming home. You and I can't get jobs. The mortgage is—"

Her words cut off the same moment her feet stopped beside the wagon tracks in the road. She saw him before she saw the gulls, somehow, sitting on the dirt outside their front door, tossing something to a handful of the many seagulls perched about the house. The birds flapped their wings and opened their mouths to eat the treat.

Gentry's body felt bloodless.

Pearl took two more steps before seeing Winn and turning back to Gentry. She didn't say anything.

Lord help me, Gentry thought. Clasping her hands into fists, she forced herself forward. Only a few seconds passed before Winn looked over and noticed them. He stood, but didn't wave. Perhaps he waited to gauge the situation after the revelation about Gentry's father.

She wasn't ready for this. She wasn't ready for this.

They reached the first seagulls, and Pearl spoke first. "Hi, Winn." Her voice sounded heavy. Gentry kept her eyes on the ground.

"Hi, Pearl," he replied. "Would it be worth it to ask how you're feeling today?"

Gentry felt their eyes on her. Quickening her step, Gentry hurried between the two of them, barely brushing elbows with Winn, and slipped into the house.

"I'm fine," Pearl said behind her.

Gentry's hands shook as she pulled loose the knot of her bonnet's strings and set it on the table. Her thoughts whirled, seeking a fast solution. She could go into the bedroom and shut the door, but it had no lock, of course. She wanted to crawl into a cabinet and disappear. *She wasn't ready for this.*

"Gentry?" Winn pressed the door open and let Pearl enter under his arm. "Do you want to talk about it?"

Gentry kept her shoulder to him. "There's nothing to talk about."

Pearl said, "She's marrying Hoss Howland."

The four words rang in Gentry's ears, running over her skin like the thrill of touching a hot stove, raising the hairs on her arms. Her nails dug crescents into her palms, she fisted her hands so tightly.

The seconds of silence that passed were so heavy Gentry *heard* them.

The door shut, hard, and for a moment Gentry thought Winn had left, but his voice, sharper than she was used to, said, "You're *what?*"

She turned her back to him, hiding in her own shadow, digging the crescents deeper.

"You're kidding."

Pearl said, "I'm going to go change my stockings," and strode into the bedroom.

Gentry swallowed and stiffened her shoulders, trying to stop quivering. "You wouldn't understand."

"How could I *not?*" he countered, stepping nearer. She felt his presence like the heat of the sun. "I understand because I've been here. Because you've confided in me." A pause, and Gentry imagined him running a hand back through his hair. "And exactly how much have you told *Hoss?*"

Her eyes burned. She folded her arms against the cold emptiness spreading through her middle and merely shook her head. Even if she knew what to say, she wouldn't be able to say it.

She didn't turn around. Wouldn't.

Too many seconds passed. Winn said nothing. The door opened and shut again. Gentry waited several breaths before turning, but he and his gulls had gone.

The bedroom door opened. Pearl squeaked, "Gentry?"

Gentry unclenched her numb hands and pressed them to her belly. She ran out the door and around to the outhouse.

She was sick for a long time.

~~~

June 23

Dear Hannah,

I've exciting news for you! I'm to be married t

The pencil tip broke against the paper; Gentry had been pushing too hard, again. Sighing, she pulled out a small knife and whittled the pencil to a point again. After a silent supper and sleepless night, Gentry was desperate to move on. To pull the stitches on this wound tight before she tore them out.

June 23

Dear Hannah,

I've exciting news for you! I'm to be married to Hoss Howland, our neighbor. You met him at the bonfire.

Memories of Winn's arm around her as they danced around the fire sprang unwanted to her mind. She rubbed her eyes with her knuckles and continued her letter.

It's very new—we don't have a date set or any plans, really. Of course, Hoss knows less about these things than I do, and with Mother gone . . . well, what I'm asking is if you'd help me with the wedding preparations. Guide me and tell me what to do.

She couldn't afford a nice dress, of course, but one didn't *need* a nice dress to get married. Just a courthouse, and there was one in American Fork, wasn't there? If not, then Salt Lake. That was a long drive. They'd certainly have to stay the night.

Gentry wondered if Hoss wanted a honeymoon, and though she hadn't eaten breakfast, her stomach swirled. She clenched the muscles around it.

I'm not sure where to begin. Should I come to American Fork? You're welcome in Dry Creek if the trip sounds desirable to you and little Rachel, of course. Just tell me what to do and I'll do it.

Please, she thought, blinking rapidly to keep her eyes dry. *Someone tell me what to do.*

I look forward to your response.

Love,
Gentry Sue

P.S. Rooster's birthday is coming soon. Would you help me plan for that as well?

Maybe Hoss would give him a little extra so Gentry could buy the ingredients for a cake. When was the last time she'd had cake?

Her hands began to tremble again, so Gentry stretched out her arms and fingers before folding her letter and standing from the kitchen table. She wanted to get to the mercantile early to ensure the letter went out as soon as possible. She hated asking favors of Hannah, but Hannah was the closest thing to a mother she had, and Gentry *needed* a mother right now.

As Gentry reached for her bonnet, she heard quick footsteps outside the door. She stiffened as they grew louder, and the door swung open, revealing a winded Rooster.

"You only just left." Gentry clutched the letter in her hands. "What's wrong? Hoss?"

Rooster shook his head. "Seagulls."

The letter creased into the shape of Gentry's fingers.

Sweat dotted his brow. "I thought I should tell you that Winn's here. There. At the farm."

Gentry should have felt something. She knew she should have felt something, but everything inside of her was sore and sick already, and Rooster's sudden arrival had her heart pounding. "All right," she said, just as breathy as her brother. "All right, I'm coming. Pearl is brushing Bounder. Get Bounder."

Rooster nodded and left, leaving the door cracked open.

Gentry stared at the floor for a long moment. Shaking sense into her head, she shoved the letter into her pocket and hurried to the water pail, filling a cup from its depths and drinking until water filled her stomach.

Snatching her bonnet, Gentry ran from the house to the stable, where her brother was cinching the saddle.

"What's going on?" Pearl asked.

Gentry ignored her. "Why is Winn at Hoss's?"

Rooster shook his head. "I don't know anything other than it's about you." He pulled the cinch and looked at her from beneath the rim of his hat. "Have a feeling you should be there."

Gentry nodded. Rooster mounted the mare, then pulled up Gentry so she sat on the saddle behind him. Bounder lunged from the stable. Gentry grabbed her brother's waist with one hand and yanked her skirt down with the other. Her mind barely had time to order itself before Hoss's blue farmhouse came into view.

Rooster halted the mare, and Gentry slid off, brushing off her bodice as she hurried to the house, noting a dozen seagulls perched on roof and porch. They scattered as she ran to the door. She didn't bother to knock.

At first the house sounded quiet, but as she stepped over the simple carpet on the floor, she heard men's voices coming from the kitchen. Pulse hammering, she moved toward the room with some measure of stealth, freezing when Winn's voice touched her ears.

"—only reason," he said.

Hoss's lower, brusquer voice replied, "And what's wrong with stability? You've obviously offered her none."

Gentry's face heated until she was sure her eyebrows would light on fire.

"Perhaps she would reevaluate if I made her an offer."

She stopped breathing. Would he? But it didn't matter. Her choice was made.

"Any offer you have to give is pointless," Hoss said, reiterating Gentry's thoughts. "She's accepted me, and that's the end of the story."

Gentry shook her head. Were they really standing here, discussing her like she was some sort of fair prize?

She thought she heard Winn growl. "Have you even considered what she actually *wants*?"

"Have you considered what she actually *needs*, boy?"

Gentry's pulse thudded against every inch of her body. She couldn't believe—

Winn snorted. "Boy? At least I wouldn't give her a minimum twenty years as a widow—"

"*Winn Maheux!*" She rushed into the kitchen. Hoss stood at the far end of the table, gripping the back of a chair in both hands. Winn stood near the stove, his white sleeves rolled up to his elbows, arms crossed over his chest—arms that dropped the instant Gentry arrived. Both men's eyes widened as their faces turned to her.

"How *dare* you!" Gentry hissed, her attention on Winn. The corners of her eyes burned. "What right do you—do *either* of you—have discussing me or my needs or my desires?"

He was trying to convince Hoss not to marry her, wasn't he? Gentry's fury extinguished in a great huff of breath. Why? *Why can't you understand?*

She looked from Winn to Hoss to Winn. Hands and voice shaking, she said. "I can't talk to either of you right now."

She turned on her heel and charged out the door. One of the men called after her—maybe both? The storm rushing through her veins and the thudding of her feet warped the sounds. Rushing through the front door, which she'd left ajar, Gentry beelined to Bounder. Only once she'd topped the saddle—skirt barely covering her ankles—did she notice her brother standing to the side of the house. The men came to the front door, but she didn't turn to see their expressions. To meet their eyes. Face and eyes burning, she kicked Bounder into a gallop and sped home faster than any enchanted seagull hoped to fly.

Pearl ran out from the garden as Gentry neared. Gentry dismounted so quickly she nearly twisted her ankle. Her hem caught on the saddle, and she yanked it free.

"What happened?" Pearl asked.

Gentry shook her head, wiping the back of her wrist across her eyes. A lump pressed against the walls of her throat.

If she tried to explain now, she'd start crying, and she was so tired of crying. She was so tired of everything.

Pearl grasped Gentry's elbow for a brief moment before taking Bounder's reins and leading the mare back to the stable. A single seagull flew overhead, landing on the stable roof ahead of her.

Gentry gritted her teeth. "Don't you dare let either of them in the house, Pearl." She retreated into the shade of their small home. Her hands trembled, and her mind kept replaying the few sentences she'd heard exchanged over and over, inventing the missing pieces for better or for worse. Her head began to throb. She poured a cup of water and spilled some of it on her breast when she drank.

Hoss knew now. He'd sounded defensive, hadn't he? Gentry wasn't sure, given time to reflect. What else had Winn said to him? What if Hoss broke off the fledgling engagement? Gentry would never be able to look at him again. Then again, after the bank foreclosed on the land and the house, she wouldn't have opportunity to.

Wincing, Gentry set down the cup and pressed her fingers into her stomach, trying to ease a sudden, stabbing pain there. She searched the cupboards, but of course there was little selection. She forced herself to gnaw on a crust of bread. The first swallow hurt, the second not as much.

What should I do? she wondered. Wait for Winn to leave and then explain herself to Hoss? Would Rooster say anything? And Winn! *How dare he!*

Her headache slid down to her chest, or maybe her bellyache climbed up, and Gentry collapsed into one of the kitchen chairs, ignoring the way it tilted, one leg shorter than the rest. Winn. Winn didn't want her to marry Hoss. He'd gone there himself to talk him out of it. Part of Gentry embraced the heavy sort of glee that came with knowing Winn might really love her the way she loved—

"No," she whispered, dropping her forehead to the table. She'd already considered this. She's already decided. She was *engaged* to *Hoss Howland.*

A few gull cries brought her head off the table. Moments later the door opened and Pearl poked her head in, eyes bright but her mouth twisted, as though her features warred with one another. "I think Winn is—"

"I'm locking the door if he is." Her voice came out like she had a head cold. Pearl frowned, hesitated, then stepped back outside.

A breeze blew in through the glassless window, carrying on it the cries of seagulls. The breeze settled, as did the birds. Gentry heard Winn's voice, but she couldn't pick out all of his words. Her stomach twisted and lodged high into her ribs. *I can't do this right now. I can't do this.*

"She doesn't want to see you," Pearl said. "She said she'll lock the door."

"And lock you out too?" Winn asked.

Gentry imagined Pearl shrugging. "I'm gardening."

Standing so swiftly her chair nearly toppled over, Gentry hurried to the front door and locked it. Moments later, a knuckle wrapped on the door's other side. "Gentry," his voice was soft, "let me talk to you, please."

"Just go." The lump in her throat squeezed the words and pitched them high.

"Gentry," he repeated, a little stronger. Gentry didn't answer. She crossed the length of the small kitchen to where Pa's ledger sat on a shelf. She opened it, the last several pages filled with her handwriting, not his.

Winn's footsteps retreated, and Gentry folded in on herself as she clutched that damnable ledger.

What else am I to do? she thought, maybe prayed. Did

that count as a prayer? Holding her breath against another ache in her abdomen, Gentry tossed the ledger back onto its shelf and rubbed the heels of her hands into her eyes.

"I knew I put this here for a reason."

Gentry whirled at the sound of Winn's voice, finding him leaning against the clay sill of the glassless window cut into the wall he had built.

The urge to wail pressed against Gentry's teeth. She swallowed it. "You have no right to meddle with—"

"I have every right," he interrupted, his voice annoyingly calm.

"Leave it to a man to say such a thing." Gentry blinked back the threat of tears. "I can't get by like you do, Winn. My family can't get by. I can't pay the mortgage. We can barely afford to keep Bounder—"

"Gentry." He straightened, a piece of golden hair falling over one of his golden eyes. "I can help you. I *want* to help you. I want you to be able to lean on me—"

"Winn," her voice sounded like a child's, "you can't even hold onto your own jewelry."

He paused, reaching one hand to his ear. Both lobes only held one earring each; he hadn't recovered the gold lost in the battle against the geyser. He couldn't afford to replace them.

"So you'll only marry for money?" he asked, quieter. "I dare you to tell me you love that man."

"It doesn't matter if I love him," she said, but she wasn't sure if the words were loud enough for him to hear.

"I've been *trying*, Gentry. I'll take you back to California. Salt Lake City. Anywhere you want to go. I'll rebuild every wall of your house and exterminate every insect in your garden. Do you really think I couldn't take care of you?"

"And Pearl?" An unshed tear blurred part of her vision.

"And Rooster? They can't live in a house of birds, Winn. They can't drift across the continent like you do."

"Then we'll settle. We'll build a house closer to Hannah, or—"

"Winn." She shook her head. "Be honest with yourself. Are you really the type of person to *settle*? To stay in one place, to work the same job year after year?"

He didn't answer right away, and in the ensuing silence, Gentry heard her heart crack like cold glass held to a flame.

"Let me in," Winn pleaded. "Let me help you. Let me *be* there for you, *and* Pearl and Rooster. Gentry," he leaned back on the sill, "don't you trust me?"

The question danced around her ears like magic she couldn't see. She had tried to put the pieces together in a way that worked. Of course she had tried. But they didn't. No matter how she turned or forced them, they wouldn't form the big picture. The one she needed.

Eyes cast to the rag rug, she murmured, "I can't."

A hush filled the house, unbroken even by the cry of a gull or the buzz of a fly. Gentry stared hard at the floor, nails digging into her palms again.

Silence, then the soft sound of shifting, of cotton pulling over clay as Winn stepped away from the window.

"Then we have nothing to discuss." His voice wasn't his own.

Gentry swallowed; the lump in her throat pushed back. A breeze filled the space. She looked up, but Winn and the seagulls were gone.

~~~

Vegetable broth and bread for supper again. Gentry started it early and leaned over the pot, stirring with a sluggish hand, watching little bits of overcooked carrots swirl through the steaming water. Her arm hurt from stirring, but she didn't want those little bits to settle. Didn't want to see her reflection across the top of the meager meal.

Rooster came inside from watering the horse. Sweat plastered his hair to his scalp despite the cooling evening. Gentry should draw a bath for him. Put herself to work hauling in the water. Heaven knew the crops needed an extra drink when he was done.

Pearl set the table. Gentry finally pulled away from the mesmerizing broth and filled bowls and sliced bread. It wasn't sweet, like her ma used to make it, but it was good enough. They ate in relative silence, though Pearl did ask Rooster how his day went. Neither she nor Gentry mentioned Winn's visit, and neither Gentry nor Rooster talked about the morning interruption at the Howland house.

Rooster took care of the dishes, and Gentry readied the pail to go to the well before it got too dark. A knock sounded at the door. Gentry stiffened. Pearl answered it.

"Evening, Miss Pearl," Hoss said. "Hope I'm not visiting too late."

Gentry clutched the pail.

"Just finishing supper." Pearl fiddled with the doorknob. "I've got to study my arithmetic."

"Is that so?" he said. "Think your sister's got a minute?"

Pearl opened the door wider, revealing Hoss standing in the doorway, still in his soiled farm clothes, though he'd trimmed his beard. Pearl said, "He wants to talk to you," as though Gentry hadn't just heard him.

"I'll get the water." Rooster took—pried—the pail from Gentry's hands. "Pearl, help me get it."

Pearl frowned. "But you don't need two—"

"My arm hurts." He grasped her lightly by the back of her neck. "Excuse me, Hoss."

Hoss nodded and stepped aside, letting the two youngest Abrams slip by.

Resisting the urge to wring her hands, pop her knuckles, *anything*, Gentry said, "Please, won't you come in?" and lit one of the candles for better light. She set it on the table where Hoss sat—right where Pa used to sit. Gentry hesitated, wondering which chair to take, if she should take one at all. Her stomach gurgled, but at least it had food to satiate it this time.

She chose the chair to Hoss's left. Smoothed her skirt. "I suppose I should apologize for this morning."

"Ah, Gentry, don't be saying that." Hoss slipped off his hat and set it on the table in front of him. It didn't look as worn as Gentry remembered; perhaps it was new. "I came here to apologize to *you*. Haven't felt right all day."

Gentry's eyes flickered from the hat to the tabletop to the candleholder. "I didn't exactly knock."

"You don't need to."

A moment of quiet fell, but Gentry couldn't tolerate another silence, not today.

"Then I'll apologize on Winn's behalf." She watched light flicker off the brass candleholder. "He's just a friend of ours." *Who I might not see again.* "A recent friend, almost more of an acquaintance." *Who's done more for me than anyone out here, but life has never been fair, has it?*

Hoss nodded. "I met him in American Fork."

Gentry licked her lips. "I suppose you know about Pa."

He sighed. "I do. Winn told me, and Rooster confirmed. I didn't know, Gentry. I'm awful sorry for you."

Gentry merely shrugged. "It does put us in a predicament. I-I don't know exactly what Winn told you, but it's not as bad as all that."

"Gentry," Hoss reached his hand toward her on the table,

but both hers were in her lap, "I know I'm not certain things. I'm not as young as I once was, maybe not the handsomest fellow around—"

"Hoss—"

"Now hear me out," he insisted. "I'm not a lot of things, but God knows I try. I wasn't raised on a silver spoon; I know how these things work out. I know a woman needs stability, especially out here."

Gentry's gaze flicked to Hoss, who stared at the table as he spoke.

"What I'm saying," he went on, "is I'm not certain things, but I work hard. Came out here with the pioneers and started this farm all on my own, got the right licenses and such. Not that you need to be caring about licenses. Don't matter what that fellow said, whatever the reason for you accepting me. Heck, wasn't much of a proposal, was it?"

Gentry's lips quirked. "I suppose not."

"I'll work hard for you, promise I will." He finally met her eyes. "I still mean to marry you if you still mean to marry me. I just," he paused, "I know fondness when I see it. I know it in you and in that Winn fellow. I just need your word that I won't have to be competing, is all."

Gentry nodded. "I already—"

"I want you to think about it a bit," Hoss cut in. "I've got a sister, maybe I mentioned her before. A little like you, in a way. Only reason I know a thing about women." He chuckled, but the mirth died quickly. "I want you to think on it."

The muscles in her jaw ached. She answered Hoss with only a nod.

"Well, that's that, then." He hesitated. "Before I go, you mind playing a number for me?"

A few of her nerves dissipated. "On the fiddle?"

"Right. I'd love a song to see me off."

Gentry's heart had little music in it, but she retrieved the pinewood case and slid the fiddle from it, unable to deny such a simple request from a man so willing to tolerate her and her woes. She tuned it carefully and asked, "Any requests?"

Hoss shrugged. "Anything, really. I'm not savvy with song titles. Never studied music, myself."

Chewing her lip, Gentry's head spun through a list of songs. The names of the cheery ones wouldn't stick, so she chose "Believe Me, If All Those Endearing Young Charms." She played it through twice on the fiddle, drawing out its long notes, closing her eyes and trying to imagine herself somewhere else.

For some reason, the song only filled her with regret.

CHAPTER 16

Rooster got paid, and the cupboards became a little fuller. The new potatoes were coming in well, and one tomato plant had survived, though it was no higher than Gentry's knee. Tuesday, Wednesday, Thursday, and not one seagull touched the sky over Dry Creek. Friday, Saturday, Sunday, and Gentry knew Winn had likely gone for good, whisked away to wherever his magic took him. She would never have a chance to apologize, to take back her hard words, or to ponder the *what if* of that past decision. She tried to console herself with what had brought her to this path in the first place: the facts. Winn couldn't provide for her and her family. He *couldn't*. Not the way things were now. And even if Winn conjured some astounding job and appeared at her side right now to marry her, how could Gentry be happy, tying him down? A man with an occupation couldn't fly away on the wings of seagulls, couldn't cast spells under the watch of his colleagues, and couldn't rush off at a moment's notice to calm the quaking earth, righting the wrongs brought on by greed and gold. Gentry would rather never see Winn again than lead him down the same broken path her parents had taken.

Of course, she didn't have the luxury of choice anymore. What she *did* have was a positive answer for Hoss—one she had, thus far, neglected to tell him. She was waiting for the

239

right moment—the moment where her stomach stopped twisting, the moment when her heart changed, or, maybe, the moment her mind suddenly forgot about a golden man and his birds.

She glanced outside, touching the locket around her neck. No wild magic looming in the yard today. If she gave one of the ghostly creatures enough gold, would it eat her thoughts for her, leaving her in an ignorant and blissful stupor?

Shaking such thoughts from her head, Gentry tried to focus on the day's chores. Just a little more time, then she would go to Hoss. Find a way to connect the *yes* in her head to a *yes* on her tongue. A little more time. God could grant her that much, couldn't he?

But there wasn't much time to be had. Pearl rode Bounder in from the mercantile and handed Gentry the letters. The first, of course, was a notice from the bank with a typed receipt of how much they owed on the land and the extra debt they'd accrue if payment wasn't made. Despite the long summer days, time certainly seemed to shrink.

The second letter, however, was from Hannah. Forgetting the bill for a moment, Gentry tore it open, her spirit instantly lifted by the smooth lines of her dear friend's handwriting.

June 27

Dear Gentry,

What fantastic news! And such a surprise! Congratulations! I remember the man. Quiet fellow, stick pull. Not the blonde one, right? Winn? I really must hear the story of this change of heart. Of course I'll help you with the wedding! You could get married right here in American Fork by Bishop Cowls. Is there a fabric shop in Dry Creek? I don't think there is. Please come to American Fork and we'll see to a dress. And don't start with me, Gentry Sue. I'm talking to Willard about budgeting some fabric, but if it doesn't work out then we'll repurpose mine. I still have it! And we're close to the same size, aren't we? Or we were, before these babies came along. Come to American Fork, and we'll get everything in order.

Caleb is so excited! I don't think he completely understands you're getting married, but I'm explaining it to him. His big sister, married! He'll be an uncle soon enough, and at two years old! How fun this will all be. Oh, and Carolyn sends her well-wishes! So do all the kids, minus Frederick. You know how he's been lately. Moody. He'll grow out of it, I'm sure.

Oh, of course! Please, please tell Rooster that Willard's found a place for him! He can start work in two weeks' time. Willard's got a room he can share with two other boys while they get things started, and they can finalize the pay after that—

Gentry lowered the letter. A place for Rooster? Two weeks' time? Shared room? Gentry skimmed the rest of the letter, seeking some answer, but there was only an invitation to attend church should she stay for the weekend. Pinching the parchment, Gentry rushed out the door and toward the stable where Pearl was brushing down Bounder.

"Pearl, do you know anything about Rooster taking another job?"

Pearl's fair brows drew together. "Did the mill spot open up?"

Gentry shook her head. Leaning against a post of the stable, she reread the letter. Pearl finished with Bounder and tried to read over Gentry's shoulder, so she just handed her sister the note in full and walked back to the house. She could go to Hoss's and find Rooster—but he would be home in a few hours, and Hoss . . .

She didn't finish the thought. She went into the house, paced to the soaking laundry and back, then went outside to check on the crops.

Pearl jogged to her, the letter bouncing with each step. "Maybe he's converting."

"He's not converting." Crouching, she pulled some weeds, then some more. "We'll just have to wait. Did you finish the writing assignment I gave you?"

"I lost it."

"Then copy that letter." She ripped a weed from the soil. "Use the back of the envelope; we're out of chalk."

After accumulating sore legs from the garden and hanging the laundry to dry, Gentry boiled half a head of cabbage and paced, waiting for her brother's return. She left the door open to better see the road to Hoss's home, and when Rooster appeared on it, she snatched the letter and ran out to meet him.

"Ryan Rooster Abrams!" she called as she ran, stopping a pace in front of him. She shoved the letter into his chest. "What is this?"

Brow cocked, Rooster took the crinkled letter and looked it over. "Wedding plans?" he guessed.

Gentry pointed to the second to last paragraph. "*This*. What does Hannah mean?"

Rooster's gaze dropped as he read. His lips parted into a smile, then a grin. Yipping like a dog, he hugged Gentry and spun her around, losing the letter between them. "This is great!" he shouted, laughing, and the sound both startled and warmed Gentry. How long had it been since her brother had laughed?

Gentry found her feet. "What? What?"

"The printing press!" He grabbed his hat and waved it over his head. "Willard set it up last month. I mentioned something about it."

Gentry's eyes bugged, and her blood buzzed within her veins. "You did not."

"I didn't want to say much." He searched for the letter and found it on the ground. He snatched it and read it over once more. "I didn't want to get your hopes up."

Gentry shook her head. "You're going . . . to work for Willard Hinkle? In Salt Lake City?"

"Comes with room and board, see?" He held out the letter as though Gentry hadn't already memorized it. "I'd come home a weekend or two a month. This is perfect!"

Gentry's shoulders slumped. "So . . . you're leaving?"

Her brother blinked. "Gentry, the job pays eight dollars a week, and that's just for start. If the paper takes off, it could be more. Up to twelve, even."

Gentry's jaw hung.

"There's a demand for it, and more and more people are moving out west," he explained. "Willard has a whole network planned."

Mouth dry, Gentry shook her head. "You're joking."

Rooster grabbed a stray piece of hair framing Gentry's face and tugged on it. "What do you think I've been doing all summer?" His face grew serious, and for once he looked more like their mother than their father. "You're just like Ma, you know. Taking too much on yourself. Did you really think I was going to sit by and watch us starve? When Hoss took us to Salt Lake, I was asking around then too, and at the bonfire in American Fork, but nothing was paying—are you all right?"

The image of her brother blurred, and Gentry blinked it clear again. "You've been . . . you've been . . ."

Lowering the letter, Rooster put his arms around Gentry again, around her elbows, and rested his chin on her shoulder. "We're not little kids, Gen," he said, soft. "We're capable, me and Pearl both. When are you going to learn to depend on us? Maybe Pa left, but we're *real* family. We're staying, always."

Gentry blinked rapidly to keep her eyes dry. She took in a deep breath and let it out, a laugh catching its end. Pulling back, she said, "The mortgage, it has late fees . . ."

"We'll pay it off." His smile widened. "Or sell it."

"S-sell?" Gentry repeated. "But Pa built this house—"

"Come on, Gen." He placed a hand on her shoulder. "Don't you want to live around people? Don't you want to leave the bad memories behind? We don't have to, of course, and we gotta ask Pearl, but we could move to Salt Lake City. Maybe American Fork; be closer to work and to Caleb."

She nodded slowly, shivers running up and down her arms. "Perhaps. Perhaps we could."

Rooster's hand moved up to her head, and he rubbed her scalp as though *she* were the younger sibling, then elbowed her back toward the house. Pearl came out, shielding her eyes from the sun, looking toward them.

"What did he say?" she shouted.

Gentry smiled—a true, genuine smile—and snatched her brother's hand. "You tell it. It's your good news."

"It's *our* good news," he countered as Gentry jerked him forward, breaking into a run. She ran, and she laughed, and for once she ate her meager supper without the slightest hint of sickness.

⁓

Hoss answered the door on Rooster's last day of work and leaned against the frame, seeming unsurprised to see

Gentry there. Gentry opened her mouth to speak, but Hoss beat her to it.

"He's going to Salt Lake City tomorrow," he said.

Gentry pressed her lips together and nodded. Hannah's letter was two weeks old now. Two more weeks of Rooster's farmhand wages, two weeks to prepare him for the trip north. Two weeks to make the decision to sell the land back to the bank so, in six weeks' time, Gentry and Pearl would go to Salt Lake City too.

Two weeks for Gentry to pry her white-knuckled fingers off her self-declared responsibilities. Two weeks to come to the decision to break off the brief engagement with the kindest man in Dry Creek. Two weeks to forget Winn, who had been gone for two and a half.

He knew, of course. Hoss. She saw it in his eyes, in his posture. In the way he said, "When a woman takes so long to give a man an answer, he starts to figure it out on his own."

Gentry wrung her index finger in her fist. "I'm sorry, Hoss." She hadn't meant to do this on his doorstep. She wanted it to be more proper—as proper as one could be, breaking a man's heart. "I do care for you, but with all that's happened . . . I need to do what's best for our family. Keep what's left together."

"You all could stay here," he offered, the words weak.

She smiled at him. "Next time you're in Salt Lake City . . ."

He nodded. "I'll come knocking."

It shouldn't have been as easy of a conversation as it was, Gentry thought as she walked back to her father's house. She shouldn't have been forgiven so easily. *In the end, I don't deserve someone like Hoss.*

A shadow passed overhead—a passing seagull. Gentry's heart leapt as her fingers reached for the necklace already pressed against her collar. Of course, the bird had no shimmer to its feathers. God had unleashed a vigorous rain on the territory two days ago, encouraging the gulls to venture away from the lake. None remembered their magic.

She sighed, stepped around a tumbleweed. Her stomach had settled, and now that she'd spoken to Hoss, her nerves were calm as well. But her chest ached. How odd it was, that a broken heart would actually feel like one.

She'd hoped to forget Winn, to get over him just like the boys she'd fancied back in Virginia. But time didn't heal her foolish heart. It infected it, and each passing hour made it ache that much more. She wouldn't call herself foolish—had Rooster not had success with work, Hoss *would* have been the right choice, even if Gentry didn't want him to be. Hoss had been her only option.

Her step slowed, stopped, and she looked back over her shoulder, the Howland farm now just a blur behind her. Her only option. Wasn't he?

Trust me.

Do you trust me?

You're safe, trust me.

Gentry pinched her necklace between her thumb and forefinger. How many times had Winn told her to trust him? Didn't she?

Her last words to him ran through her memory and chilled her. *What if I had?* she thought. *What if I had trusted him?*

What if she had trusted Rooster? Pearl? Hannah? Hannah had scolded her once for being prideful. Rooster had chided her for thinking she had to save them all on her own.

Her knees weakened and she swayed, but she caught herself before tumbling. She never trusted any of them, did she? Even her own instincts. When Pa left, she had *known* where he was really going, hadn't she?

Her shoulders knotted, and she forced herself to walk. "I made the wrong choice," she whispered, looking into the sky until the sun made her eyes water. Pretending it was the sun that made her eyes water.

I made the wrong choice.

～～～

Though Rooster was usually absent most of the day, the house felt strange without his presence in it. Though there was little threat to be had in Dry Creek, Gentry found herself double-checking the door lock at night. She thought to pull apart one of the window boxes just to board up the glassless window in Winn's magic-made wall, but she'd never be able to drive nails into its brick-like surface.

The second bed was free, but Gentry and Pearl still shared theirs. Food stretched a little farther, and nine days after Rooster arrived in Salt Lake City, he sent a letter home that had eight dollars in it, along with a note about how it was in the city and how everyone thought he was Mormon.

That night Gentry made her ma's recipe for velvet chicken soup—a dish she hadn't prepared since the night Winn stayed for supper. It filled Gentry's belly well but didn't taste the way it should, the way she remembered it tasting. It didn't relieve the pressure beneath her ribs or the visions of gold that laced her dreams.

Laundry became an easier task now that it was just her and Pearl and neither of them worked in dirt as often as Rooster had. The planned move meant the crops would be left behind, so they no longer needed tending. With so much spare time, Pearl raced Bounder about in the evenings and explored the desert that led to the Oquirrhs. Gentry planned for the move and practiced fiddling—Hoss still wouldn't take the beautiful gift back. Even when she played a cheery song, its notes were laced with guilt. When she could tolerate the sensation no longer, she used the last pages in Pa's ledger to write letters to Rooster and Winn. Of course, she couldn't mail the latter.

Just under four weeks before the move to Salt Lake City, in the morning while Gentry mucked Bounder's stall, she heard the faintest cry of a seagull. Starting, she dropped the pitchfork and turned, searching for the source. She saw nothing.

"One moment, girl." She rubbed Bounder's nose before venturing out of the stable. No recent rains, but it wouldn't be the first time she heard the ghostly sound of Winn. Still, her pulse quickened, and she searched the landscape for any glimmer of wild magic.

She found the creature on the back of the stable, perched on the corner. It took off just as quickly, but Gentry thought, maybe, she saw a shimmer at the tip of its wing.

She held her breath, watching the white and gray bird until it grew too small to see. It could have been just a trick of the morning sun or a blur from flapping, but Gentry dared to hope. Could the bird be one of Winn's? Could he have forgiven her?

"And why would he?" she asked herself, punctuating the words with a sigh. She hadn't apologized. As far as Winn knew, she had already wed Hoss. And better for him to believe that too. Were his arms ever to open to her again, how would she explain that she wanted him for him, and not because Rooster's prospects had changed their fortunes?

She returned to mucking the stall, her thoughts gliding on the breeze left by the seagull's wings. How could she tell him? Even if Winn ever did decide to visit Dry Creek, she wouldn't be here. He wouldn't know where to find her if he cared to look. She couldn't post him a letter. She could hardly ride west and hope to stumble upon the Hagree and leave a message with them, praying Winn might fly by again and receive it. Gentry had been a stupid and self-centered woman, and now she had to pay the price.

Gentry's pitchfork stilled. She stared at the fresh shavings half scattered in Bounder's stall.

The price.

She touched her necklace.

Wild magic. It's always here, if you're in the right place.

Gentry might be useless when it came to protecting her loved ones from the throes of the mine, but perhaps she could do this.

She hurried to the house, where Pearl drew on her slate. Poking her head into the front room, she said, "Pearl? I'm going on a walk. Will you be all right?"

Pearl nodded, focused on her work.

Closing the door, Gentry focused on the Oquirrh Mountains. She saw nothing magical about them now, but when wild magic did cross her vision, it was almost always near them. Winn had warned her about feeding gold to the ethereal creatures, but if they helped her, it would be worth the risk.

So she walked. She didn't ride; she didn't want to risk missing something. She walked away from the house, away from the invisible border of Dry Creek, until the sagebrush thickened and the soil roughened. Night beckoned magical things more than day did, but Gentry certainly wouldn't be able to see where she was going in the dark, not to mention the chance of running into something far more harmful than an earthy spirit. She studied the branches of each sagebrush and tree she passed, studied a mouse as it scurried across her path and the flight of a bee searching for its next flower. She stopped where her self-made path grew rocky and scanned the area, searching, hoping. Seeing nothing, she changed course. It wouldn't be hard to get back home with such low and sparse vegetation around her. Nothing to block her view of town, but perhaps that was the problem. She was too close to town. She kept climbing, the sun shifting slowly with her, as if trying to get a better look at where she was headed.

She reached a small copse of trees, studying their leaves to see if any shimmered like the branches at the Hagree camp did. Wiping sweat from her forehead, she sought out birdsong and examined wrens, but their feathers were free of magical glow. Her legs cramped as she trudged into her second hour of hiking, but on she searched, wandering closer to the mountains and up a foothill.

Had she not developed such an aversion to the creatures, she might not have noticed the black insect the length of her thumb sitting beside a patch of wild grass, its long legs crooked and ready to jump, its dark body reflecting the now afternoon sunlight. Sunlight that morphed into a halo surrounding it.

Gentry held her breath and took a few steps away from the bug, not wishing to startle it. Crouching, she watched the creature, its antennae twitching, mandibles sputtering around a blade of grass. Magic, and not wild.

It's bribery and imagination, Winn's voice whispered in her memory. *They hear your thoughts, when you want them to.*

Would this creature listen to her?

Hello, Gentry tried, attempting to think the word loudly. *Can you hear me?*

The locust continued on as normal.

"Hello," she tried again. "Little locust, can you help me?"

The bug nibbled its lunch.

"You said anyone could do it, didn't you?" she whispered, her heart beating out the letters of Winn's name. With fingers tipped with cold, she unclasped the necklace from around her neck and stretched her arm forward, letting the locket dangle.

The locust's antennae stilled. In that moment Gentry knew. It was *listening*.

The ability to truly listen creates a bond stronger than gold.

Gentry closed her eyes and breathed slowly, in and out. She tried to focus on the insect before her. Tried to wash away the memories of its kind destroying her garden. She listened, hearing her own pulse and the soft rustle of sagebrush as a warm breeze stirred.

Opening her eyes, Gentry studied the locust. She quelled her disgust and tried to find beauty in its dark form. She listened, but heard nothing. She prayed the bug would at least notice the effort.

"If you understand me, I'll make a trade." She pinched the chain hard between her fingers. She thought of Winn, of his face, his hair, his clothes. His birds and his bird house. "Winn Maheux." Gentry enunciated each syllable. "I need to find him."

The locust turned toward her.

"I know the going rate," she added, "and this is a lot of gold. But I'll give it to you, if you can take me to him. Do we have a—"

Buzzing sounded from the sagebrush around her, growing more intense with each heartbeat until it drowned out her thoughts completely. Locusts she hadn't seen suddenly appeared around the plants, taking to the air, swarming as they once had over her crops. Swarming around *her*.

Gentry bit down on a shriek, squeezing her eyes shut and covering her head with her free hand. She forced the other to remain outstretched, even as hundreds of legs crawled over it and nibbled at her fingers. Small tugs dragged on her necklace and pried her fingers open, claiming chain and clasp. The pattern of the insects' song filled her ears, yet it sounded . . . different. Not simply the buzzing of a mindless swarm. It had cadence. Melody. Almost like a speech Gentry could never hope to understand.

She thought of Winn and his seagulls. The story he told her when they visited the Hagree. Their connection.

Gentry opened her eyes and found herself consumed by darkness. Thousands of locusts surrounded her without a gap between them. They churned, forming a living tunnel before her. A tunnel of shadows, vibrating and humming. Though no matter how hard Gentry squinted at the tunnel's sides, she couldn't make out the shapes of wings or legs. Only hear them.

She peered ahead. Light—not sunlight, but a muted glow not unlike the light within Winn's house, the light that glowed in the corners from unseen places. She walked toward it, though the distance she gained seemed to be a quarter of what she should gain, as though the ground moved backward as she covered it. The glow stretched wider, and after a long moment, Gentry stepped out of the tunnel and into its warmth.

Crisp orchard grass crunched under her feet. She found herself in a grove of aspens and pine, surrounded by the white blossoms of asters. The rocky face of the mountain was gone; she couldn't even feel its incline beneath her feet. Turning around, Gentry sought the tunnel, but it had disappeared.

The sounds of the forest—sounds that reminded her of Virginia—fell upon her like heavy rain. Hums and buzzes and shrieks, songs and shrills. A musical dissonance. She peered at the gaps between trees overhead. No sun, only that pale light.

Her time with Winn had certainly had its effect on her— she was not as panicked at this sudden change in scenery as she would have been only months ago. There was a strange pressure to the air, as though behind this illusion of greenery the locusts breathed as one. Bated breath. Waiting. For what?

What do you want me to do? she wondered. She thought to call out, but restrained herself. There was a strange reverence to these charmed woods, and the sound of her voice would break it.

She took a step forward, studying the asters, searching for movement in the grass. She found none. She peered to the trees and beyond and now saw long, green paths between trunks. A path lay in every space between the trees, leading in varying directions. Identical. Or were they?

She spun slowly, taking in the glade.

Once I learned to listen to their spirits, I understood.

Gentry closed her eyes and listened to the noise. Thunder, chickadee, wasp, cricket, owl, wind. She held still, skin tingling. Hog, rain, hummingbird, wolf, jay.

Locust.

She recognized the pattern amid the noise, the rhythm that had rattled her bones as she ran out to her garden in panic and fought the creatures to save her crops. She recognized its undertones among sounds that should have swallowed it.

She kept her hands at her sides. Inhale, exhale. She moved forward until her toe hit a tree root, and she opened her eyes.

A green path.

The rest of the glade vanished, leaving only shadow behind her. One green path stretched ahead, glowing and colored by the shade of unseen boughs. She moved forward, her heart pumping hard and slow in her chest. Her footfalls made no noise, and each step carried her farther than it should have. Despite that, the path stretched on and on, with no end in sight. Gentry knew everything she saw was a trick, some unknown element of magic, yet her body grew weary with the distance, and she soon found herself out of breath.

All at once, the path fell away, leaving her in a grove smaller than the first. No trees composed its walls, only shadows. No grass or earth covered the ground, but a path built from flecks of gold. In its center rested a single locust somehow familiar to her, and Gentry knew it as the one she'd first approached on the hillside by her home. Indeed, it crouched upon the pendant of her mother's necklace.

The creature hummed at her. Waited. The choice hovered in the space between them, unspoken and heavy.

Gentry knelt and reached forward until its antennae tickled her fingertips.

Then she woke up.

～

Blue sky, blotted by a single, feathery cloud, filled Gentry's vision. She stared at it, blinking, for several seconds until she came to herself.

Starting, Gentry sat up, her spine protesting the sudden movement. She had lain sprawled against the side of the foothill, a half-buried stone digging into her hip, her foot shoved into the center of a small sagebrush. Down the slopes lay her home and the stable, the half-ruined garden. The feathery cloud passed in front of the sun, offering her a semblance of shade.

The locusts announced themselves with soft buzzing.

They gave her a small berth, perfectly circular, their

bodies blanketing the rest of the inclined ground in shimmering black. Their presence turned the foothill into obsidian, there were so many of them. An entire swarm, yet she could not bring herself to fear it.

Something pricked Gentry's palm. She opened her hand to find the clasp to her ma's necklace there, its shape imprinted against her skin. She wondered at it, holding the token between thumb and forefinger. Only the clasp, but she pocketed it and pressed her hand against the fabric, grateful.

The creatures buzzed again, waiting. She had given them gold. And they had given her ... what? Friendship? Trust?

Do you trust me?

The memory of Winn's question stabbed into her heart like a cold metal spike. He should have been here for this. How she *wanted* him here.

She moved forward to kneel; the swarm buzzed and shifted with her. She steeled herself. "I would ask a favor of you." She didn't know if she had to speak aloud or not, for Winn never did. Then again, she wasn't Winn, and these creatures were not his seagulls.

The swarm hummed.

"I need you to search for ... two ... people for me." An image of her pa wafted through her thoughts, making her body heavy and cold, despite the summer sun. She pushed him away. She had made choices. He had made choices. Whatever choices were left were each their own. Gentry would not choose for him.

She leaned close to the swarm and whispered "Winn Maheux," and then another name, a name that might help her plead her case, in the long run. But it was Winn's name that lingered on her lips, soft and cold like snow. "Please. Please try."

The hum of the locusts intensified until the foothill itself began to shake. Their bodies rose into the air as one, a great storm cloud of wings and legs. It soared skyward before splitting off into three groups that repelled from one another, each taking a direction: west, north, and southeast.

Gentry stood, heedless of the dust littering her skirt, and watched the locusts soar until her eyes could not tell their swarms from the blue of the sky. She reached into her pocket and pinched the clasp of her mother's necklace, offering a prayer to whatever deity would listen.

She picked her way back down the slope. Her belly grumbled, ready for lunch. Her neck felt uncomfortably bare.

It took her over an hour to reach the stable, and she leaned against Bounder's door while she caught her breath and stretched her legs. Bounder nuzzled the rim of her bonnet, and Gentry patted the mare's jaw. She closed her eyes for a moment, breathing deep to alleviate the tightness in her chest, but she had to settle for a dull, lonely ache.

I met Winn because he was already in Utah Territory. Surely something will bring him through again. Maybe not to Salt Lake City, unless he needs work. And I'll look for him. I'll listen for the quaking of earth or follow the rumors of geysers and look for him, and someday, someday, *I'll tell him how sorry I am. That I love . . .*

She pressed the palms of her hands into her eyes. Bounder nudged her bonnet. "It'll be all right, girl," she whispered. "Somehow, it will be all right."

Faint buzzing tickled her ear. Lowering her hands, Gentry looked at the door to Bounder's stall and saw three locusts there regarding her with interest. Their wings glimmered with magic. She didn't touch the golden clasp in her pocket, yet she saw the telling shimmer. Her eyes had been opened. What would Winn say, to know of this strange bargain she had made? To know she could see these creatures the way he could, without special enchantment?

"Hello," she whispered. "Thank you for your help. You're welcome to stay, but don't touch my crops. Those are for my family. And be sure not to linger underfoot."

The locusts hummed to each other. Or, perhaps, to her.

~~~

Six days since she walked into the dreamlike grove of the locusts. Six days since she gave them her mother's necklace. Six days since she whispered Winn's name and they carried it across the desert on buzzing wings.

Six days, and they hadn't returned.

Gentry leaned on the sill of the glassless window, staring past the garden and the stable, where Pearl brushed down Bounder to get her ready for the long trek to Salt Lake City. Gentry watched the line where the sky met the desert, her fingers drawing circles on the magic-hardened brick that, at its heart, still encompassed Winn's earring. The only piece of him she had left, and soon Gentry wouldn't have that, either.

She'd been silly enough to consider digging the memento out, but of course her family still lived here, and it would have done no good to have the assessor come by and see they lived in a three-walled house instead of a four-walled one.

Gentry rested her chin against her palm, watching the cloudless sky. In her mind's eye she imagined a seagull crossing it, then another, and another, and then Winn appeared for some reason she couldn't fathom. Maybe because he'd forgiven her, or maybe because for some reason he figured she would never really marry Hoss and had come to her senses. But that sky stayed clear of both bird and bug, and the emptiness of it radiated deep in her core, a hunger that couldn't be satiated with food.

Perhaps some choices couldn't be unchosen. Perhaps there was no redemption for her. Perhaps she deserved that.

"Do you . . . need help?" Pearl asked.

Blinking herself to her senses, Gentry turned from the window to her sister. They were nearly packed, with some of the furniture already loaded in the wagon. Once the house was emptied, their supplies were set, and they got word from the assessor, Dry Creek would be only a memory.

"Sorry." She stepped away from the window. She had tasked herself with beating out the rag rugs, and here she was moping again, daydreaming, whatever she should call it. She scooted an old chair off the carpet and picked it up. It left smears of dust on her sleeve.

She tried not to notice the sympathetic look Pearl gave her. It was in the arch of her eyebrows and the slouch of her shoulders. Though Gentry hadn't spoken of it, she knew both her siblings recognized her heartsickness. Pearl was more astute than Gentry gave her credit for, and she missed Winn as well. Each time Pearl mentioned him, Gentry felt like her spirit shrank inside her body. She'd collapse on herself, thinking too much of him. Yet she could hardly bring herself to think of anything else, other than what a fool she'd become.

She glanced out the window again, searching the empty sky. What if the locusts never came back? What if they found Winn and he coerced them to go on their way? Could he hate Gentry that much?

She shook her head as she dragged herself from the window. Crossing to the stove, she checked the bread sitting atop it. Cool enough to wrap.

"Pearl." She tied the cloth into a tight knot atop the bread's crust. "Would you take this to Hoss, please?" A simple parting gift, but he would like it.

Pearl came without complaint and took the bundle in her

arms. After she'd gone, Gentry hauled the old rug outside, her mind quickly picking up where it had left off.

No, Winn wouldn't hate her. He wasn't capable of hate. Yet a world where he never forgave her, never saw her again, was becoming more and more realistic. Gentry played with the idea of moving on, venturing out in Salt Lake City, finding some nice Mormon boy to marry, but none of it soothed her or kindled her hope. Better that she stay independent and grow old looking after Rooster and Pearl.

She shook her head and tossed the rug over the clothesline, disturbing a locust hiding in its slender shade. "Be of use, Gentry," she muttered to herself. Retrieving a stick, she beat the rug senseless until her arms ached and she coughed dust from her lungs. Then she folded the thing and stuck it into the back of the wagon.

Wanting a walk, Gentry tied on her bonnet and ventured toward the mercantile, wondering if it was at all cooler in Salt Lake City than in Dry Creek. Certainly the lake made it cooler. Would winter be harsher to compensate?

She went to the window on the side, and Mr. Olson tended her, pulling a single letter from her family's cubby. She still felt a twang, seeing mail for her, wondering if, by chance, her pa had written after all. That it was all a big misunderstanding, that he was coming home, that he'd struck gold. Anything. But Gentry turned the letter over and saw the address of the assessor. At least the disappointment had whittled itself down to a speck. Soon, in time, she'd stop hoping for her pa's handwriting altogether.

"Thank you." She turned back for the house, opening the letter with her thumbnail. They were behind on mortgage payments, so there was to be no return of funds on their family lands. But everything else seemed to be in order, and after a few more of Rooster's paychecks, the Abrams would be unburdened of their father's holdings and be able to truly start anew.

She'd not reached halfway home when the ground rumbled beneath her, causing her to stumble. She dropped the assessor's letter and stooped to grab it, only to have the earth shake again like a great beast was rolling over beneath the ground.

Her pulse raced as she straightened, trying to find her footing as gentle trembling stirred the dust around her. She saw a shimmer through it, an uneven road of subtle sparkles that wove westward. She heard the hum of one of her locusts before she saw it land on her shoulder.

Setting her jaw, Gentry hurried home. The earth bucked again, knocking her to her knees, then resettled into a purr that shook the sparse trees and the scant buildings around them. Gentry had no gold save for the clasp of her mother's necklace, which she kept in her pocket. Even so, she didn't know how to calm an earthquake.

She reached home, and the ground settled. She searched for Pearl, but she had likely holed up in Hoss's home during the quake.

Gentry peered westward. The shimmering road had vanished, but she knew where it led. The mines. The people attacking the earth without realizing the consequences. Surely the quakes and geysers didn't appear near the gold itself, else even the least believing of men would make the connection. Wouldn't they?

With so much gold in California, anything that remembered magic would probably be drunk on it. The thought brought images of her pa to mind, which she pushed away.

The first quake, the one that introduced her to Winn, had been as far as American Fork. Surely they reached Salt Lake

City and beyond. For how long? Even the voice of God wouldn't persuade every gold hunter to give up his livelihood and go home penniless. So men would continue to mine gold from the veins in California, bleeding out the earth, until none of it remembered it was once so much more.

And Gentry and her family had to suffer the consequences until the deed was done.

The locust on her shoulder hummed.

Or do we? she wondered, and her hands balled into fists. She couldn't stop the mining, no, but couldn't she slow it, at least a little? Grant her loved ones—and the earth itself—some respite?

She turned toward the bug on her shoulder. Its antennae twitched.

"How many more are there of you here?" she murmured. The locust hummed, and in the back of her mind, Gentry thought the word, *Enough.*

She licked her lips. Squared her shoulders. Sucked in a deep breath and hurried into the desert, away from Dry Creek, until she was sweating and aching and sure no one could watch her.

Turning to the locust on her shoulder, she whispered, "You want gold?"

The insect buzzed.

She nodded. "Take me to the mines."

The song of the swarm bellowed through the hot air. Locusts appeared as if birthed by the earth itself. They hit like a thunderous wind, slamming into her, scooping her off the desert soil and tossing her into the air until Gentry couldn't tell one direction from the other. She bit down on a scream. Trust. She had to choose to trust.

A nauseating sensation of weightlessness assaulted Gentry, and suddenly the sky was everywhere, patches of blue winking between so many bodies of black. The locusts formed a tight, vibrating bowl around her, thousands of legs clinging to cloth and skin alike, all of them glimmering with the sheen of magic. Gentry struggled to adjust or shift, sit or stand, to gain her bearings.

She dropped suddenly, and for the space of a breath she fell, untouched by any of the locusts. Then the insects scooped her up again, spinning her until Gentry had to squeeze her eyes shut and grit her teeth to battle the dizziness swirling through her body. Tendrils of wind pierced the dense cloud, whipping by her like switches. The magic sped her through the air. Covering her head with her arms, Gentry closed her eyes and tried to breathe deeply. She was under the ocean with a storm coming or trapped inside a boulder rolling down the steep slopes of the Wasatch.

There was a rhythm in the buzzing, a sort of cadence to the flight of the locusts. Gentry tried to focus on it, to steer her mind away from the speed and the height. She searched for patterns within it, and when she discovered one, she listened for its beginning, over and over. The sun hid its location from her, but the minutes flit by through the tiny holes in her locust-made net. Minutes, minutes. A quarter hour. Two. More, she thought, but the song of the locusts warped time almost as much as it warped direction.

After what felt like hours, the vibrant song of the swarm began to slow, and Gentry knew her destination neared. *Gently, please!* she begged, as the swarm spiraled and deposited her on the top of a red-burnished butte. The sun had shifted slightly in the sky, but moving so far west, it had to be a later hour than it appeared.

Gentry inched toward the edge of the butte on shaky legs; it wasn't so different from flying in the torrent of gulls, but she didn't have Winn to hold onto, not anymore. An ache zipped down her center, but she steeled herself and took in her surroundings.

The locusts had dropped her on a butte above the mining efforts, not terribly far from where the Boston Company had been, if Gentry's fleeting glimpse of Californian geography was right. A diverted river passed through the cliff's shadow. Long, curving sluices bordered with men desperately panning edged it, along with tents and forts and a spiderwebbing of canals. Gentry had grown up in the city, surrounded by the workings of men, but seeing the mining now, through her gold-enchanted eyes, made her recognize the scars marring the earth and the deadness of the soil, for none of it had the shimmer of magic.

They would never stop. This was a bandage, that was all. Yet she had no desire to hurt these ignorant people. First, she had to scare them and buy this bruised and battered land a little more time.

Winn should have been here.

She let herself smile. Despite the mess she had made with him, at least she was finally doing something herself. Finally able to take action for the better, so she hoped.

Around her feet crawled the locusts, antsy for another feeding, another command. She didn't know how much they would do without bribery. Their relationship was too new, but Gentry was ready to learn.

She'd stay here and let them do the work, for they had the true power. She was, as Winn had said, only a conduit. Gentry took a deep breath, letting the air inflate her chest. She stepped closer to the edge of the butte. Reaching into her pocket, she pinched the last piece of her mother's necklace between her fingers.

"Save this if you can," she begged them. "There is gold enough for all."

But she had to prompt them, so she dropped the golden clasp at her feet. The insects immediately swarmed for it, antennae and legs feathering against her shoes. This time, she spoke with her thoughts. *Half of you, fly down to the river. Swarm, buzz, crawl. Scare them away.*

She visualized half of the locusts doing just that, and to her amazement, they responded. Half of the black insects rose into the air and from behind the butte, a cloud of pestilence. The buzzing radiated in Gentry's bones and numbed her ears. They flew as though each was part of a larger creature, and they barreled down the mountainside toward the river and miners. Gentry could barely hear their screams of alarm over thousands of wings. She thought of the time these very creatures swarmed her small home, and her heartbeat quickened. Through open patches in the swarm, she saw men dropping pails and shovels, running downstream as they swatted at the insects.

She reached out to the others with her thoughts. *Can you hear me? Please, fly down to the river. Break the sluices and the dams.*

The rest of the swarm poured over the side of the butte like sludge. Gentry felt their song humming through her muscles, and, deep in her throat, she sang with them. The black locusts spread out like oil, chasing straggling men from the water. The supports holding the walls for the diverted river began to creak.

Then Gentry noticed her hand. The veins glowed with gold. She traced the lines, feeling their warmth against her fingertips. Did her eyes shine too?

A loud cracking echoed against the butte. One of the dams buckled, releasing a great current into the natural river bed. The force shoved waves up and over the banks and into the tents. Locusts gathered tight as spearheads and dive-bombed the sluices, penetrating the wood. Others chewed on supports like termites, knocking the slides to the ground, flooding the area.

A gunshot rang into the air.

Gentry backed away from the butte's edge. She may have been noticed. That shot might have been meant for her, and a rush like snake venom raced through her limbs.

A mill wheel fell from its supports and crashed into the new waves. Tent canvases bubbled in the growing depths. The remaining miners fled for dry ground, running to stay ahead of the surging river.

The butte trembled. That, Gentry knew, wasn't her doing.

Something deep under the deadened earth was stirring.

"Time to go," she whispered, and she tried to push the thought out to the swarm. They responded, returning to the butte and swirling around her. Many of them clutched bits of gold in their legs or carried whole nuggets between them.

"Thank you," she murmured, the words mingling with their song. "Let's go back to Dry Creek before the mob reaches us."

The locusts agreed—she felt it in the cadence of their buzzing—and they swooped beneath her, flying her across the desert, away from the descent of the sun.

CHAPTER 17

Caleb ran around in the yard before the Hinkle's house, waving his half sister's rag doll around in one hand as Pearl chased him, growling like a mountain lion and laughing. Gentry watched them from a soft chair in the front room of Hannah's home, some knitting forgotten on her lap. They would intrude on the Hinkles' hospitality only a day more before venturing north to Salt Lake City and to the rented spaces prepared for them. In the meantime, Rooster was helping Willard with equipment or orders or something to do with printing that went over Gentry's head.

"I know heartbreak when I see it." Hannah's statement drew Gentry's attention away from the window and the children at play. She stood in the doorway, little Rachel bundled and asleep in her arms.

Gentry smiled. "She'll be too heavy to carry soon enough."

"Don't go changing the subject." Hannah crossed the room and sat on the bench beside Gentry. "There's another wedding in your future."

"I'm the one who called it off."

"I know." Rachel stirred, so Hannah began rocking side to side. "I also know that's not why you're heartsick."

Gentry sighed and looked back toward Pearl. "What do I have to be heartsick over? I've got Pearl and Rooster, and good job prospects, and a new home waiting. Not to mention generous friends."

Hannah smiled. "I had a beau of my own when I was a little younger than Rooster, before I met Willard. I loved him. At least, I thought I did. Feels so long ago now, it's hard to remember."

Gentry met Hannah's eyes. "What happened?"

Hannah shrugged. "He was a Methodist. I was due west. He didn't want to come, I didn't want to stay, in the end."

"A sad parting," Gentry said.

She nodded. "But for the best, in the end." She looked down at Rachel with such sweet affection, Gentry felt like she was intruding.

She set her knitting aside. It had been so long since she'd had yarn to knit that her work looked sloppy, anyway. "I'm going to get some air."

"I'll start dinner in a couple hours."

"Be back to help you." Gentry offered another smile before stepping out the door. She tousled Caleb's dark hair as she passed. She'd forgotten her bonnet, but she didn't feel like heading back to fetch it now.

She knew her way around American Fork decently well and retraced a path that led to the cemetery. Memories of moving shadows and blob "monsters" tickled her thoughts, and she smiled genuinely. What an adventure that had been. And her adventures weren't over. After settling in Salt Lake, she would still listen for the rumbling of the earth and chase it down as Winn had, somehow. As long as she could find the gold, she could take care of her loved ones and calm the brewing tempests. But, as Gentry knew, gold was not easy to come by. Perhaps God intended her to resign as a homebody. Not the worst of fates, she supposed.

"Nasty things! Shoo, shoo!"

The woman's cry made Gentry pause in her walk. She spied her waving a broom about a half-built porch at a few locusts taking perch there. A few *shimmering* ones.

Her breath caught. She peered ahead, past the cemetery, searching for a private place. Down the road, a farm without other homes near it. She ran, her skirt fluttering behind her. *To me, please!* she begged, for she knew these locusts were not the ones who had taken her to California or followed her to American Fork.

Her lungs and legs burned by the time she reached the farm and the stalks of corn growing along its crooked fence. Heat bloomed beneath her blouse and in her cheeks. Bending over, she breathed deeply, trying to steady herself. Moments later, the familiar hum of the locusts brushed her ears, and dozens took home in the corn leaves nearby her, antennae flicking back and forth, wings stretching as though excited.

Gentry straightened and, keeping her voice low, asked, "Were you successful?"

The creatures buzzed, bodies glimmering even without the sheen of the sun.

Her heart flipped and twisted. "Which one? Who did you find?"

They buzzed, and unbidden in her thoughts, Gentry saw the image of a seagull.

Tears sprang to her eyes. They had found Winn. They knew where he was. But was it too late?

Gentry shook her head, hope nearly choking her. She had to try. She would never forgive herself if she didn't try.

She loved him.

"Please, can you take me to him?"

As the locusts leapt from the cornstalks, Gentry realized she hadn't asked how far he had gone. She'd promised Hannah to be back to help with dinner.

But sometimes promises had to be broken for better ones.

The locusts became a cloud around her, and soon her feet left the ground. She zoomed high into the air, certain someone would see her. Yet in the darkness between the insects' bodies, Gentry could barely see anything herself.

She flew with the power of a hundred eagles across the desert, not west, but south. Tendrils of wind whipped through spaces between locusts and danced around her limbs. Gentry hugged herself and tucked in her knees, trying to make herself smaller, centered. The shimmer of magic encompassed her, fueled by the rhythm of locusts' wings. Without more gold, this might be the last time Gentry traveled such distance with such power, so she absorbed the song around her, memorizing its unspoken words.

In a burst of weightlessness, Gentry managed to orient herself downward and spied rust-colored desert passing far below her. The gusts stole her breath away as she looked ahead through a star-shaped gap in the locusts, beholding the largest canyon she'd ever laid eyes on. It stretched for miles in either direction, a gaping maw carved right into the stony earth.

The cloud dropped and propelled forward, heading right for it.

"No!" Gentry cried. She grappled for something to hold on to but felt only the flitting of wings under her fingers. "No, not there! Let me down! *Let me down!*"

The cloud swept upward. Blinding sunlight pierced the star-shaped window just before it closed. Gentry tumbled backward, feet over head, before weightlessness assaulted her once more. The cloud tightened around her, and Gentry's backside thudded against something hard. As swiftly as the blowing out of a candle, the locusts lifted from her and spiraled down into the mouth of the great canyon, which gaped not twenty feet from her, stretching endlessly, as though the earth itself had broken in two.

Gentry gasped for air, her chest and shoulders jerking with each intake. Her skirt puddled immodestly about her. Fingers dug into hot, dusty soil, gripping small handfuls in fists. Her bonnet barely held onto her neck and dangled between her shoulder blades, and pieces of hair flew wild about her face.

She stared at the canyon until her heart slowed enough for her to differentiate one beat from another. Her body felt too cold and too hot at once. She blinked, her eyes dry.

Slowly she got her feet beneath her and stood, her joints stiff and shaky, her torso light. She took a step forward and paused.

The locusts had fled into the depths of that canyon. Gentry no longer heard their song.

Was Winn ... was he down *there*, or had the insects stranded her here, not understanding her wish or no longer caring to fulfill it?

She slid a foot forward, sliding her shoe across the red-tinted dust. Moved the other. Held her arms out as though she walked a tightrope, eyeing the edge of the canyon the entire time. She inched forward bit by bit. When she stood a few paces from its lip, she dropped to her knees and crawled to the edge, peering over.

The canyon plummeted deep into the earth, its base drawn by a slim, silver river over a mile below. Its walls were not straight but rocky, almost stair-like in many places, with stone layered in a way that made Gentry think of stacked flapjacks. Beige and rust and sienna, they seemed to lean toward that narrow river. She'd die before ever reaching the water, broken apart on the menacing cliffs.

She didn't see the cloud of locusts nor a single gull. Swallowing, she trembled.

"Winn?" she whispered. Coughed. Gripping the edge of the cliff, she swallowed once more and shouted, "Winn!"

His name echoed between cliffs, and in the sound she heard the desperation of her own voice. The call faded, leaving her alone once more.

She backed away from the cliff a few feet and lifted herself onto her knees, peering about her barren surroundings. Nothing. There was *nothing* here but the great chasm. A chill coursed down her spine, contrasting with the merciless heat of the sun against her hair and shoulders. How would she get home?

Setting her jaw, Gentry crept to the canyon lip once more. Filling her lungs to bursting, she shouted, "WINN!"

The canyon shouted back, "Winn! Winn! Winn. Winn . . ."

Silence.

Gentry fisted her hands and blinked to keep her eyes dry. "I'm sorry," she murmured into the depths. "I'm so sorry. Oh, Winn, if only you knew how much I—"

Her words caught as she saw a glint of white down below, coming toward the lip. Gentry cried out in joy—a seagull with a shimmer about its wings. She leaned as far over the lip as she dared and waved, beckoning it to her, begging, *Please, please, please.* A weak laugh erupted from her throat when the bird did, indeed, sail toward her. It flapped with some difficulty until it rose above the lip and landed. A small rolled paper was tied just above a webbed foot.

Gentry carefully reached shaking hands toward it, and when the bird didn't shy, she grasped its leg with gentle fingers and untied the red thread holding the note in place. Unrolling it, she read its simple message.

Do you trust me?

"Winn." A tear traced the length of her cheek. She flattened the note in her hands, searching for something more in its corners, but they were blank. She turned the paper over and found one more word: *Jump.*

"You're kidding." She looked from the note to the seagull, which flapped its mottled gray wings and leapt back into the canyon. Gentry watched it disappear against the silver river.

Her gaze dropped back to the paper and reread, *Do you trust me? Jump.*

She read it again, and again, and again. Scanned the canyon cliffs below. Even with a running start, she'd never get far enough to make it to the river . . . and at such a height the water would be hard as stone. The locusts had vanished; she couldn't ask them to buoy her. Surely Winn didn't expect her to actually . . .

The paper shivered in her hands. *Do you trust me?*

Don't you trust me? he'd asked it, last she saw him.

"Yes," she whispered, crumpling the note in her quivering hands. Her eyes stung, and her heart throbbed. "Yes." She backed away from the lip and stood on numb legs. A chill crept up her fingers, wrists, and arms. Her brain buzzed. She retreated another step, another, another. Knotted her skirt around her leg so it wouldn't fly up. "Yes," she repeated, letting the note fall from her hands.

She gazed into the cloudless sky. Reached for her necklace, but found only her bare neck.

"Yes," she squeaked, and she ran toward the canyon.

CHAPTER 18

Gentry ran faster than ever before until the ground disappeared and her feet kicked only air.

She fell, the silver river slicing through her vision, the air snapping and whistling in her ears, her skirt whipping as she soared past the first cliff. A large outcropping filled her vision, and in its rust-colored stone Gentry saw the blur of her life, of Virginia and Utah, and forgot them all at once.

Then white rushed at her with the sound of beating feathers and crying gulls, soared with the heat of a geyser. The birds flew around her, passing her in her drop, spiraling around her feet—

And two arms caught her, knocking the air from her lungs. She stopped falling, braced by forearms and hands that glowed faintly with gold. The birds flew in a tornado around her, and Gentry desperately fought for footing until she could turn around and come face-to-face with his golden eyes crinkled at the edges with a smile, and Gentry laughed and cried and threw her arms around him, burying her face into his neck.

"I'm so sorry." Her words flowed fast and jittery. "I'm so sorry. I made the wrong choice. I thought I had to . . . it's not because of Rooster. I knew before that. I knew all along."

She pulled back and stared into Winn's eyes as the

beating of seagull wings tousled his golden hair. "I love you, Winn," she said. "Please forgive me. Oh, Winn, I—"

He kissed her, and Gentry was falling again, but this time she didn't flounder. Her hands swept to his jaw, and she kissed him with all the energy eddying inside her, kissed him until her heart settled and beat with steady excitement. Kissed him until all she tasted and smelled and *thought* was Winn.

Her feet touched solid earth, and she leaned against him, tangling her fingers in his hair. The gusts stilled. Winn squeezed her waist, and Gentry pulled back with a sigh.

Winn grinned. "I knew you did." His eyes brightened, and he clasped her hands in his. "Gentry! You used *magic!*"

She chuckled, her head still floating with the birds. "I did. I didn't know how else to find you."

He tugged her forward and kissed her once more. "I would have come back eventually."

"We left, Winn."

He leaned back. "What?"

"To Salt Lake City, where Rooster will work for Willard Hinkle—my friend Hannah's husband," she explained. "We left Dry Creek."

"And Hoss," Winn added.

She nodded, trying to resist the girlish smile blooming on her lips. "And Hoss."

He embraced her, lowering his chin onto her shoulder. Gentry slipped her arms under his, resting her palms on his shoulder blades.

"I'm so sorry," she whispered. "What I said, I didn't mean—"

Winn rested his forehead against hers. "You are more than forgiven, my lady. And I must apologize for acting out of turn as well."

"You didn't . . ."

"I recall a very angry Gentry Abrams storming away from that farm who would beg to differ."

Gentry stared into his gold-flecked eyes and grinned. "I jumped into a canyon for you."

He laughed. "You jumped into a canyon for me. But enough of this nonsense." He stepped back and looked her up and down. "We need to settle things so this doesn't happen again."

Gentry shrunk back. "I promise I won't—"

"In that I lay my claim and insist you marry me and only me, Gentry Abrams," he finished.

She laughed, a new lightness in her chest—or, rather, the absence of a pressure she hadn't realized was still there. Like she was a child again, light and carefree and *happy.*

Still, practicality nagged at her. "I don't know if you're the type of man who settles, Winn. You said so yourself. You haven't found anywhere you belong."

He swept loose hair from her face. "I have. Salt Lake City. That is where you said you're going, right?"

Gentry blinked a tear from her vision and nodded.

His hands cupped her cheeks. The tear must have escaped, for he brushed his thumb just under her lashes to wipe it away.

She leaned into his hands. "I have so much to tell you. And California! I went back with the locusts. We made such a stir—"

"That was *you?*"

She grinned.

He swept loose hairs behind her ear. "A bolder woman I've never seen. But you didn't answer me."

"I do trust you."

He smiled. "Not that. I believe I proposed . . . in a manner of speaking."

Her skin tingled until Gentry felt sure she glimmered with magic herself. "A proposal requires a declaration, Winn Maheux."

He studied her eyes. Brushed her chin with his fingers. Bent down and brushed his lips against hers. The rest of the world fell away, and for an instant, Gentry forgot she was ever part of it.

"A declaration that I am bewitched by you, Gentry Abrams," he murmured. "And that I love you. Say you'll have me."

She opened her eyes, and the goldness of him filled her vision.

"I'll have you."

CHAPTER 19

"Oh my!" cried their next-door neighbor, a forty-something-year-old woman named Annabelle. She clutched a broom in her hands, paused in the sweeping of her porch. "Look at all of them! Shoo!" She waved her broom at the Russian olive.

Gentry, planting some radishes in a sunny spot outside her rented apartment, followed Annabelle's gaze and spied the shimmering bits clinging to a branch. *If you're going to come into the city, you have to stay out of sight,* she chided them. "Oh, I'm sure they're just passing through," she called over as one of the insects climbed her skirt. She tucked a few stray hairs—their roots tinged gold—behind her ear.

"You should have seen them in the summer!" Annabelle wailed. "Nasty things. There may be more. Goodness. Harold! Harold!" Annabelle dashed inside to find her husband.

Gentry pinched a smile between her lips and glanced skyward, searching for seagulls, but she found none. Winn would be here soon, and these creatures needed to be gone before he arrived. *Thank you,* she thought. *Now you,* she looked at a distinct glimmer in the tree, *hide in this bush, just for a little while.*

The locust shimmered in response.

Annabelle burst out of her small home, hand clutching her husband's sleeve. She spun, eyes wild. "They were *here!*

They were just here. Gentry! You saw the locusts, didn't you?"

"One or two grasshoppers," she said.

Snorting, Harold pulled free of his wife's grip and retreated back into the house. Gentry did likewise.

Breakfast awaited.

~~~

"So he's trying to get it done fast to prove he's worth keeping," Rooster spoke around a mouthful of potato hash, "and he pulls the ink roller too far back and gets it on his pants."

John, Rooster's colleague and bunkmate, snorted and clapped a hand over his mouth to keep his half-chewed food behind his teeth. Gentry rolled her eyes and smiled, piercing her fork into the center of her egg, watching the yellow liquid seep out over the tines. For now, Rooster kept his separate apartment down the road, but they'd taken to having breakfast and supper as a family, often with one or two of Rooster's friends attending. Hannah, Rachel, and Caleb joined them this week as well, Hannah having come to Salt Lake City to help Gentry with wedding plans.

"Could you pass the pitcher?" Winn asked while wiping a napkin across his chin. He often joined the meals as well, albeit sporadically. Once he found steady work nearby, his attendance would grow more regular.

Gentry handed him the pitcher and laughed when he grabbed her wrist instead of the handle and refilled his cup in a somewhat sloppy manner.

Pearl asked, "Did it ruin his pants?"

Rooster swallowed another bite of hash. "What do you think? Best part is he didn't realize he'd done it till Willard said something. He was walking around all day with a black streak across his trousers!"

John coughed and drank some water before saying, "How do you not feel that?"

Rooster shrugged. "I think he'll stay on, though." He leaned forward and peered out the window. "Probably should set out soon." He shoveled the rest of an egg into his mouth before grabbing his dishes—and one of Hannah's scones— and taking them to the sink. His friend followed suit. Rooster called, "See you," and hurried out the door.

"Bye!" Hannah shouted after him, waving even though Rooster wouldn't see her.

"More." Caleb banged his fork against the edge of the table. Hannah broke off a piece of her scone and handed it to him.

Winn took Gentry's plate when she was finished and set to washing the dishes as she wrapped the meager leftovers from the meal. She was starting to get used to having a full belly every morning and every night. Pearl began packing her bag for school—the Mormons had assembled a real school here, though Pearl would attend for only another year or so. Hannah handed Caleb a book to entertain himself with and took to feeding Rachel.

Gentry moved to the sink and rested her cheek on Winn's shoulder. "I have a surprise for you," she murmured as he scrubbed the rim of a cup.

He cocked an eyebrow at her, the earring in his right ear glimmering—the same earring that had held up the side of the old Dry Creek house. Gentry excavated it the morning of the move. She'd managed to convince the wall to stay upright by offering it gold scraped off the mouth of a cup from her mother's china—one Pearl had hidden in a chest before Gentry had taken the rest to American Fork.

"Oh?" he asked.

Straightening, she tugged on his elbow. "Dishes later. Come."

Stepping around him, she stooped and opened a low cupboard door, pulling from it a simple paper box. She hurried outside ahead of him, searched for the creature in question, and quickly caught it beneath the box's lid.

Winn stepped out of the house and walked to her. "What's this? My birthday is three months away, Gentry Sue."

"Here." Gentry grinned, her ribs quivering just a little. She wasn't entirely sure what Winn's reaction would be—hopefully good. Hopefully.

Lines wrinkling his forehead, Winn took the box and lifted the lid to see a long locust inside, its antennae wiggling.

His lip turned up at one corner. "Oh, Gentry," he said, tone dry. "You shouldn't have."

"Winn." She cupped his hands in hers. "This locust thinks it knows where your father is."

His brown eyes flitted to hers, wide and searching. His lips parted ever so slightly. For a long moment he didn't speak, and neither did Gentry. She worried the inside of her lip.

"I . . ." he croaked. "How?"

"My ma's necklace." She nearly whispered. Salt Lake City was so much more crowded than Dry Creek; she never knew when someone was eavesdropping. "I thought . . . well, he'd be getting older now, maybe not travelling as much. And these locusts are small and common; they can get into places your gulls can't. I sent them out when I started looking for you. Last night, they came back."

They both looked down to the locust at once, to the faint shimmer of magic coating its body.

Winn swallowed. "Where?"

"North," Gentry answered. "That's all I know. You

don't . . ." she paused, trying to read his face, but she only saw confusion and surprise there. "You don't have to go."

"No, I . . . want to." He lowered the box. Nodded. "Today. Come with me."

"Now?" Gentry asked.

"We'll take the gulls." He gingerly set the locust down and clasped both of Gentry's hands in his own. "Who knows how long we have until we lose him again."

"It might not be him, Winn."

"Maybe not. I've been disappointed before." He looked down at the locust and grinned. "I can't believe you did this."

Gentry lifted her nose. "I do try."

"You're amazing." He kissed her. "I love you. Let's go."

"But Hannah—"

"She can pick out tablecloths for the supper or whatever it is she wants." Winn waved a dismissive hand. "I'll saddle Turkey, you pack lunch. We'll have to walk a bit to make sure we're not seen."

Gentry laughed. "All right. North we fly."

~~~

Gentry wouldn't have guessed they were in Canada if Winn hadn't told her after they landed. Southeast Canada, in a town Gentry couldn't find the name for. A town that, while a little on the cold side, made her think of Virginia.

The locust led them to a rather well-to-do home with white siding and dark shingles that was surrounded by a white-painted porch and a door with faded blue trim. The windows all had glass, shutters, and tawny curtains. The home wasn't on as much land as Gentry would think a three-story house would demand.

"This is where you grew up?" she asked, tucking loose hairs beneath her bonnet.

"No," Winn answered, and he left it at that. Squeezing one of her hands, he led them up three stairs to the front door, where he rapped loudly with his fist.

Gentry bit her lip. Seconds passed. What if no one answered the door?

But a moment later the knob turned, and out peeked a woman of thirty years or so, a white lace cap over her dark hair, a long white apron covering a yellow dress. "Yes?" she asked. "Can I help you?"

"I'm terribly sorry," Winn said, "but is this the residence of Ira Maheux?"

The woman looked startled.

"If not—"

"No, I mean, yes, it is," she said, and Gentry detected a slight accent to her words, but one she couldn't place. "It's just . . . no one ever comes for Ira."

Her pulse quickened.

Winn's grip tightened. His skin lost some of its coloring, and for a long moment he didn't reply. The woman frowned and fidgeted with a button at the front of her dress. Gentry was about to break the silence when Winn asked, "May I see him? I'm . . . his son."

The woman—a nurse, perhaps?—startled once more, but she tried to cover it with a nod. "Of course, he's upstairs. Might be sleeping, but I'll check. Come in."

She stepped aside to let them in. When Winn didn't move, Gentry kissed his shoulder and gently pulled him through the doorway.

The house was as nice inside as it was out, with smooth floorboards and woven rugs. A few candles compensated for the evening light. Two other men, one old and one young, played cards at a far table. Gentry wondered if this was some sort of retirement home. She wasn't sure how old Winn's father was, but she knew Winn had no siblings.

Up one flight of stairs, then another. The woman stopped at the first door they reached on the third floor and knocked lightly before cracking it open.

"Mr. Maheux?" He must have been alert, for the woman opened the door farther. "Your son is here to see you."

"Son?" the man within repeated.

Winn released Gentry's hand and pushed past the nurse. Gentry followed him, entering a wallpapered room with a canopy bed and white night table with matching dresser. A reading chair sat in the corner. Both the shutters and the curtains on the window were open. The man on the bed was balding, his hair half white, half pale blond. A thin beard in need of trimming covered the lower half of his face. Gentry guessed him to be about sixty-five.

His eyes, dark just like Winn's were, fell upon his son before switching to Gentry. He looked back and forth a few times before focusing on Winn. A crease dug its way between his eyes.

"Hello, Da." Winn slid his hands into his pockets. His shoulders trembled ever so slightly, despite the casualness pressed into his tone. The nurse retreated from the room, and Gentry hovered near the door, unsure of her place. "It's been a long time."

Ira Maheux pushed himself up on his pillows, rubbed his eyes, and stared at his son. "Winn? By God, Winn, is that you?"

Winn managed the smallest of smiles.

Ira tried to get up, but he winced and settled back against the pillows. "Forgive me, this arthritis won't let me be." He glimpsed Gentry, but she would be a later question. "Winn, I barely recognize you. You've ... you've grown up." He paused. "We haven't met before, have we?"

The question sent a shock through Gentry. How would he not know? But then it dawned on her. Ira Maheux's ailments were not purely physical. His mind must have lost its sharpness too.

Winn must have noticed. He shook his head. "This is the first time."

"Thought maybe ... you were dead."

"Not dead."

Ira glanced at Gentry before speaking again. "No ... you're too smart to die in no man's land." He coughed. "But I ... Lord in Heaven, boy. Where have you been? I-I went back for you, but they said you'd run off ...."

Careful not to creak the hinges and draw attention to herself, Gentry slipped back into the hallway to give the men some privacy. There was a window seat down the way, and she sat on the cushion, peering out over the greenery of Canada, wondering for a brief moment if it were even legal for her to be sitting there. Someone had left a children's book titled *Pip's Daring Escape* on the cushion. Gentry picked it up and thumbed through the illustrations.

Time passed—enough for the light coming through the window to take on a blue hue—and the door to Ira's room opened. Winn stepped out, looking around until his gaze found her. He motioned for her to come, so Gentry set the book down and hurried over. Taking her hand, Winn pulled her into the room.

"This is Gentry." He pulled her closer to his father's bedside, leaving the door ajar.

Ira offered Gentry a faint smile she couldn't help but return. "And that other lass?"

286

"I believe she's the nurse," Winn answered, and Gentry bit the inside of her lip to keep from frowning. Was the woman who had led them to the room new, or did Ira simply not remember her?

Winn's father nodded. "And you two are getting married, hm?"

"That's the plan." Gentry beamed.

He squinted at her. "What was your name again?"

"Gentry," Winn and she said in unison. Winn tightened his grip on her hand, and Gentry wondered what they had spoken of while she was gone. His mother, obviously. Maybe what had been happening the last decade in their individual lives. Did Winn tell him about the magic? Had he needed to repeat himself? She'd have to ask later.

Ira raised a hand—it tremored slightly—and pointed to the dresser across the room. "There, mm, one of the drawers. Under some handkerchiefs. Black box."

Winn passed a quick glance to Gentry before releasing her hand and following Ira's instructions. He shuffled around the contents of the first drawer before pulling out the box in question. As he did, the room shook, rattling a glass left on the night table. Gentry moved to the doorway, grabbing it for support, waiting for the earthquake to intensify—but it lasted only a moment before fading.

Here too, she thought. *Repercussions from California are reaching the other side of the continent.*

"Oh." Ira covered a cough, eyeing the black box. "What's that?"

Winn didn't show any signs of discomfort, but Gentry thought she could feel uncertainty dripping from him like condensation. She stepped away from the doorframe, closer to him. "You asked me to fetch it."

Ira cocked his head, squinting. "Oh. Winn. Winn, yes. Open it."

Winn glanced once to Gentry before lifting the small lid from the box. When he did, he paled. "This is mother's."

"Kept it all this time. I do have some sentiment in me." He cleared his throat, then coughed again. "Might need to be resized, though."

Winn met Gentry's eyes, and Gentry saw a shimmer there that wasn't the gold flecks of magic. She guessed the small box held a ring, though Winn closed it before returning to her side and taking her fingers again, weaving his own between them like their hands had been created to fit together.

"I . . ." Ira's expression drooped. "I'm sorry, lass. What was your name again? Mary?"

"Gentry." Only she answered this time.

He nodded. "Bit masculine, isn't it?"

Winn's lip quirked at that.

"Don't know if you need it, but you've my blessing, son." Ira scrunched handfuls of his blanket. "I don't know if you want it, but you have it. I don't suspect you'll be sticking around, but these bones of mine aren't going anywhere anytime soon. You know where to find me."

Winn nodded. "Thank you."

Ira smiled before addressing Gentry. "I hear this is your doing."

"Not really," she said.

"Modest." Ira nodded. "If Winn is anything like his boyhood self, he'll need a modest woman."

Gentry smiled. "I don't have any concerns."

They stood there in silence a moment before Winn met Gentry's eyes. There was a sadness in his gaze, a sort of resignation. Gentry squeezed his hand and eased him toward the door. Best to go while Ira's wits were strong.

As she touched the doorknob, however, Ira said, "I didn't mean to hurt you, boy."

There was clarity to his voice. He didn't look at them, but at his aged hands. "Thought I could do something good with the loss." His voice caught a little, but he didn't cough this time. "Was heartbroken. I loved her. I thought, maybe, if I could do good with what she'd left behind, I wouldn't feel so . . . empty."

His eyes glistened, and he rubbed them with both fists for longer than what could be comfortable. When he pulled his hands away, he seemed mesmerized by his own fingers—or perhaps by the raised, blue veins beneath them. When he looked over again, his brow scrunched, gaze narrowing in on Winn. "Are you the new doctor? You look like my brother."

To her surprise, Winn nodded. "You're doing well, Ira. Best to get some rest."

Ira confirmed the assessment by settling back down against his pillow.

Twilight encompassed the sky when Winn and Gentry left the house, both of them silent. It was late now and would be even later by the time they returned to Salt Lake City. Hopefully, none of her neighbors would notice. Perhaps it was for the best that Rooster lived in his own place too.

The earth rumbled again, and Winn paused, taking Gentry's forearm in his hand to steady her. But, like before, the quake was gentle and ended quickly. Winn frowned, turning west—toward California. It was while watching his taut expression that Gentry had a thought.

"That's it," she whispered.

Winn turned back to her. "What?"

"The mining," she said. "We can't stop the mining. But maybe . . . maybe we can fix things from the other end." She considered. Gentry was still unfamiliar with all aspects of magic, but if there was any way to—

Winn's knuckle under her chin drew her from her thoughts. "What are you thinking?"

She was thinking of Ira. "We could make them forget. Not everything is magically awake. The bits of earth upset by the mining are, though. But what if they were to . . . sleep, like the rest of the world? Would the quakes and the storms and the geysers stop?"

Winn blinked at her, a slew of emotions crossing his face. Confusion, calculation, sadness. She recognized that last one the best. If all the earth went to sleep, there would be no magic left for those who knew its secrets.

Still, he answered, "Maybe. Maybe, Gentry. I . . . I'd have to talk to the Hagree." He turned away from her, deep in thought. Gentry didn't dare interrupt him, even when a minute passed, then another. Finally he said, "I should talk to the Hagree. Soon. Tomorrow."

Gentry ached to go with him, but she knew being away another day—possibly more—would hurt Pearl, and likely her own reputation. As they walked away from the town, to a place where distance and darkness would cover the tornado of Winn's birds, Gentry held fast to his hand and simmered in his unusual silence. Perhaps she should have waited to tell him her idea; he'd had too much placed on his shoulders for one evening, and even now he walked away from a father who, though sincere in his regret, struggled to remember him.

They reached tall grasses near a winding stream, and once the seagulls flocked and spun them into the air, Gentry held Winn in her arms and kissed away his sorrows, their night-clasped journey illuminated by veins of gold.

CHAPTER 20

"You can't add lace!" Gentry blurted as Carolyn, holding two pins between her lips, sorted through her basket of sewing supplies for trimming. Hannah, Rachel planted firmly on her hip, grinned and swayed to keep the baby happy.

"You don't like lace?" Hannah asked, an amused glint to her eye.

Gentry turned on the stool she stood on, dressed in her half-finished wedding dress. It was a simple design with long sleeves despite the summer and a high neckline that closed with a small white button. Carolyn had just been pinning the hem when Hannah made her extravagant suggestion.

"It's too much," Gentry insisted. "You've already done too much for us." Rooster had been able to purchase the fabric for the dress—a soft white cotton—and the Hinkles had jumped at the chance to help her sew it. Winn was to start work in the quarry this week . . . once he returned. He'd been gone three days already. What if the earth had leapt from its rest and swallowed him and Gentry was debating the use of lace she'd never get to wear?

Her heart sank.

"My goodness, we don't have to use lace." Hannah's amusement died as she took in Gentry's face. "I just thought it would be nice. It's not terribly fancy lace. Homemade—"

"Sorry, sorry." Gentry shook her worries free. "I was thinking of something else."

Hannah offered a sympathetic nod. "They'll hold the job for him."

That wasn't what Gentry was worried about.

"Hm." Carolyn had found the thin strip of lace in question and pulled it from the basket. "I don't think there's enough for the skirt, but maybe the sleeves?"

The door opened just then, and Pearl, her cheeks flushed with exercise, stumbled in. She opened her mouth to speak, then looked her sister up and down. "Oh my! You look like a princess!"

Gentry half successfully hid a smile. "It's just like my other dresses, just white."

"Is not," Hannah countered, gesturing to Pearl. "Look at the extra panels in the skirt. Doesn't it make it look so full?"

Pearl nodded. "I can't wait until I'm married."

Hannah snorted and switched Rachel to her other hip. "Soon enough, soon enough."

Carolyn stepped over to Gentry, holding the lovely off-white lace up to the dress's sleeve. "What's got you running?"

"Oh." Pearl straightened. "Winn's back."

"He is?" Gentry nearly fell off the stool. Jumping down, she fumbled with the buttons on the back of her dress. "Carolyn, help, please."

Hannah laughed. "He's not going anywhere."

But Gentry shook her head. "I have to talk to him. Pearl, can you get my dress? In the corner?"

Pearl spun around until she located Gentry's dress. Gentry shimmied out of the wedding gown and threw her old clothes on.

"I'll start on the hem," Carolyn said, "but we need another fitting tonight!"

"Thank you!" Gentry pecked Pearl on the head with a kiss and rushed from the Hinkle's home, nearly tripping on a loose toddler as she went. It wasn't until she burst outside into the cooler desert air that she realized she hadn't asked just where Winn was.

"I'll start on the hem," Carolyn said, "but we need another fitting tonight!"

"Thank you!" Gentry pecked Pearl on the head with a kiss and rushed from the small apartment in the back of the Hinkle Printing Press, nearly tripping on a loose toddler as she went. Both Carolyn and Hannah had kindly come to Salt Lake City to aid in wedding preparations. It wasn't until Gentry burst outside into the cooler desert air that she realized she hadn't asked just where Winn was.

Probably at her and Pearl's shared apartment. Unless he'd gone back to the cabin he and Rooster had started building. No, the little apartment. That was more sensible.

She ran in that direction, absently noting the glimmer in a nearby shrub that whispered of one of her locusts. She offered a brief greeting to two women she passed on her way and nearly hanged herself on the clothesline she'd set out that morning.

Winn sat on her porch eating a peach.

Gentry stumbled to a stop in front of him, catching her breath. "You're all right." He offered her a small smile, then his peach, which she waved away. "Tell me what happened."

"Inside." He tipped his head toward the door. He stood, and Gentry followed him into the small kitchen where they all dined every morning. Winn leaned against the table.

"They're taking it to the keepers," he said once Gentry closed the door.

"The keepers? Who?"

Winn shook his head. "I admit even I'm not sure. I've

heard them mentioned once or twice before, but Waga never took me to meet them and never explained in detail. I don't know how much he himself knows." He set the half-eaten peach down and folded his arms. "I'm sorry I didn't send a bird. They talked for a long time."

"Did they agree?"Winn nodded. "Waga believes it will create a rippling effect. With enough gold, we command something to sleep, and the effect will spread outward, eventually covering the entire planet. Faster with elements directly tied to the earth—rocks, rivers, trees. And faster, the more ripples we make. But the Hagree must take it to the keepers—the ones who first gave *them* the secrets to magic. They'll have the final call. Until then, we wait."

Gentry pressed her lips together and took Winn's hand. "I'm sorry, Winn."

He offered her a small, sad smile. "It won't hurt them, forgetting. It simply breaks their ties with man."

"Your seagulls—"

"It's likely they won't forget before our lives are through, so Waga believes." He tightened his grasp and pulled Gentry close to him, wrapping her in his arms. He smelled like the desert mixed with butternut. Gentry settled herself against the crook of his neck. "In the end, it will help a lot of people."

"I'm still sorry."

"I'm not." He pulled back just enough to see her face. His eyes sparkled with remnants of gold. "There's too much good in my life to be sorry."

She smiled. Kissed him chastely on the lips.

He kissed her again on the forehead. "I suppose I should report to the quarry. A few weeks there, and I might win the next stick pull."

She laughed. And realized Winn was right. They had too many blessings to be sorrowful over the loss of one. Still,

Gentry wished she could change the world to fit Winn's desires. Wished she could show it the unseen wonders that lurked in the sky and the mountains. Wished she could make every last miner in California listen.

Then again, if they were anything like her pa, they wouldn't.

~~~

One Month Later

A seagull squawked somewhere outside—likely perched on the eaves of this house or the next, since there wasn't an abundance of trees near the small two-room cabin. Gentry rolled over in her bed and pressed her face into her pillow, stray hairs from her braid tickling her cheek. Beside her, the mattress shifted, and a breath later, warm fingers brushed the strands behind her ear. She curled into the touch until lips pressed against her forehead, convincing her to open her eyes.

Winn loomed over her, propped up on one elbow. His mussed blond hair looked soft in the blue, predawn light seeping through the curtains of their new home. He must have woken earlier, for he wore a loose linen shirt. He hadn't worn one when they'd fallen asleep yesterday, nor the night before, after their small, blissful wedding.

He swept more hair from her face, letting his fingers linger on her jaw. Gentry lifted her hand from the blankets and twined her fingers with his, smiling against his mouth when he leaned down to kiss her.

When they broke apart, he whispered, "It's time."

It took Gentry a moment to understand his meaning. She thought of the seagull outside her window; Winn's normally didn't make a peep until well into the morning, per Winn's request. The sad glint had returned to her husband's gaze as well, one she hadn't seen in his light brown orbs in weeks.

She sat up. The sleeve of her nightgown slipped over her shoulder, but she didn't bother to fix it. "You've heard from the Hagree."

He nodded. "I hope you're up for a little travel. The sooner, the better."

～

Once the birds set her down, Gentry took in the smattering of ponds, their grayish water reflecting the pale blue of the October sky. She wouldn't have recognized the place had Winn not told her the name. The Egret—the same place the geysers had so angrily lashed out at them, driven to madness by the never-ending gold mining. It looked different in the light of day.

The waters were eerily calm, the place too quiet. Even the seagulls didn't rustle so much as a feather. It was as if the place knew what was about to happen, knew Winn and Gentry had come to release it from its magic. At least, any magic that could be manipulated by man. Even the breeze held its breath.

The Hagree's messengers, a small herd of deer, had brought with them hewn nuggets of gold, unpolished and uncut, still mixed with the earth from whence they'd been taken. Whether these had been in the Hagree's stores or taken from the mining in California, Gentry wasn't sure, but it was enough to bespell the Egret waters and a few more places. They would start here, then move out, causing ripple after ripple until the gold ran out and the earth, slowly, settled into a peaceful slumber.

Winn's hand pressed against the small of her back. She turned to him, but his eyes—burning gold from the magic that had brought them here—watched the waters. Leaning into him, she asked, "Do you want me to do it?"

He blinked, the spell between him and the ponds broken. "No, I should." He offered her a small smile, then retrieved two larger nuggets from their bag of gold. Gold that could buy them a great deal of comfort, if they wanted it.

Winn approached the first pond, one of the largest. A locust landed on Gentry's shoulder, buzzing a peculiar song.

"We won't forget," she whispered to it. "I promise."

Its antennae tickled her neck.

Winn dropped the nuggets into the pond, and Gentry saw magic tint the air: a shimmer of knowing, almost pearlescent.

"I command you to rest." Winn's voice carried on the whist air, strong and clear. "To recede from the minds of mankind. To recover from your wounds and your strife. Forget your bonds and your oaths, and be at peace."

Even in the bright morning light, Gentry could see a faint gold glow tracing Winn's arms. The pond shimmered as if in response, and the glow died away, first from the pond at Winn's feet, then the one to its right, its left, until Gentry could see no trace of magic from the waters, only that which hovered around the gulls and her locust companion.

Pressure laced the air to the east. Gentry turned, scanning the endless sky. Something else was upset. Something beyond this territory.

Winn's fingers laced with hers. He seemed to be at peace, just as the waters that surrounded them.

"Shall we?" he asked.

Gentry nodded, and the seagulls leapt to the air around them, flying in unison, building a torrent that would whisk them to their next destination. But regardless of where they would go or when the earth forgot its ties to man, Gentry knew one thing for sure.

With Winn beside her, she would never be without magic in her life.

AUTHOR'S NOTE

There's an old writing adage that says write what you know. This time around, I took that advice to heart. Having been born and raised both in Utah and as a Latter-day Saint (LDS or Mormon), I determined my own home would make a good setting for the type of story I wanted to tell. Fiction revolving around the California Gold Rush is not rare, but telling it outside of California makes this novel a little different (that and the birds that turn into a house).

I strove for more historical accuracy in this book than in others I've published, but to make the story I want to tell work, I played around with a few things. One of these is the year the story takes place—or, rather, the vagueness of the year. I intentionally left the year off the letters in this book so I wouldn't have to nitpick between things that happened in 1851 versus 1852, and so on. The California Gold Rush spans the years of 1848–1855; this book nestles within that time period.

Another sleight of hand in this tale is the city names. Originally, Gentry's story happened in the town of Fountain Green. However, after finding some contradicting information, I determined to make her town fictional and name it Dry Creek—an apt name for the home of anyone who's ever lived in the second driest state in the nation. The second is American Fork, which during this time period was called Lake City. However, having both a Lake City and a Salt Lake City in the same book got to be confusing, so while American Fork was not called such until 1860, for the sake of simplicity, I pretended that was the name it was originally incorporated as.

I also want to take a moment to discuss two cultures alluded to in this novel, the first being the "Hagree." I have always loved Native American culture; I studied Native American literature during my undergrad at Brigham Young University. Given that Utah Territory was vastly unsettled by

Westerners, I knew Native Americans were to be part of this story, and I wanted to tie them to Winn's past. I did not, however, want to assign fictional lore to any real Native tribe, and so I created my own. The Hagree are entirely fictional and are not intentionally based on any existing Native American peoples.

The other culture referenced is that of the early LDS Church. Some pioneer history is intertwined in Gentry's hope to sell china to the Mormons for their temple (which was completed in 1893 and took forty years to build). The first LDS temple, built in Kirtland, Ohio, before the pioneers' journey to Utah, used broken glass, pottery, and (mythed) fine china in the building's stucco. Kate Ensign-Lewis's article "3 Myths About the Early Church You Thought Were True" on *LDS Living* does a great job of describing what may or may not have been used in the building of the Kirtland Temple.[1]

There is symbolism in both the seagulls and the locusts in this book. In 1848, shortly after LDS pioneers settled in the Salt Lake Valley, a swarm of insects (now referred to as "Mormon crickets") descended upon the pioneers' crops and began destroying them. Fortunately, flocks of seagulls soon appeared and began devouring these crickets, saving the pioneers' crops. This was considered a miracle sent by God, and it allowed the Saints to become self-sustaining.[2]

Veins of Gold stretches across three genres and is simultaneously a quiet and a quirky tale. I hope you enjoyed reading it as much as I enjoyed writing it.

---

[1] Kate Ensign-Lewis, "3 Myths About the Early Church You Thought Were True," *LDS Living*, 2011, http://www.ldsliving.com/3-Myths-About-the-Early-Church-You-Thought-Were-True/s/64388.

[2] Richard W. Sadler, "Seagulls, Miracle of," in *Encyclopedia of Mormonism*, ed. Brigham Young University (Provo, Utah: Brigham Young University, March 28, 2008), http://eom.byu.edu/index.php/Seagulls,_Miracle_of.

ACKNOWLEDGEMENTS

This book was a bit of an adventure—a story I came up with while trying to match a previous genre, but it ultimately took up a life of its own and became something different. Something that didn't quite fit in with other books, yet a story that still claimed a little piece of me. I want to foremost thank Heather Moore for helping make this book happen when the doors began closing. She was an unexpected helpmeet that I didn't (at first) realize I needed.

Thank you to my agent, Marlene, who helped me clean up my manuscript and who gave me permission to take a back road with it, all while continuing to look out for me and my best interests.

Thank you to my husband, Jordan, for all his support, and to my sister Alex and my assistant Amanda for helping me with kids while I wrote and edited. And edited. And edited.

I need to give another round of applause to those who helped me get this book into shape. My alpha readers, Hayley, L.T., Danny, Rebecca, Laura, and Juliana, and my beta readers, Caitlyn, Leah, Whitney, and Kim. Also to Michele, who agreed to give me a last-minute dev edit, and to Kristy, who wields a red pen like it's Excalibur.

As per tradition, thank you to my Father in Heaven, who looks out for me and who has blessed me with any and all talent found within these pages.

CHARLIE N. HOLMBERG is the *Wall Street Journal* bestselling author of The Paper Magician series, which *Publishers Weekly* called a "promising debut." Short-Listed for the 2015 ALA Fantasy Reading List for *The Paper Magician*, she is also the author of *Followed by Frost*, *The Fifth Doll*, and *Magic Bitter, Magic Sweet.* Charlie is a board member for the *Deep Magic* ezine of science fiction and fantasy. She is represented by Marlene Stringer at the Stringer Literary Agency.

Visit Charlie online: CharlieNHolmberg.com

Made in the USA
San Bernardino, CA
01 March 2018